"Many Irish
Blessings Your
Way.
Slainte!

Loretta A. Murphy

The Pipes Are Calling

Loretta A. Murphy

PublishAmerica
Baltimore

ISBN: 1-4241-4826-X
PUBLISHED BY PUBLISHAMERICA, LLLP
www.publishamerica.com
Baltimore

Printed in the United States of America

This novel is dedicated to the brave men and women of Ireland who crossed the Atlantic Ocean in the famine years and to the all the loved ones they left behind.

Acknowledgements

With heartfelt thanks

to the many dedicated "bards" of the Anthracite Coal Regions for "passing on" the real stories of the Mollies through the long dark years. *Without you, the truth would have been lost.*

to Kevin Kenney, who really did "make sense" of an extraordinary period in American history in his non-fiction book *Making Sense of the Molly Maguires.*

to Bill O'Brien, who fueled my fire to tell the tale of the O'Donnell murders by sharing his pictures and newspapers archives with me. *You have earned the title of "Seanachai."*

to the men and women of the Ancient Order of Hibernians for keeping the Irish culture alive

and finally, to my family and friends who love me and humor me in all my "Irishness," *go raibh maith agat*. You mean the world to me.

"Danny Boy"

O Danny Boy, the pipes, the pipes are callin'
From glen to glen and down the mountain side
The summer's gone and all the roses fallin'
'Tis ye, 'tis ye must go and I must bide…

But come ye back, when summer's in the meadow
Or when the valley's hushed and white with snow
I'll be here in sunshine or in shadow
O Danny Boy, O Danny Boy, I love ye so…

And when ye come and all the flowers are dying
Though I am dead as dead I well may be
Ye'll come and find the place where I am lying
And kneel and say, an Ave there for me

And I shall hear, thou soft ye tread. above me
And all my grave will warmer, sweeter be
And ye will bend and tell me that ye love me
And I shall sleep in peace until ye come to me

And I shall sleep in peace until ye come to me…

Chapter One

On Opposite Sides of the Pond
The Story of Maggie and Galen

Auburn hair brushing her face, the thin jean-clad woman flipped briskly through the genre organized racks at *Sound World*. She was not annoyed, just impatient. Bingo! There it was...**New Age/World/Celtic**. Rather a hodgepodge range of musical interests, wasn't it?

She was hoping to find the CD she'd heard about on her favorite radio show, *The Thistle and the Shamrock*. Just to look. Not to buy. Impulses reigned for the moment, the woman continued to scan the alphabetically arranged rows. A rap song banged on in methodical rhythm, like the dull headache of a hangover.

Thank God Irish music thrived here in America. Well, maybe not exactly *here* over the speakers at *Sound World*...but in today's music scene. Ireland and her musicians were generally well represented. It was one sane alternative to the daily diet of rap and rehashed classic oldies ingested by today's listener. *That* was certain fodder for brain death.

Maggie Carroll hoped a little sojourn into this musical den of mainstream mediocrity would not be fruitless. Some stores dutifully stocked endless compilations of Irish drinking songs all which included yet another remake of the Irish Rovers' infamous *Unicorn Song*. Maggie was crossing her fingers for at least one complete row of CD's put out by several different artists. The more rows, the better the odds of hitting pay dirt.

She was not disappointed. Son of a gun. *Sound World*, loud overcrowded haven of rap-rock-soul that it was, could take a bow. It had a surprisingly impressive collection of Irish performers. Exactly *three* rows deep and devoted entirely to Celtic music. So far, so good. *Altan*...then the B's... *Brigid Boden, the Bog Rovers*...now, C's...*Claanad, the Coors*. Maggie dug deeper. She was a woman on a mission.

Desperate? Desperately seeking a copy of *The Chieftains'* new release.

There it was ... that little nagging twinge of guilt. *Wise up Maggie Carroll*. You are a middle age mother with two kids and a mortgage. This CD was next week's lunch money.

Would she never grow up?

Oooohhhh. *But I do so want it.*

Right. That itchy little desire for sweet indulgence spread up from her belly. She *could* have it...but only at the expense of one bill or another. Was it worth it? The small treasure hung before her suspended like the proverbial carrot in front of the horse's nose. Maggie sighed

Money was tight since the divorce. The kids always needed something. Her eyes filled with tears, but only for a minute. She wouldn't trade her kids for the world, not even *two* worlds. But, hell, wouldn't it be nice one day to wake up and not have to worry about what hat she was going to pull the electric bill money from *this* month?

Her Irish blood thickened. No sense feeling sorry for herself. She squared her shoulders, sniffling back the tears. In a far corner of her mind, she heard Grammy Carroll's voice, full of old country, no-nonsense practicality...

Stiffin' that lip, Lassie, before it freezes like that. Why, 'tis a fool's folly to want what you can't have, girl. Those that are the happiest are those most content with what God gives them.

And, praise and begorra, look at that. As if on cue wasn't God giving her exactly what she sought? Yes, *here it was.* Yes, yes, yes! The thrill of the chase peaked. Maggie's heart raced. She held the Holy Grail in her hand.

To have or not to have...

Damn. They were back. Whenever internal conflict reared its nasty little head, Maggie could count on her Good and Bad Angels to give her conscience a run for its money. Maggie checked to be sure. Yep. There they sat, challenging each other from atop her opposite shoulders. It was bad enough to come from a culture that had enough fairies to fill an encyclopedia, but the Irish had the angels to deal with as well.

Maggie tightly closed her eyes. She might as well take her comeuppance now—before she actually spent the damn money.

Bring it on, you two hooligans.

The Good Angel grinned at her. Imagine that. Jiminy Cricket starring as the Good Angel and Tinker Bell in the role of the bad one in a new Disney film produced by the Little Sisters of the Immaculate Heart of Mary. It gave Maggie the willies.

Each whispered little conspiratorial messages in her closest available ear. The Bad Angel was wearing her blue Celtic war paint and ready to kick ass if necessary to make her point. The Good Angel, brandishing his time-honored weapons of self-righteousness and well-placed guilt, was simply a pain *in* the ass. Where was a fly swatter when you needed one?

Alright, Maggie decided, enough of the sermons. I'm a big girl. For crying out loud, I'm practically old. Back to business...*Chieftains' CD...no Chieftains' CD.*

The Good Angel was whining on and on good naturedly—sounding suspiciously, well, like her grandmother if the truth be said. *Do the right thing, Margaret...blah blah blah...the cable is overdue...blah...blah...you already have every CD they ever released.* Yadayadayada. Sis, boom, bada.

And not to be outdone...in the other ear...*yes, Maggie, but we're talking about new Chieftains' music here. We love new Chieftains' music...*

Oh dear...she felt the two little horns prickling her scalp, ready to pop up, like iris bulbs in spring. A fiddle and pipe played soundtrack in the background. She felt herself being drawn over to the dark side. Tinker Bell a.k.a. the Bad Angel grinned demonically.

Maggie shrugged. Nothing to get excited about—just a typical day in her overworked conscience's mental tug of war with itself. It was just a CD. What was the big deal?

Uh-oh. Reality check. The Bad Angel was winning by a length *Sigh.*

It wouldn't be the first time. Feeling guilty as a schoolgirl, she said a half-hearted prayer of repentance that the consequences, since consequences there most certainly would be, wouldn't be…*couldn't be*…all *that* bad.

As if possessed by a force outside her body, her fingers slid toward the zipper on her purse…

Maggie Carroll teetered on the brink. The black abyss of succumbing to temptation's sultry invitation beckoned seductively. Besides, she'd already repented her sin before the act. Shouldn't that earn her points? There must be some clause about that in the *Handbook to Committing Sin and Depravity.*

Ah, the heck with it.

It wasn't like she'd have to go out with a tin cup and a monkey. There was plenty of food in the pantry and if the Chevy ran out of gas, well…

Well, she'd…she'd…do what? Her mind searched for a plausible solution. Of course! Why she'd steal change from her "Pennies to Ireland" jar! Murmuring a silent prayer to the Saint of Single Mothers…*whoever* she might be, Maggie cast her lot in with the Bad Angel. Tinker Bell grinned in conquest and stuck her tongue out at Jiminy.

Show off. Maggie shot her nemesis a glare. She would have slapped her for gloating, but then the people up the aisle from her would have probably called the cops.

The small square of hard plastic tucked under her arm, Maggie headed for the checkout. Her good angel was really going to have do try a little harder if he was planning Maggie's salvation.

On the drive home, listening to her new acquisition, Maggie concluded the Chieftains definitely worth both eating leftovers *and* paying for ten gallons of gas in pennies, dimes, and nickels. She sang along softly. The old ballad, "My Bonnie," took on new life with an altered arrangement here and there. The next reel, "The Irish Washerwoman," stirred her left foot into a light tap.

She couldn't help herself. American as apple pie, Maggie Carroll was born and raised in the small northeastern Pennsylvania coal town of Greenville. It was a poor rural area. Once upon a time, this area of anthracite coal country had been rich with the mining industry. The lands were attractive to the many migrating in from Ireland—Maggie's ancestors among them. The green rolling hills were a reminder of home.

Maggie loved her home and country. But...silly as it sounded, from childhood, she'd felt a bond with Ireland. Only if she'd been born on Erin's native soil, could she have loved the Irish culture more. Soon after her divorce, she'd taken back the family surname of Carroll. She hoped her daughters would understand. It was no reflection on either they or their father, but on Maggie's pride of her cherished heritage.

She knew some but not much of her family's genealogy. Her own mother's attempt to trace their Irish roots came up blank. Locating where *from* exactly their branch of the Carroll line heralded in Ireland was at a dead end. Frustrating as the search was, Maggie knew her mother reveled in every minute of it. Maggie remembered the day the older woman had come home literally beaming. In her hand she clutched a copy of her great-great grandfather's last will and testament as proudly as if it were a museum piece.

The census from 1880 showed this grandfather Danny Carroll's birthplace as Ireland. Nothing else. There were no records of any passage aboard ship. The paper trail ended as scantily as it began. It was as if her great-great-grandfather appeared from nowhere onto American soil. His papers showed he'd been in the country for a number of years before he finally naturalized. It was much later, long after he had become a citizen, that he had married their great-great-grandmother Mary Theresa. Maggie often wondered about their story. Had they known each other in Ireland? Was it a grand romance?

The thing was...Ireland was a piece of her, a passion that Maggie craved with a longing that was a little hard to explain to others who didn't feel it. Secretly, she wished she'd been born there. Some days, she almost ached with a physical yearning. A bond to a country she'd never even set foot onto. And yet, she was not alone. She knew others who felt it too. Irish blood recognized Irish blood.

She met them at festivals, over Celtic music sections in the record stores, and the occasional *session*. During St. Patrick's Day parades and the like. The Irish managed to congregate one way or another. Years ago, she and a few friends had gone bar hopping one Paddy's Day in a long black limo. They'd had the time of their lives, getting drunk with one band after the next, singing Irish songs at the top of their lungs between bars.

Many a moon ago that was. *Deep sigh.*

It was another life then. When Maggie was younger and could get away with things of that sort. She hadn't the responsibilities of a job and children yet. *Why hadn't she gone to Ireland then?*

She hated second guessing herself. Maggie frowned a little, her good mood temporarily dampened. *Coulda...Woulda...Shoulda.* The three step sisters of discontent. Yeah, she *should* have gone over years ago. It was her one dream. And yet always, she had one excuse or another. *What if she had gone?* Maybe in her 20s or early 30s. Would her future have been different having put a tentative toe into what was left of her gene pool on the fair Isle of Erin?

She knew it was foolish. Silly. Still, there were times she felt it...the unexplainable sting of tears at a photo of an Irish hillside or a certain lilt of a brogue. A sort of homesickness. For a place she'd never been?

Good grief, Charlie Brown. She needed a life! Well, she had a life...maybe she just needed a better one.

Even so, secretly she knew in her heart she'd get there. Someday. Maggie wouldn't be able to help herself. Someday...between water bills, parochial school tuition, orthodontic bills, and the next major crisis. Whatever *that* may be. Someday.

Until then, she had her daughters...and the Chieftains. Paddy Maloney and the lads would have to do their part for Ireland until she could get her hands on the real thing.

————

Seamus Devlin ran his ungloved hands through the thick red beard he sported every autumn. The brisk air at the small Donegal County airport made you know you were alive. Irish weather was as temperamental as its women. Seamus leaned against the cold damp bricks for only a moment before he ducked inside the terminal building for a bit of warmth.

The plane was due in soon, hopefully with his older brother on it. Perhaps the prodigal son would be able to negotiate a cease fire. Once he knew there was a war on, of course. Seamus rubbed his numb hands together briskly. It would be grand to see his older sibling but Seamus was secretly a tad selfish if the truth be known. He was more than glad to be unloading the burden of his parents' latest lapse into lunacy onto Galen's broad and capable shoulders.

Naturally, 'twas best Seamus be the first one to break things to Galen. Gently. He needed to prepare his sibling for what was back at the house. Ma was not, well, not herself since Da's episodes of chest pain. She was looking all spooked about the eyes. And Da!

Why, your man refused to slow down despite what Doc Mike had told him. The infernal arguing between his parents had the house in an uproar.

And that was putting it bloody mildly.

When Galen experienced the magic of the three ring circus that had put down stakes in the Devlin sitting room, Seamus was half afraid he'd take the next plane back to the States. Seamus didn't suppose his big brother would take kindly having to get back on another flight so soon. Galen hated flying. Had he more time than bankroll, his brother would have gladly spent the extra money on the QE2.

Not that he'd miss the cash, the sly dog. Galen Michael Devlin had the cunning of a fox when it came to sniffing out a business opportunity. His fresh and honest approach had won him the spot of right hand man for Mattie O'Carrick, one of Ireland's biggest travel brokers. Mattie had an eye for talent.

Early in Galen's career, he was thought an easy mark by the big boys in London and Dublin. They'd chuckled slyly, thinking they'd died and gone straight to heaven as the country boy from Donegal approached the bargaining table. But they underestimated the fresh faced lad. When the dust settled, Galen had given them a whole new respect for country boys. The O'Carrick called him his Trojan horse as a joke.

Galen Devlin *was* a deceiving sort. He overplayed the bumbling country bumpkin routine to a hilt. No one who knew him took the act seriously but to those who *didn't* know him... Seamus smiled. He suspected Galen occasionally felt a twinge of guilt, using his humble upbringing to throw off the hounds, but as his Da would say, all was fair in love, war, and business.

He recalled the comment of Ballycraig's resident sage, Ol' Man Sweeney, on the very subject. *When the pot calls the kettle black, Lad, they've been keepin' cozy in the same oven.* The old man provided a running commentary on Galen's business activities with a wisdom only the elderly are able to drum up with any regularity.

"Guilty? Go on with you, now, Galen, me boy-o. A fair fight is fair enough. If one of our own is not fer us, then who? Have ye not said it yerself, and on more than one occasion I might add, that they'd swindle us blind here in Ballycraig if not fer you and a few others watchin' out for the home folk."

"Do you think the O'Carrick himself pays you for naught but yer pretty face?" The old man chuckled warmly, prodding Galen with an affectionate poke of his walking stick. "The old ones would say you were thrice blessed by the fairies, Galen. Blarney, wit, and wisdom. You might try occasionally using it to say, eh...find yerself a lassie to bring home. Yer sainted mother is beginning to think you'll never make her a grandmother."

Seamus recalled Sweeney had rolled his eyes, throwing a side glance at the younger lad. "Is it any wonder the girls swarm around yer ma's door like bees round the hive? Well, if they be a-waitin' for him to pick a wife, Seamus, I'd say you'd best snare one for yerself, Lad. Before yer brother loses his boyish charm."

Seamus grinned, remembering the row between Katie O'Shea and Nora McClafferty last time Galen was in between business trips. He and Galen had a good laugh about it on the phone, but Galen was in for more than he bargained for this trip home. Dennis Devlin was but one of the troubles he'd face come disembarkment.

Katie and Nora were at Mass only yesterday, separately pumping his mother for Galen's estimated time of arrival. Peg Devlin led them on a wild goose chase before begging off home with a headache. This trip home, the two fight cats would be primed for a rematch. Jesus, two summers ago Nora started a rumor that Katie had plastic surgery to poof out her lips...or was that liposuction to depoof her thighs?

Never the mind, Seamus figured. Loser take the spoils. He was neither opposed to surgically poofed lips or suctioned thighs as long as he wasn't the one doing it or having it done. More than glad to supply the girls with a few well laid bread crumbs of information, Seamus would shamelessly plead ignorance. Imagine that, both girls showing up like that at the airport. Coincidence?

Well, there were those two other planes due in today with passengers from New York...

And anyway, it wasn't like Seamus told the girls exactly which one Galen was *on*. Feeling warmer and rather frisky, he winked at pretty Katie. Lovely as always, dressed in a bright blue hooded cape, the Irish beauty posed nonchalantly by the exit gate with her wolfhound, Phooka. Seamus was particularly partial to that exact shade of sky blue.

Sighing appreciatively, Seamus swung around to wave at the saucy competition. There she was. Darlin' Nora. All dolled up in red cashmere and high heels, Miss McClaffety was wreaking havoc by her mere presence. The local menfolk were falling all over themselves trying to snitch a glimpse on the sly from their wives. Seamus gave an equally appreciative whistle. Under his breath of course.

Heaven knows, it was tough enough having a tall, dark, and handsome big brother. A lad had to look for the silver lining where he could find it. Seamus inwardly cringed as he watched yet another of his male counterparts wince from a well placed feminine elbow to the ribs. My, my. Nora did look hot today.

An elbow was more than fitting punishment for lusting after the likes of Nora McClafferty. Worth every jab and one for good measure. Yes, it was tough having a tall, dark, and handsome big brother, but there was the odd perk or two. Sauntering over to Katie, he put on his most handsome Devlin smile.

"Why, Katie O'Shea! How pleasant meeting you this fine fall day an' you looking so fetching to boot? A shipment coming in for your father? Really? And fancy, our lad Galen due in as well. Shall we wait with each and other then?"

———

Galen Devlin sat with both hands braced solidly on his knees. Turbulence. The frequent flyer's pothole. Everything would be fine. Right. Fine. Jaws clenched, his stomach seized up a bit with every bounce. He just might throw up, in which case he would be totally mortified.

In response, he automatically said a Hail Mary with silent lips. The Catholic school boy in him remained obedient. More was required to ward off potential air disasters. Galen muttered a quick Our Father and added a Jesus H. Christ just to be sure. His mum would be proud.

In the wake of September 11th...it didn't hurt to be vigilant.

The rumbling feeling subsided on cue. Galen breathed a sigh. Those Hail Marys were powerful stuff. And a little turbulence was a sight better than the *other* worries he'd had about flying over. Bombs, terrorists with box cutters, shoe bombers.

Christ, what was the world coming to? He'd thought of sailing. A few days extra, yes...but with the troubles in the air these days and the long security lines. Galen felt relieved to have the privilege *and* the money to do as he pleased *had* he decided that route. Odd for an advertising executive in a multimillion dollar travel related firm to be so squeamish, but Galen never had the stomach for flying. Even *before* the Twin Towers went down.

His boss, Mattie O'Carrick, didn't care. Or didn't seem to. Mattie flew a lot. When he wasn't traveling by jet, it was by the seat of his pants. "The O'Carrick," as the locals christened him, cared little for irrational fears or sanctimonious regulations. Mattie was fond of saying that rules had no meaningful purpose but to frustrate those who choose to live by them.

Last Fall, Mattie had been back in the air as soon as the President reopened the skies. But then, Mattie, an Irish American pilot who flew bombing missions in Viet Nam during the '60s, liked to live dangerously. His adventures didn't end after Nam. He'd married an Irish heiress and made millions on her investments.

"I'd be a damn fool to worry how you get from Point A to Point B as long as you get there."

Mattie's long white hair and dark sun glasses gave him the look of a rakish aging rock star, especially when he flashed that toothy O'Carrick grin. Knowing Mattie, he might well have played in a rock band or two on the way to the top. Or even more likely, been a roadie to somebody like the Stones.

"Just keep the famous Devlin dough rolling in, you hear, Lad? Galen, you're shrewder than most yet honest to a fault. It's a lethal combination. Your talent and my lovely wife Lizzie's voluptuous bank account keeps us solvent here at O'Carrick Traveling Tours. Hell on Hot Wheels, take my private yacht if it tickles your fancy. Just get there in one piece."

Galen planned to do just that. Not the yacht. The getting there in one piece. The events of September 11th in New York had given him much food for thought. The last few months found him craving friends and family. He strained to glimpse the Irish coastline through the misty clouds. It would be good to be back. Hearth and home called.

He needed time to recover from the drama in the States. Some well-needed rest while planning his next sales campaign for the American telly. Ireland was suffering sorely from the decrease in tourism since the Trade Center disaster. O'Carrick Traveling Tours needed a shot in the arm.

"Galen, it's not the kiss of death…but times have been better." Matt O'Carrick's tone was friendly. "Take a breather with the family before you come back to New York, but come back…with some fresh ideas. We need to recoup our losses from the past two quarters."

Galen stretched his long arms and rolled his neck. Maybe being back at Ballycraig was just what he needed. The dust of New York's Manhattan district was still in his nostrils. He'd be glad to be rid of it. To see Seamus…Ma…even Da, the old scallywag. He felt a renewed energy already. Galen Devlin was homesick. He hated to feel it, even worse, to admit it.

Worse yet, he was lonely. It had nothing to do with how many people he saw each day or how many places he traveled. Sometimes Galen was most lonely when he was out with a crowd. Figure that. Silly…he envied the couples he saw in restaurants, in the pubs, on the streets…

Ah, he was waxing sentimental. Good thing he had Seamus. The boy had more girls' phone numbers than a dating service. By more than fond speculation, he knew his handsome red-haired baby brother would already have scored them each a date for the Friday night early show at the cinema.

God, he hoped it wasn't Nora McClafferty or Katie O'Shea. Ma had written they'd had one heck of a row over him last time he'd been back to Ballycraig.

His ego restored, Galen smiled. It was a fine thing to be going home.

————

Tommy Terrance O'Toole stretched his short limbs and basked in his newly developed plan to sail to Tir Nan Og. He watched the goings on of the young lass, Maggie, in his magic globe. Tommy heaved a sigh. This was not to be easy. Nooo, not in the least.

His bones were weary with the toils and troubles of Men. Every ache reminded him. He longed to pass over. It was his time, and long past. Tommy was becoming dull-witted and impatient with the state of human affairs. If he did not soon sail…what would become of him?

Why, praise Mauve, he might be forgetting where the grand fairy ship, the *Celestial,* docked for boarding! A string of *what if's* interjected themselves into his consciousness. If only he could turn back time…

Sadly, he could not.

Finally, though, the pieces were falling into place. Queen Mauve had not deceived him! It was about time…about a hundred and twenty-eight years time to be exact. Long he had waited to redeem himself in the eyes of the beautiful Fairy Queen! His memory tugged at him to recall his foolishness and the greed that left him stranded on this side of the Mist.

Stranded like a rat. His memory was returning. Queen Mauve had told him it was part of the glamour. He had to atone for his deeds. Funny, 'twas that stealing it back part that had caused the biggest stir among the Fairies...

Tommy rubbed his ear, remembering...

The mental block drew back a few more inches, like the curtain on a stage. His head ached a bit as repressed memories came to the surface. Tommy remembered the day as if it were yesterday.

Danny Carroll had found his gold by trickery and wit...and Tommy Terrance had by trickery and wit ...*stolen it back*. Tommy Terrance sulked a bit, remembering the irate Fairy Queen as she dragged Tommy, gold spilling from his pockets, before High Counsel.

"Fool leprechaun! Meddling and finagling in affairs where he has no business being. If not for his nonsense, he'd have no sense at all. Master O'Toole here saw fit to have broken the age old covenant between Man and Fairy. A promise is a promise, *to give one's word sacred*. Tommy Terrance O'Toole lost his gold to young Danny Carroll fairly and squarely. Young Danny set him free as the Law clearly demands."

The Queen turned her wrath back on to the cowering leprechaun. Her long and elegant fairy finger pointed directly at him. Tommy never forgot the look of pure bright rage in her usually gentle eyes nor the sheer terror he'd felt in his chest. It burned him even now.

"Fool! Look in the crystal...you greedy creature...young Danny can not pay the rent on the cottage and was arrested by the English. See! Now he has set sail for the Americas, aboard a ship with prisoners. Do you not see the women crying at the docks?" Mauve's face grew suddenly dark. Looming tall above the cowering leprechaun, she was a terrifying sight..

"But, bbb...but, your Eminence, 'twere my gold first. I meant no harm! He had no right outwittin' me of what was mine!"

Tommy thought a minute before going for broke. "And besides, your Eminence, is he not just a poor farmer? What difference could a poor..."

The Queen picked him up again by his ear and shook...hard. Tommy swore his already pointed appendage stretched a bit. Eyebrow raised cooly, she looked Tommy straight in the eye. He never felt such fear. Tommy still felt her burning wrath.

"You short-sighted, short-legged, empty-headed... *You made a tryst and he bested you.* The Code of Honour amongst Fairy and Man is at stake here. Look in the Crystal, you fool! Fate *meant* him to win that gold from you ...so that he and that young lassie, Brigid Devlin, could keep the farm. A farmer! Lump headed leprechaun...do you not know what he does besides tend sheep and sow?"

"But...!" Tommy started to speak...but quickly shut up out of fear. She was the Queen of the Fairies and he would rather not be turned into either a sheep or a sow at this stage of his long and ill-fortuned life.

"Your blithering idiocy lost one of the Sons of Mollie to the Americas. As if we could afford to lose one more good man. Has not the Famine taken enough from Ireland's fair land? Fool fairy! You with one stupid act singlehandedly set back the independence of Ireland!"

Tommy could also still, a hundred and twenty-eight years later, feel the flush of embarrassment and shame that overcame him at that moment. Queen Mauve was right. So, it was no coincidence that young Danny had been bright enough to guess his riddle and find the gold. And with the blessings of all Fairieland no less.

Tommy Terrance had known Danny Carroll long enough to know he was an Irish patriot, who loved kin and country above all else. So Carroll had been meant to stay in Eire and fight the good fight. He looked into the crystal and saw the truth. Young Danny's fairmindedness and courage were to have been instrumental in winning Ireland's freedom.

Tommy's foolery had sent Danny packing on a debtor's ship to the Americas, risking never to return to his beloved Irish soil. A tear slid down the wizened face of the fairy. He felt as responsible for the bullets that still fell on Irish soil as were the bull headed leaders on both sides. Irish fighting Irish for a freedom not yet gained.

Tommy wiped another tear and blew his nose in his pocket handkerchief. No sense blubbering over spilt milk. That was then, and this is now. There was no way to undo the past, but he could help change the future. Mauve had shown him all of it in her Crystal.

Until Tommy Terrance O'Toole atoned for his evil doings and general interfering with the Future by making right what he had wronged, he was stuck on the mortal side of Immortality. He longed to pass over the Mist to be with the family. Tommy missed his wife and his family. There were so few leprechauns, or other fairies for that matter, left on Irish shores these days. Most, like he, were not left by choice.

But...there was Hope. The Queen had not left him without Hope. Even though he should have sailed for Tir Nan Og long ago, he knew the Missus would still be waiting along with his mam and pap. More than likely they'd all be ready to give him a rap upside the head for his foolishness and meddlin'. Affairs that were none of his business had gotten him in trouble more than once in his long life.

Never mind that. Tommy Terrance O'Toole was up against one this time, to be sure. The Wheels of Fate were rolling in his direction, true enough...and if he could avoid getting run over, he might sail before his next birthday.

No, it would not be easy. But then, nothing ever was now, was it? There was a kink or two. For one, the lass, Maggie Carroll, needed to get to Irish soil so his plan could move along. And Galen Devlin was another thing altogether. *Ah, well.* He'd consider *that* obstacle when he met up with it. Tommy Terrance's black mood slowly brightened into a broad sunny smile.

'Twas hard for even the most formidable opponent to keep a good leprechaun down. Thumbs in suspenders, Tommy braced against the winds of his imagination. He breathed in, almost feeling the ocean spray against his cheeks. *Ahhhh*...he could feel himself there even now. He, Tommy Terrance O'Toole Himself, on the grand fairy sailing ship, the *Celestial*. Face in the mist, finally on his way to Tir Nan Og.

Reality brought him back. First thing's first. The *Celestial* would have to hold her sails on. Tommy had a rendevous to arrange and precious little time to waste. True...he had never tried to conjure his way across an ocean before but...never mind. He'd figure something out or his name wasn't Thomas Terrance O'Toole.

———

Maggie Carroll picked young Siobhean up at daycare and sped home, where, if all things were perfect in a perfect world, thirteen-year-old Rosaleen would be arriving home from the school bus. The Chieftains played merrily, uvllian pipes and bodhran mixing in a lively tune. Maggie cruised along, singing with the music. The day was bright, late November, winter coming but not yet descended. A grand and golden day.

Oh Danny Boy...the pipes, the pipes are calling...the sweet strains of the old ballad flooded the mini-van. For probably her hundredth time, maybe more, she felt the stirring. Silly, yes, but no matter. Whenever an artist did the song, male or female, Irish or not, Maggie shed a tear. This time was no different. Her heart strings tugged. Sentimental silliness?

Perhaps, but there was a part of Maggie it touched. A part that she'd forgotten existed. The part of her that longed to ditch her life as she knew it...and all for a hope and a dream.

Had Danny Carroll left his home for a dream?

Sudden melancholia flooded her mood. Why hadn't she taken more risks in her life? Something always held her back. Fears. Worries. Money. But mostly, she admitted honestly to herself, it was the fears. Afraid to leave one security for no security. Afraid to uproot the kids for a crazy notion that could turn out to be nothing more than a pipedream.

She reflected on her irrationalities. Would anyone care if she up and left? Well...the girls naturally. But the kids would adapt. Ireland would be a glorious place for them to grow up. She could use her nursing degree in Ireland...certainly the Irish had medical problems like everywhere else in the world. There was probably a nursing shortage just like here. Hey, maybe they had sign on bonuses. She could sell the blasted house...pay off the credit cards, buy a cottage on a hill...

If she were going to dream, she might as well go for the gusto. Why, she might even write a few songs. If she lived somewhere other than dumpy old Greenville, Pennsylvania, perhaps she'd find her muse.

Inspiration...that's what she needed.

Whatever happened in Greenville these days anyway? Nothing to pique the imagination, of that she was certain. Years ago, when coal was the center of the economy, things were different. Back in her grandfather and greatgrandfather's day. Schuylkill County was hopping then. Big business, rich millionaires, sensationalistic murders, labor conflicts and hanging trials.

Heartbreak and mayhem. Lots to sing about.

The most excitement Maggie had recently was deciding whether or not to try out for the annual community theatre's production of *A Miracle on 34th Street*. The production didn't spur Maggie to song especially since no one was available to play piano for the auditions. Maggie was offered a part but rehearsals clashed with Rosaleen's schedule so she bowed out.

So much for the cultivation of her artistic talents. No wonder she was restless these days...

Siobhean murmured softly and stirred in her nap. Like clockwork. Maggie remembered when Siobhean was born, in the years BD...Before the Divorce. She and Jared had laughed at the unfailing miracle of the mini-van as a sleep induction aid. At age four, it still worked on Siobhean. The little one still needed recharging following a busy day's play at Donna's Darlings Daycare. Equally revitalizing for Maggie was the fifteen minutes of found peace on the twenty-minute trip home.

A horn blared nearby. Maggie snapped back to reality.

And I shall hear, though soft you tread above me...

Frankly, didn't life just suck sometimes? Poor Mrs. Danny Boy's mother! Or worse yet, his girlfriend! Put all this effort into life, she philosophized dejectedly, and the payoff is some philandering significant male other comes back to walk all over your grave and cry the blues. Tsk, tsk, and as surely as they walked all over you in life. Just like a man!

Maggie was 42, divorced, and broke. She knew all about the walking all over you part. Worse yet, she had two young kids depending on her. Turning the corner of Coal and Railroad Streets, she mentally took stock of her situation. It could be better...

But dammit, it sure could be worse.

Thanking the Big Guy Upstairs for her healthy family and employment, she knocked on wood and thought up an impromptu prayer that things stay that way. Still...

If nothing ever changed and everything stayed the same...

There were things she hoped for someday. Like her trip to Ireland. She had wanted to go forever but had it happened? No. Her chances of getting to the Emerald Isle anytime soon were slim. Heck, getting there anywhere before the year 2020 was slim. She did the math. Let's see...

La de da, gee by then, Siobhan would be out of college. Rosaleen, hopefully, started well into her career as either say, an investment banker or a rocket scientist. Maggie wasn't sure either profession was ready for her thirteen-year-old genius. She'd sworn to warn the public only if national security was at stake.

Her fantasy blossomed. Yes...let's see...

There she was, at the airport. Her luggage perfectly packed. One carry on and a suitcase. More than that would be pretentious and reeked of tourist. Yes...motherly obligations met, children secure in their career paths, Maggie would hop on board Aire Lingus non-stop for the Land of a Thousand Welcomes. And her cottage on the hill. The cottage on the hill was for writing. Maggie would do nursing for a while...until her first book sold...

It would be like a Lifetime movie. Hopefully she wouldn't be sporting a grey-haired bun and wearing sensible shoes when she got off the plane. She'd hate to have to have her first kiss of the Blarney Stone be while leaning over the back of her wheelchair.

Oops...back to her fantasy...

Yes, from Ireland, she'd monitor Rosaleen's career...her first born by then should have landed either on top of the corporate ladder or Jupiter's sixth moon. Siobhan was too little to predict a career but Maggie would have her eye on her, too. Yes, if all things were perfect in a perfect world...

Sigh. Calgon, take me away. Tucking the dream away carefully for another time, she cruised into the driveway of their small house just as Rosaleen, scowling with the weight of her overstuffed Gap bookbag, entered the walkway. Her sonar kicked in as Maggie scanned the potential damages. Being a mother was no cake walk. It took x-ray vision, Popeye muscles, and the patience of Mother Theresa.

"Mommeeee...I'm hungry!"

Siobhan wailed from the back seat, her nap rudely interrupted. Ireland, it seemed, would have to wait for another day. Hamburger Helper and a salad were taking precedent. Maggie pushed *eject.* The Chieftains were silenced, along with her dreams.

"Mommy...you should see what Billy Dixon did to Rachael Holmes...and guess what, I aced my social studies...what's for supper...?"

Content, if not fulfilled, Maggie prepared for her evening at home.

———

Galen Devlin was thankful to be back in the folds of his family. Well, to a degree. Mind you, Galen didn't mind helping with any obstacle thrown in his family's path. Seamus had made it clear within ten minutes of Galen's departure from his flight, in no uncertain terms, that he needed help with a problem at hand. When the "problem" turned out to be none other than the senior Devlin refusing to listen to the good sense of Doc Mike or anyone else for that matter, Galen considered turning right back around for New York.

"Pigheaded fool of a father we have, have we not, Galen?"

Aye, Seamus had made no bones about it. Their mother was at her wit's end trying to get their thickheaded Irish father to follow the healthy heart diet that he had no choice but to follow. Peg Devlin had drawn her line in the sand and once Peg Devlin set her mind to a thing, that was pretty much that.

"I will not, in any certain or uncertain terms, sleep with that egit father of yours ever again until he listens to that doctor. Galen, don't you look at me like that! Your father is two cards short of a deck and always has been. Seamus, stop your infernal giggling. It's not as if you're some shining example of physical health. When was the last time *you* got off the sofa and exercised?"

27

If it wasn't his family, Galen would be laughing. But, considering that he expected a quiet haven to plan his next marketing strategy, this was *not* the home sweet home he'd envisioned. Christmas dinner had been a nightmare. Galen decided that the fighting in Belfast must have relocated to the family's kitchen. In fact, dodging bullets might have been safer. The barrage of verbal animosity being fired back and forth across the Devlin kitchen table was brutal.

"Fer cryin' out loud, Da. Will you not eat the bloody diet food before she's down to Father Burke filing for an annulment?" Pleading, Galen turned his attention to his errant father. "Have you no thought for the family name, Pa? I'm too old to be the product of a divorce and who'll get custody of Seamus?"

His mother glared at him. There was no justice. As if it weren't bad enough that his mother and father were acting like Kathleen Turner and Michael Douglas in the *War of the Roses*, his foolish brother had gone and arranged a date with the *most witless* females available in Ballycraig. Beauty being in the eye of and all that, Galen couldn't fault their looks. It was their IQ's that were questionable.

Had things changed so much here at home? Perhaps he was being naïve but he had expected to leave fake fingernails and the fetishes of New York fashion back in the States. Ballycraig's women seemed to be behaving as foolhardy as those he'd left in the city. Galen felt a big let down. He wasn't sure why. His disappointment was vague and it left him restless.

He'd been nostalgic for the simple comforts of rural Ireland. After the hair-raising ordeal in New York he needed to relax and rejuvenate his creative side. He'd hoped for a nice date or two, a few laughs with a female who had more substance than a New York billboard ad.

Perhaps he expected too much. The womenfolk of Ballycraig were panting over urban comforts like Tommy Hilfiger and painted enamel pinkies with no less passion that any female New Yorker. It was a mad world. Even Ireland was not safe. Galen wondered if he could stop it from turning, just for a few minutes, and bail out.

"Peg Devlin, I won't eat rice with my beef and you may as well take that rabbit food and give it to that long-eared, red-eyed furry creature belongin' to Fergus Lally's lad. Have I not told ye, Peg, I bloody hate rice. 'Tis potatoes and corn and gravy I want. And…be quick with it, woman!

Oh God, they were at it again. Galen cringed as the sound of the cast iron fryer hit the stovetop. Dennis Devlin should have quit while he was ahead. It was the "be quick with it, woman" that did him in. Peg Devlin flew out of the kitchen, past her oldest son, and toward the coat rack. Flinging a few choice words backwards, she grabbed her makintosh.

"Make yer own supper, you big headed galout of a man. And feed Seamus while yer at it. Galen, start the car. You're takin' your sainted mother out to dinner at Lannahan's before she says or does something she'll more than likely regret."

Galen knew better than to agree, disagree or profess neutrality. He got his coat like the dutiful son he was and trailing behind his mother's wrath and muttering, flashed a half grin back at his forlorn father. Dennis Devlin might be thickheaded, but he wasn't stupid. He'd seen his darlin' Peg with her Irish up. There was no cure except to let her work it out.

Preferably as far away from the Devlin household as reasonably possible.

Dennis Devlin shrugged at his son. Galen shrugged back, as quizzical as his father about the ways of the female species. Meddling in the affairs of fairies, priests, and women only led to madness. It was best to let such things alone to sort themselves out.

———

"So you see, Ma, we need to recapture our losses from those past two quarters. Travel is at an all-time low. People are moving but it's business related for the most part. My job is to come up with some ideas to stimulate a sluggish market to overcome its anxieties and travel to Ireland."

"Specifically, to Ballycrag, right?"

"That's right." Galen sipped his wine thoughtfully. How long it would be before a brain storm would hit him this time? His last campaign, "Spend Christmas in Ireland," had been a huge success, bringing in business at a time when seasonally tourism was at a natural low. The pitch, focusing on the charm of a traditional holiday celebration in the bed and breakfast trade, was a study in simplicity. His boss had been well pleased—enough to toss in a bonus that had paid off his parents mortgage and laid a tidy sum into lining his ever-growing nest egg.

"Galen, what about..." Peg Devlin's speech slowed as her eyes traveled to the main entrance. His mother's interest became temporarily distracted by the arrival of one of her fellow cronies from the church choir. Her voice lowered to a conspiratorial stage whisper. "Oh my, but look at what the cat dragged in the door..." Then louder, "Well, don't be a stranger, Maude Tyler!" The older woman slid out of her chair and away from Galen. Thank the Lord. He was left free to daydream.

The sounds of the pub became a pleasant background murmur as mentally soothing as white noise. It was imperative that whatever angle his new campaign took, Ballycraig remain a benefactor of his efforts. He would dutifully reapproach his oldest allies...the bed and breakfast owners, the restauranteurs, the hotel and hostel owners...for input and fresh ideas. Independent of his plan, good as it might be, the local folk had their finger on the pulse of the current tourist trade. The insight they provided to him was invaluable. For better or worse.

What would make people want to fly to Ireland after September 11th? The faithful still came...the diehards, so wizened from tour buses and buffet meals, they barely noticed the guarda barricades and chalk outlines in the streets of Belfast even during the worst days of the troubles. Nothing stopped the little old ladies of the Catholic Daughters and their gentlemen in the Knights of Columbus as they made their pilgrimages to the Old Sod.

Like the tour group from South Brooklyn sitting diagonally from their table. Galen grinned at a grey-haired matron clutching a purse the size of a suitcase. An en route terrorist to the Emerald Isle had better think twice before taking on the ladies of St. Patrick's of Hibernia. That purse alone could take out three Al-Qaeda in a single swipe.

All jokes aside, Galen knew there was an answer. Fearful of air travel himself, he knew exactly what was keeping people home, not just from travel to Ireland, but in general. He had his work cut out for him. Searching his memory, Galen sought an idea that hadn't been done. At least not recently.

Golf tours were a dime a dozen and that segment of the tourist came hell or high water. Ireland's moderate latitude made it a mecca for golfers longing for the green—of the golf course. Golfers and snow-haired grandmas being shepherded along by their white collared pastors kept more Irish children in milk and shoes than their out-of-work fathers would like to admit.

Tourism was Ireland's bread and butter. The steady stream of immigrants that poured out of Ireland in the late 1800s had produced countless offspring reared on stories of the little people and misty magic in the glen. The Blarney Stone was still a number one attraction. Galen had spun a fantasy campaign a few years ago off one of the local castles. "Win a Storybook Stay in a Real Irish Castle" had won him a trip to the East Coast to meet with Disney executives to discuss a movie based on his concept.

He felt a rush of creative juice. Pulse quickening, Galen knew he was on to something. Mind racing, he looked for something to write on. What about other reasons why people travel to Ireland? Galen jotted down points neatly along the fold of his napkin. Family ties, culture, the music, the scenery…the same reasons, different for each person, a longing all the same…

"Oh…Danny Boy…the pipes…the pipes…are callin…"

The old song flitted softly through Galen's thoughts like a spring butterfly in the rose garden. Lately, Galen had found himself humming the melody. Galen found something about Danny Boy's tune and lyrics haunting. It had always been one of his favorites. Really more an American tune than an Irish one, he mused.

He wondered, as with so many of the other traditional pieces, about the story threaded through the song. Was it an old lover waitin' and watching for her stray love, Danny, to come home? Or a mother praying for a son to arrive before she takes her last breath?

31

He suddenly got it. The idea he'd been waiting for surfaced. Snatching up his mother's cocktail napkin, he furiously jotted down more random thoughts. The old sod…pipes calling for home…coming back across the sea to reunite with family left behind. Galen's excitement grew.

What better than ties to the past to bring them round? The Trade Center Disaster had left people scrambling for meaning in their lives, to connect with family and friends. What say O'Carroll Traveling Tours bring the lot of them back home? Those staunch Irish-American Danny boys and girls clinging to Ireland's myth from across the sea *deserved* a chance to tread softly on the graves of their ancestors. Galen Devlin and O'Carroll Traveling Tours would see they had that chance.

Galen was being neither sarcastic nor mercenary. He grinned. It was just…well, he often saw life from the viewpoint of a telly commercial. It wasn't being capitalistic. Cold hard American cash was one shade of green of which Ireland could use more. His parents struggled all of their lives to keep the proverbial wolf away from the door. Galen's successes had brought some respite from money worries, but he forgot not the value of a dollar nor the depth of an empty pocket. He cared little for money itself, but a great deal for what it represented. The tourist trade paid the bills and paid them prettily.

Yes, Galen thought to himself, green…the color of Ireland…the color of money…the color of spring. That's it! Galen's creative juices kept flowing. A timeline formed in the back of his mind. The campaign would hit the magazines and internet by January…they'd have the winners ready to announce for Patrick's Day.

Galen loosened his collar. If he were a cartoon character smoke would be pouring out his ears by now. An artist possessed by his muse, he fired off ideas faster than he could write. Frantically scribbling, Galen allowed the entire contest to take shape. Contestants would have to describe in a brief paragraph or two how the "pipes" were calling them back to Ireland. The most poetically poignant would win a deluxe trip for two to the land of a thousand welcomes. The rest of the lot would be unable to resist the call and book a trip through O'Carrick Tours.

Galen knew it would be a record-breaking campaign. The O'Carrick would be well pleased.

––––––

By the time Peg Devlin returned from visiting with her croney, her industrious son had outlined his new advertising campaign and placed a call to the New York office. Pleased as punch with himself...if he didn't mind saying so...Galen was leisurely sipping a hot toddy. Normally an observant people watcher, he failed to notice that a fellow diner had been watching him all through dinner.

Unbeknown to Galen, the Wheel of Fate had turned another notch.

There was a smug expression on the face of the short, gnarled old gentleman seated to the rear of the eatery. Half veiled by the shadows at the darkened table, he leisurely sipped a Killian's Black and Tan. Ah, 'twere a wonderful thing to be able to give life a bit of a nudge now and again.

Tommy Terrance O'Toole could almost hear the gulls and feel the salt spray. Tir Na Nog was closer than ever. That twist of thought manipulation—with a wee dusting of blarney thrown in for good measure—was a mite easier than he'd figured it. He hadn't wanted to do more than plant the seed or the lad might have thought it too easy. Sipping his ale, Tommy mentally packed his trunk in preparation for his departure... Ah, there was much yet to do. He'd worked up a grand thirst.

Tipping his mug for the last drop, Tommy kept his good eye on the lad who was buying his ticket to paradise. Galen Devlin wouldn't be such an easy lock to pick in their future dealings, but, ah, then where would the challenge be? Laying a handful of gold coins on the table, the little man slid out of the tavern unnoticed.

Galen, as he and his mother prepared to leave for home, noticed the cluster of uniformed waitresses crowded around a back table. He thought little of it. Had he looked more closely, Galen might have seen the glitter in the eyes of the stunned young serving girls.

The three waitresses quickly sorted the coins into three even piles before scooping them into their pockets. Unaccustomed to such good fortune, doled out, no less, in old coins fit to be in the museum at Dublin, the girls knew better. Smugly, they kept their backs together as they filled their deep uniform pockets. Honor among thieves.

———

Thank God the Christmas holidays were over. Maggie scrunched the last of the wrapping paper in the huge black plastic bag when the phone rang again. Sighing, she let the machine get it.

Maggie was tired of both Harrison *and* his phone calls. Frankly, she wished he'd give it up already. It was him, leaving yet another message on her machine. That made four today she'd had to erase. Annoying but strangely satisfying. Guilt was a wonderful thing. Harrison had messed up big this time and his conscience was prodding him to apologize.

Well, Maggie was having none of it. The days of wine and roses were over. She hit play.

Maggie...pick up ,please...I just want to talk to you. Click. Beep. Erase.

*MAGGIE...I know you're there...I just want to apologize...*Click. Beep.

*Maggie...I never had a thing to do with that woman. You have to believe me...*Click. Beep.

Like hell she'd believe him. If it didn't cost so much, she'd get a private number. Served her right for going out with a pretty boy. Harrison constantly needed a new admirer. His antics left her on the sidelines, feeling like a fool. Her alleged male friend managed to preen his feathers in front of the entire female social circle at whatever gathering they attended. Harrison's last little escapade at the hospital's Christmas Ball fund raiser left Maggie with a bone—a long bone—to pick.

Wait...make that *two* long bones. Her ex's blond Goddess for that night's event spanned a leggy 5'9". Maggie found she had not one drop more of patience to put up with even one second more of his nonsense.

Giggling blondes and alcoholic stupors left her cold but like a karmic moth to the porch light at the center of the universe, Maggie had kept going back for more. This last little flame unfortunately singed her wings just one too many times. She left the Ball solo with car keys in hand. Harrison could take a flying leap home for all she cared.

It hadn't been all bad at first. Was anything? After her divorce, Maggie shied clear of the male species. Harrison had started out as a pleasant diversion. For the next three on again, off again years she and Harrison had been together, things were at best, say, temperamental. Maggie even thought she might marry again…for a while.

She sighed again.

Yeah, right. On the relationship scale the bad times far outweighed the good. Before the Blonde Goddess, it had been the Raven Haired Harlot, and before that the Brunette Bimbo. Frankly, Harrison and his high maintenance ways had been on probation for a while. After last Saturday night, the final verdict was in.

Harrison was history. GUILTY…of philandering and aggravated deceit. Sentenced to life without Maggie. No parole. Sounded like the lyrics of a country song. One of those twangy ones she hated in particular.

H-I-S-T-O-R-Y
You're a dirty rotten scoundrel
You can kiss my butt good-bye…
Sentenced to a life without me
In a jail with no parole
You're a prisoner of love
Guilty clear down to your toes

The phone rang again.

Maggie knew she couldn't keep dodging his bullets forever. Hopefully he would eventually suck onto to some other unsuspecting female host. In the meantime, she'd let Mr. Answering Machine do the dirty work.

"Mooooom…I need to be at dance practice in an hour."

That figured. Maggie checked her watch. She was to be at the school for parents' night twenty minutes ago and planned on Rosalie babysitting Siobhan. Figured again. Maggie was convinced, based on Murphy's Law of Irish-American relativity, that the chance for two non-related school functions to be on the same night was higher if said parent also attended night classes and/or worked. This called for Plan B. That meant she'd drag Siobhan and look sophisticated, right out of *Working Mom*, like she planned it that way all along.

Oh, the trials and troubles of the single mother. Maggie felt another song coming on the tip of her tongue. "Oh! the trials and troubles of a single mother...Wouldn't change it even if I had my druthers..."

Jeez, those country lyrics were a cinch. They pretty much wrote down whatever thought came next. Words bubbling up from one's subconscious. Shades of Grimm...it brought to mind the toads and frogs that spilled out of the mouth of the bad sister in that old fairytale her mother used to tell her.

"MOM!"

Yeah, and if she could write music to go with those lyrics, she'd be rich. The phone rang again. She swallowed back a horned green toad that was threatening to rear his ugly head from between her vocal cords.

"Mother!"

"Oh, for crying out loud, Rosalie. The machine will get it. Come on, grab your sister. I'll drop you on the way to the school."

———

"Hey, Mom...look at this. I'm on *VIRTUALERIN*.com. There's this cool contest. You oughta do it."

Maggie paused from buttering the toasted cheese-to-be sandwich. Like mother, like daughter. She smiled. Her Irish was infectious and hereditary as well. Now her kids were cruising the bookmarks for her "travel to Ireland" sites. She absentmindedly wondered what the prize for this give-a-way was. Connamara marbles maybe.

Not that she'd be in the running. Maggie Carroll described herself as unlucky based on a long losing streak. She did not win sweepstakes, lotteries, or fifty-fifties. Her cereal box never held the trinket promised on the outside and if the coupon for the item on sale was in her purse, it was always outdated. It seemed she was as unlucky at winning money as she was at love. It was rather like a curse.

Stooping over her teenage daughter, she read, in a bold Celtic font, spanning across the screen amongst merrily dancing shamrocks:

ARE THE PIPES CALLING YOU BACK? TELL YOUR STORY AND WIN YOUR DREAM TRIP...JOURNEY TO IRELAND AND RECLAIM YOUR HISTORY...

Maggie read on. The premise was simple enough, even for the unlucky like herself. Write in and convince the marketing director at some travel agency that you longed to go to Ireland. She searched for the usual disclaimers...especially for the small print announcing "all winners will be selected by random...that is a one in eight trillion infinity chance of winning..."

Discouragement before things even got started. Always left her feeling like what was the point...in a sea of entries, what were the odds?

But there wasn't a disclaimer. Maggie checked twice. In fact, the contest seemed pretty straight forward.

> Are you longing to visit Ireland to find your roots or perhaps simply to fulfill a secret wish? If you are of Irish ancestry and have never visited the Old Sod, you are eligible to enter our one of a kind St. Patrick's Day giveaway. Fill out the entry form below and send us your tale in a hundred words or less. And while you're at it, download our brochure...O'Carrick Traveling Tours...we're all things Irish.

"Mom, you could do that. Why don't you enter?"

Maggie was jogged back to the present. "Yeah, sure, why not? You go ahead and download it for me, sweetie. I'll look at it after supper."

Rosalie downloaded the entry form before following her mother into the kitchen. The smell of melting butter reminded her it was tomato soup night. "How 'bout I do the soup, Mom?"

"Sure thing, Kiddo."

The two cooked companionably, side by side, discussing the internet contest. Rosalie stirred the soup thoughtfully. "Why *do* you want to go so bad, Mom? What would you say to win?"

Maggie thought for a moment before answering her daughter. She tried to sum it into words but it didn't come easily. Her love of Irish…all things Irish…had been there as long as she could remember. There were stories about great grandparents from the old country, whispers of family legends and forgotten secrets. It was a like homesickness without ever having had the home.

Her subconscious held memories that floated to the surface with varying degrees of clarity and coherence. There was a blurring of Irish-American cultures that softly framed her childhood. When her grandmother dropped names, it was with references to some town named Ballycraig where some relative of somebody lived.

Until she was about eleven, Maggie thought "Bloody English" *was* the Proper Noun used to describe the British. Green was worn on St. Patrick's Day because to wear red meant you were a "Dutchie." To wear orange was the worst…it marked the dreaded Orangeman. Bing Crosby singing "An Irish Lullaby" could silence a room. If, God rest his soul, he sang "When Irish Eyes are Smiling," it warranted tear shed.

Maggie knew she was Irish. There was never any question of her heritage, but so many pieces of her family history were lost. There were never many answers either…as if a huge eraser had rubbed away any paper trail of the past. For all her love of Ireland, her own grandmother shared little of their Irish heritage beyond a few vague family tales. How Maggie wished she'd been old enough to have picked her grammy's brain before the matriarch passed on. Maggie knew her great grandfather, Daniel Carroll, was an outlaw of some sort, sent to the Americas to work off his debtor's sentence. But that was all. Nothing of substance. The rest, well…

There were whispers of hangings and murders and bloodshed. Sein Fein and the Mollies. A hand cut off as it forced open a bedroom window. Maggie shivered. Good Lord. A young girl's fantasies and fears. She shook off the chill.

Very little fact to back it up or cast doubt. No tangible evidence about anything. Maggie would like to know more. No one else in her family seemed to have this nagging pull to go back to where their roots buried deep into the earth. Back to Ireland. Maybe there she'd find the answers.

"Oh, Rosalie…there's a feeling deep inside me that tells me I need to go there. To complete a circle. I can't explain it except to say that something's drawing me, like gravity. Isn't it odd?"

Listening to her mother, Rosalie was thinking. No, it wasn't odd. Not any odder than the usual parental weirdness displayed by her birth mother. Other mothers baked cookies and belonged to the PTO. Her mother sang Irish songs out loud to the CD player in the car while Rosalie's friends in the back seat rolled their eyes. Other mothers decorated in Pier One, Early American, or Oriental. Her mother decorated in multi-shades of green and still had St. Patrick's decorations around on the 4th of July.

But, for the sake of peace, Rosalie smiled sweetly and held her tongue. At thirteen, she may be inexperienced in the ways of the world, but she recognized an opportunity to suck up when she saw it. Come to think of it, she wouldn't half mind a trip that got her mother out of the country for a week and a half.

Naturally, her mother would never make her go on a plane. September 11th remained a frightening reality even though Rosalie was far more optimistic about flying than her mom. Nah. She hoped so anyway. Going away in the middle of the bleakest days of March, to some awful rainy European country that expected you to eat sheep meat once you got there didn't sound all that enticing a trip. On the other hand…a few sugarplum visions of blissful independence, a string of school night sleep-overs, and an unchaperoned party complete with boys danced around her head.

"Gee, Mom, what makes you think that's odd?"

———

That night, the house quiet, Maggie sat down and semi-composed her wishes and dreams into some long hard thoughts. She had told her daughter the truth earlier. She was not blind to her darling adolescent's rolling of the eyes, but never mind that. The point was Ireland. She wanted to go so bad, she could taste it. To put it into words…now there was another story.

Dreams. That was a start. She'd dreamed it in dreams. Maggie wrote slowly, capturing what fragments and wisps she could. But then it came. Flowing faster as her fingers tried to type onto the keyboard what began flooding her mind. It streamed from her consciousness like rivets of spring water cascading down the side of a mountain. Where exactly it was coming from, Maggie hadn't a clue. If it made sense, she figured it was a good start.

And so she read.

I've dreamed of it in dreams so long it has become a reality…one of visions and songs and tales spun during long dark nights. Ireland…the land of my forefathers and mothers. It calls me…the pipes beckon at night…during that time between wakefullness and sleep. Is it the land calling me back…or someone, something else?

I imagine the ship that brought my great-great grandparents over to the Americas…my great-grandfather, Danny Carroll, was a rogue, they say. In debt, a common criminal. What did he do to be banished from the land he loved? Had he a dream? What was his tale?

Did his leaving not of his own free will leave within me a legacy of longing…to go back, to finish something he left undone? Was he an outlaw as they say? Or was the Law of the Land the true villain?

This I know…my grandfather fought for freedom in his new home. It was said by some in the family that he joined the labor movement known as the Mollie Maguires and for good or evil, championed the rights of the working man in the coal mines of the Americas. He married my great grandmother, twenty years his junior, late in life and they had one child...my grandmother, Theresa Maria Carroll, and her one daughter, Margaret Theresa, had me.

I want to find my great-grandfather's roots, back there, in the Old Sod, and know his story. O Danny Boy...the pipes, the pipes are calling. They are calling me...

They sing to me at night, barely in a whisper at first, then louder...

> *O come back to Ireland...come back to me*
> *Come back to the green rolling hills and the sea...*
> *Come back to the music, come back to the dance...*
> *Come back to Ireland and me...*

It's my grandfather Danny's song, perhaps, as well as my own. It is not a mournful song. It speaks of hope that will not grieve for grief means all is lost. Send me to Ireland... it will fulfill the childhood dream I have not abandoned to adulthood.

> *May the magic of Ireland...summon me back*
> *Where mountain meets seaside...where present meets past*
> *Where my grandparents toiled and fought to be free*
> *Where my long ago love is yet waiting for me...*

Maggie stopped. She quickly read over her rantings. Not bad in a poetic sort of way. Her thoughts but all churned up, like butter, smooth and palatable. The travel agent ought to like the come back to Ireland part and the contest judge might look kindly on the mention of Danny Boy.

Folding the contest entry into thirds, she slipped it into the envelope and scrawled "**O'Carrick Traveling Tours...2222 Rockville Plaza...New York, New York**" on the front. Funny thing, a trip to Ireland by way of New York. Perhaps her own greatgrandfather's journey in reverse.

Talk about poetic justice.

Chapter Two

Coming Across:
Danny and Brigid's Story
Ireland, 1873

The stench in the bowels of the ship was ungodly. Danny would not have minded so much had there been a bit of air, or a ray of light. But the repetitive rocking of the mammoth vessel and the perpetual stink was a recipe for nausea. It was as sickening to his senses as the longing to be back home was to his soul. The only thing he held on to during the long days at sea was the thought of escape.

They'd dragged him, though bravely he'd fought them off. On the dusty roads for what must have been a day or two. Then into the city. Through the back alleys of Belfast, the British sergeant-at-arms collared him along, grunting as he shoved the blind-folded Danny along darkened paths.

They'd taken him, from his father's home as they'd finished Sunday tea. They'd hardly returned from church. He had heard little after they had rapped him cross the head. Mostly a loud ringing, louder than the bells at church the Sunday he and his mate, Jimmy Muldoon, skipped out of mass and hid in the belfry. But too, he'd heard Moire, his pregnant sister. Moire, screaming in the soldiers' stone faces, a-wagging her finger and demanding the gun toters release her brother at once.

Merciful Mary, they had the heart at least not to harm her. His wrists were still raw from the bindings used to cuff them together, his side still sore, bruised by the Englishman's gunpoint nudges. Despite his heartache, he smiled inwardly. Moire could be right cheeky at times. Wincing at his battle wounds, he said a silent prayer of thanks that the stern faced English blockhead with the musket must have a hysterical sister of his own back in London.

Danny wondered had Moire gone directly to Brigid after he'd been taken. She'd have been frantic, wondering what became of him. Both knew the risk Danny ran for his involvement in the war against the troubles. Arrest. Deportation. Hanging. Perhaps this was for the best. To be deported…rather than tried for his crimes as a Son.

Danny wasn't sure which was worse, but as far as he knew, there was no boat back from a trip to the gallows. At the very least, as a common criminal, he might return to Ireland some day. As a felon, convicted of crimes against England, he was a man without a country. Or worse yet, a man without a head.

But what of a man without his heart? He thought of Brigid Devlin. Would she wait for him? Would she know in her heart that he would be back as soon as he could? Danny Carroll feared little but the loss of the lass he'd loved. They'd spoken, softly, of the perils they might face, as young lovers so do, yet took little heed to make a pact. And her expecting a wedding and all, come the spring. A loud sigh escaped his lips.

"Ah, Brigid, might ye think of your rebel kindly. May I be back home and in your arms before the heather blooms."

———

He gathered from his shipboard mates they were sailing for the Americas, just out of Belfast. The *Hibernia*, with one hundred and fifty souls on the decks and below, was bound for Port of Philadelphia. It was October in the Year of Our Lord, 1873. The creaking sound of the vessel gave rise to the sneaking suspicion that its seaworthiness was questionable.

Judging from the look of a few of his fellow passengers, so were some of their morals. Danny glanced around the dark cavernous expanse of the wooden ship. He was among the best…and the worst…

Erin had to offer. Rebels, thieves, and debtors mingled with poor men, spinsters, simple maids, newlyweds…and unlucky lads like himself. In the darkness of steerage, it was hard to tell the good from the bad.

Not that it mattered. *The Hibernia* carried human cargo in its lower decks. Passage was cheap. The upper decks were reserved for a few select passengers—tourists sailing home from a European tour, businessmen traveling abroad. In its cargo hold lay a shipment of Irish linens and laces bound for market in Philadelphia and New York City.

The voyage was to take five weeks but to Danny, it seemed like five years. Day turned to night and night day. Late October was leaning past hurricane season, and despite rough seas, they'd yet to encounter truly ill weather.

The "dirty Irish," as those in the steerage were called, occasionally bribed their way to the take in the clean air of the decks. Generally, it was a pretty fresh faced lassie making promises to a deck hand who managed the feat. Once, Danny bartered to swab decks, just for a bit of sunshine. Afterward, he relished the memory of salt stinging his face and sea air in his lungs for the rest of the journey.

He replayed the events of the past several weeks in his head often. Brigid's scent was still in his nostrils, as if it were just moments ago, not weeks ago, since he'd breathed her in. The last time they were together, the morning after Mass, he'd been so cocksure of himself. Telling her he'd a surprise, flaunting their love before God and the Fates.

He had found the gold coins almost by accident that night, on the way home from a meeting with the Sons. They had set fire to the barns of an English landlord in Derrydown but it had taken longer than expected because the Sons had cleared the livestock out before tossing in the torch. Wandering home through the early morning mists, he had gotten a bit disoriented. Ah, but then, he'd seen the gold, in front of him like the beacon of a lighthouse in the night. He'd thought it the answer to his prayers.

There was enough to pay off the farm, to repair the cottage, to restock the herds of sheep and goats that dwindled as the Famine's hunger grew in their bellies and shattered their lives. Enough to buy

Brigid a bauble or two, and a real gold wedding circlet for her finger. He was thanking God for his good fortune, when, as quickly as they were in his hands, the coins were gone.

Danny's memory went as foggy as an old man's when he tried to recall finding the treasure or remember how he'd lost it. The glint of the gold filled his mind's eye. The vagueness only surrounded the event, an amnesia of sorts. He'd been so happy, ready to surprise Brigid with the news…then, something happened. The money was suddenly gone and he was home in his family's cottage getting ready for Sunday Mass. No sooner had they returned from Mass than the British soldiers were at the door, accusing him of debts unpaid, and marshaling him away…

Perhaps it was the sergeant's giving him that rap upside the head that had Danny forgetting. If it were a concussion, his memory would return. He only wished he could forget the pain of his losses as easily as circumstances surrounding the mysteriously misplaced gold coins. He was not sure how he could bear it. In that moment, Danny thought he might go daft with longing for his home and family.

Yet, as life tends to surprise itself by flourishing in the deepest and darkest of places, indeed life went on around Danny. He could not help but take notice that it did not even skip a beat. The brisk upper class activity on the main deck had little to do with the happenings in steerage below.

A babe was born to a woman from Belfast on her way to Philadelphia to meet her husband who'd found work on the docks. Couples made love, silently, beneath rough blankets, as others doing the same, pretended not to see. Thankfully, despite the stench and dysentery, no one died.

For the Irish onboard the aging vessel, leaving their homeland in varying degrees of destitution, dishonor, and disheartedness, the ship was a limbo from which they would emerge into a new life. They prayed it would be a better one. Some immigrants to the New World would make their fortunes, others meet their fate. There were no soldiers to stop them, no hunger to weaken them, no barriers to hold them back. In the middle of an ocean, courtesy of the dark backdrop of steerage, they could dream all the bright, shining dreams they wished.

Tears were shed, stories shared, futures foretold. For some, the journey was an escape from the famine. For others, it was an unwelcome exodus from home, friends, and family. Hatreds formed, but so did the bonds of friendship. Both energies had the potential to last a lifetime. Some wouldn't but many would.

The weather had been stormy since the voyage began. Young Danny's heart ached. For his family…for his beloved Brigid…for their wedding that was not to be. For his farm, passed down through generations, tilled with the blood and sweat of his father and his father's father before him. For Ireland. Daniel Charles Carroll loved Ireland with a passion in his soul. Anger burned deep for what had been done to him and his.

"What did *you* do, lad, to earn passage on this fine vessel?"

His melancholy thoughts interrupted, Danny turned his head to take in the thin dark Irishman, watching him intently from the shadows. The man leaned against a wooden beam.

"'Tis more like what I didna' do than what I did. The Queen's Lads liked me little enough before…when I could make not the mortgage on the farm, well…" Danny laughed. "Ye might say I gave them good and plenty cause to want to be rid of me. I seem to have found myself on this one-way barge bound for Hades with no more than me wits and me skin."

Despite the stench, Danny managed to grin. He had no reason to be unpleasant but he saw no purpose in divulging to this stranger any information that wasn't necessary. There were those about who made it their business to start mischief. Turncoats were not uncommon in rebel circles. Danny had learned early the dangers of a loose tongue.

The dark man grinned back. "Ye be not alone, lad. There be more of us than not the bloody Brits have reason to deport. If God can not bless them, then may He rest their souls." He hesitated, surveying the surroundings before continuing. "Then, Lad, what say you? Are you one of us?"

"It takes a Son to know one, does it not?"

For a moment, both men said nothing. The silence spoke volumes. The tall man nodded silently. Danny returned the wordless tip of the head.

The code was unmistakably clear. To those who were the Sons of Mollies, the secret lay in silence. The organization lacked numbers, but not brains. One of the most impenetrable things about the Sons was their invisibility to the British eye. A ragtag Irish rebel was difficult to distinguish from a group of ragtag Irish farmers.

The English found out quick enough they could rattle the solidarity of the Irish with an occasional traitor or two. But winning over a few sniveling weaklings was a far cry from winning the war. The fortress of Irish patriotism ran deep. Its roots fed a network of resistance the Brits would be only so happy to ferret out. Danny would keep his own council until he knew his new acquaintance with greater certainty.

The boy's sense of self-preservation heightened. His pulse quickened, eyes darted about, scanning the immediate area for anyone looking overly anxious to eavesdrop. A baby wailed in a distant dark corner, far to the stern of the ship. Time seemed to suspend itself for a moment, unspoken questions hanging heavy in the stagnant air. Then, the older man continued, softly but with an urgency of purpose.

"This is not my first trip, lad, nor my last. Know ye, there is a need for silence on both sides of the water. Oppression makes as heavy a weight in America as it does in Ireland. "

"You speak in riddles."

"I speak the truth. Can you handle more?"

Danny's interest was spiked but his trust was wary. English spies were plentiful, though not oft found in the bowels of steerage. "It takes a Son to know a Son. Mayhaps the truth would be more palatable if I knew who was serving it up."

The older Irishman smiled in amusement. Danny noted it, adding a disclaimer.

"With all due respect, Mate."

"I'm a stranger to ye, Daniel Charles Carroll, though ye be not one to me."

Danny registered silent surprise by raising an eyebrow but let the other man continue.

"The bodymaster at Ballycraig spoke to me of ye. Perhaps 'tis better, in times like ours, to have a care." He extended a hand. "Patrick Doolin."

"And, so, Patrick Doolin." Danny returned the shake firmly. "Since ye spoke my name as plain as me sainted mother who gave it to me, I'll not be repeatin' it in the way of introduction. What are you about?"

Patrick Doolin told him. The two men settled into a heated discussion that lasted until past midnight. It passed the time as well as anything aboard the great ship. The *Hibernia* rocked in the turbulent, October seas as the two men hunched together.

The huge cavity of the old ship echoed its occupants last whispered murmurs before sleep. Still, the two men remained deep in conversation. In the eerily peaceful silence of an immigrant ship fleeing famine, a deal was struck between the Irishmen. A partnership borne out of a love of Ireland, forged in hatred of English tyranny. Neither realized it would last a lifetime.

Brigid Devlin knew something was wrong when Danny didn't arrive by late Sabbath afternoon. She had not heard from him since Mass. These were dark days. Enough gossip had been heard in the village of late to know that the English were hell bent on collecting what was due them. She breathed a silent prayer. They'd never had enough on Danny to bring forth charges on his rebel activities. Dear God Above, she prayed that they had not enough now or ever.

She and Danny were betrothed, to wed the month next. She'd her mother's veil to wear, though not a dress. Fine trappings, though fine they be, were not important to the girl. It would be enough to be Danny's wife. He'd lost so much. The Hunger had cost them all dear, but the Carrolls had lost more than most. His mother, gone, wasted away, her eyes vacant even before she had passed over…his father, left with a bitter taste that turned him to the drink, leaving Danny to keep the farm going. Every month, Danny had dutifully paid the mortgage on the property.

The Troubles, the Hunger…someday Ireland's suffering would pass. They must have hope. For when things got better, Danny told her, the Carroll farm would be there for them. Some days, as Danny walked her home in the twilight, spinning tales of their future with the thread of their dreams, he would talk of the farm lovingly.

It would be theirs, he swore, and their children's after them. Free and clear of English taint. The day would come when Ireland would be free. On those nights when he was most impassioned in his speech, she knew he would be soon off with those who were fighting for that freedom in secret.

Danny never told her what the secret society did...for her protection, he said. It did not take much for her to guess, even without the Sight. She was Irish and female. She did not need to be told the obvious. Those nights, Brigid prayed a little longer and harder, saying the Rosary twice and asking the Blessed Virgin for Intercession.

A sense of dread built in her as the hour passed. She held her needle tightly like it was the crucifix of her wooden beads, willing her unspoken prayers to bring him to the door of the cottage safe and whole. 'Twere not like Danny. He should be here by now, teasing her ma and claiming to be still hungry though the dishes were not yet washed from Sunday tea.

Brigid busied herself with her needlepoint. Linen and lace for her hope chest. She'd been hoping to marry Danny Carroll since she was a wee lass. The thought of him always made her smile. Danny would call the tablecloth she was embellishing woman's foolishness. He cared more for a well turned leg of mutton than a frilly piece of fancy to cover a table but she knew he would sweetly humor her feminine touches.

They'd met after Mass just that morning, hurriedly sneaking off from their families for a clandestine moment. Danny had embraced her, in the back of the Sacristy while Father Boylan greeted the congregation leaving church by the front door. Laughingly, she'd pushed him away.

"If you shan't have me now then shall I come a-courting later, Miss Devlin? Say after tea when the tables must be cleared and the dishes washed? I shall spirit you away, I swear I shall, from your toil and woe! I have something to tell you...news, wonderful news."

Then, they kissed. Brigid was left with more than dishes on her mind when her family left church for the walk home. She was sixteen years old. Her father said these days her virginity was all a poor lass in Ireland had to offer as dowry. In that case, Brigid figured to hold on to all her cards until it was time to play them.

"No and keep those serpent hands to yourself, Daniel Charles Carroll. A married man and woman we will be a fortnight hence and *then* we'll see about those hands." The red-haired girl grabbed her betrothed and joyfully spun them round in a makeshift reel. When they stopped, she leaned up and into him with a full kiss on the lips.

"Oh, Danny, my love. Window shopping is better than naught." She had teased and winked at him. He had to chase her down the path until she'd let him catch her so they could kiss again. He'd been so excited with his news but had never told her. She didn't know what it was and now he was late.

Perhaps she'd never know. A tear caught in the corner of her eye before inching down her cheek. Something was wrong. Terribly wrong. Her fears gnawed with a vengeance, causing her tea to turn in her stomach like bile. It was happening and she was powerless to stop it.

The afternoon sun was setting when she heard the rapid knock at the cottage door. Her fingers were raw from the needlepoint she had kept at the whole afternoon. She had sewed as she chanted Hail Mary's and Glory Be's for hours. Silent prayers that her fears would be wrong.

It was Moire, pregnant and crying, with her big strapping lad of a husband, Gerald, in tow. The world began to spin in slow motion shortly after Moire started to tell her about Danny's capture. It was still spinning as Moire fixed her strong tea in between sobs and words of anger. Brigid's heart sank with the sun. There were no words to console her.

She would not see him again. So they were true, the dreams. Moire would not hear of it, but Brigid's own ma knew the Sight well enough and did not try to offer Brigid false hope. 'Twas a curse. She herself had dreamed Brigid's grandfather had gone over the side of his fishing boat a month before it happened.

Brigid, her youth optimistic, had scoffed at the dreams that plagued her the winter past. Refusing to...not wanting to believe they were true. Yet they'd crept into her sleep like vapors beneath a door.

Dreams…troubled dreams where she awoke in a sweat, with her heart pounding and pulse racing. She was running at nightfall, along the beach at Ballycraig. Down near the rocks where the selties come to sun with their young. Running and screaming. Even in her waking state, she could feel her throat seared with the harshness of her screams.

Her screams were the same every night. Over and over. Screams for Danny. Danny lost.

Brigid sighed. It was the Sight.

One could not run from it. The Sight was not uncommon in the Devlin women. It did not show in all of them and it rarely, if ever, had shown in the Devlin men. Brigid had prayed it was wrong, but it was happening. She knew it to be so. Daniel would not come back. In her visions, she saw the boat, its massive wooden hull. She could feel the weight of it, crammed with poor Irish, all of them dreaming of a fate better than the one they were dealt from their homeland.

"Brigid, are you listening…the Sons are meeting…tonight. They'll get him home again. Ye'll see…"

Brigid did see. All too clearly and that which Moire knew nothing about. She saw Daniel leave Ireland's shore. He would not perish. No, he would love her always and she him. She prayed to her patron saint, Brigid, for strength and to God to keep Danny safe.

But she knew better than to pray for him to come back to her. The Sight was clear in that. Brigid Devlin and Daniel Carroll would never meet again on God's green earth, neither in Ireland or the Americas. Their circle would stay open until another time and place. This much she knew to be so but no more. By God's will, their blood would pass on, but not together blend. Not in their lifetime.

Chapter Three

A Match Made

"Galen, what do you think of this one?"

The January chill had set into the pavements of New York City. Everything was frigid and gray, except for the mixture of subway steam seeping through the grates intertwining with the thick chemical warmth of exhaust from a thousand idling cars. The gases rose up like the mists over the Moy. Galen, looking down from the O'Carrick Manhattan offices, thought it looked as if a giant dragon might emerge from the whiteness and fly up and away amidst the skyscrapers.

"Must I?"

Galen was sorely feeling the effects of his vacation. He'd dallied in Ireland far too long. There'd been comfort in the simplicity of life back home that soothed his urban nerves. Galen had been in New York the day the Trade Center had been toppled. Living in war-torn Ireland all his life had not prepared him for the devastation thrust upon the Americans and the rest of the sane world. It was an act of cowardice, not of war.

Galen felt blessed to have been able to embrace his mother and shake his father's hand. By the Grace of God, his office had been far enough away that he and his co-workers had never been in immediate danger. Still, had Mattie's company been bigger, more prestigious…enough to have warranted an office in one of the Trade Centers…

Galen shook off the thought. Home, family, love…these were the important things in life. September 11th had taught the world that. And here he sat, reading some of the most ridiculous testimonies to idiocy he'd ever had the privilege. If only he could find one with some heart, some sentiment of nostalgia for his homeland.

"It's not another…'I believe I am the reincarnation of an Irish druidess and your contest will reunite me with my blood roots' one, is it? I'm fresh out of patience for another of those, love."

Galen's secretary, or as Martha liked to call herself, his "administrative persistence," pretended to swoon.

"You be watchin' that love stuff, you Patsy gigilo, or I'll sic Big Nate on you." Martha was 58, black as coffee, and happily married. "What happened to all them fair Irish lasses you keep tellin' me about? I thought your mama would have you married off this trip for sure."

"I told you, Martha, I'm waiting for you to divorce Nate. I shall never be happy with another."

The big woman pretended to flush with embarrassment, fanning herself with her diamond studded hand. "Honey, you couldn't afford the likes of me! Now, get that cute little tush over here, and look at this one. I'm not foolin'. This one came by snail mail but I downloaded it to make it easier to work with."

Galen bent over the monitor. The web site had been flooded with the usual number of boring, ridiculous, pornographic, and downright stupid contest entries. The downside of these things was that somebody actually had to read the lot of them and separate the garbage from the glitter. That would be Martha's job. She was damn good at it, too.

Somewhere in the middle of the stream of email after email, Martha somehow came up with enough good ones to make it turn out to be a real contest. Galen rued the day he would have to survive the New York corporate jungle without the stoic Martha by his side. He'd inherited Martha from Mattie.

Now that Mattie practiced management by cell phone, spending only a fourth of his time in the Manhattan office, he'd streamlined his entourage to include only his personal assistant, Theresa McKenzie, and her husband, Mattie's body guard, Frank. Frank, an ex-Marine, had been in Nam with Mattie. Mattie liked to refer to Frank and Theresa as his two man reconnaissance team.

Galen liked to read the first paragraph and let it gel for a minute. If it still had his attention, he'd finish the piece. He read the sentences once, then again, before walking away to stare out the window once more.

I've dreamed of it in dreams so long it has become a reality...one of visions and songs and tales spun during long dark nights. Ireland...the land of my forefathers and mothers. It calls me...the pipes beckon at night...during that time between wakefulness and sleep. Is it the land calling me back...or someone, something else?

Galen rubbed his right temple. He always rubbed his temples when he made a decision. Martha smiled. She *knew* it would get him, would have bet money on it. Galen Devlin was a sucker for romance, whether he knew it or not.

"Told you."

"Martha, you are a smarty pants."

"Yeah, well, tell me somethin' I don't know. Get on over here and keep readin' so I can go home tonight. Big Nate's planned me a late night love feast and Big Nate don't wait. It's our fifteenth anniversary tomorrow."

"Congratulations, Martha. Why don't you take off and I'll lock up? This one looks like a possible keeper...I'll finish it and print out a hard copy if I decide it's in the final ten."

"Deal."

Martha, for all her size twenty-two, moved like the wind when it involved an early quit. She was gone before Galen had even sat back down at terminal of the Dell. Galen swore the papers on the secretary's desk rearranged themselves into neatly piled stacks as she swooshed by. Mattie O'Carrick surrounded himself with the only a few trusted and loyal employees, but he prided himself on the fact that they were the best.

This I know...my grandfather fought for freedom in his new home. He joined the labor movement known as the Mollie Maguires and for good or evil, championed the rights of the working man in the coal mines of the Americas. He married my great grandmother, twenty years his junior, late in life and they had one child...my grandmother, Theresa Marie Carroll, and her one daughter, Margaret Theresa, had me.

I want to find my great-grandfather's roots, back there, in the Old Sod. O Danny Boy...the pipes, the pipes are calling. They are calling me...

They sing to me at night, barely in a whisper at first, then louder...

O come back to Ireland...come back to me
Come back to the green rolling hills and the sea...
Come back to the music, come back to the dance...
Come back to Ireland and me...

It's my great grandfather Danny's song, perhaps, as well as my own. It is not a mournful song. It speaks of hope that will not grieve for grief means all is lost. Send me to Ireland... it will fulfill the childhood dream I have not abandoned to adulthood

Galen felt a chill go cold down his back as he read the words over and over. He wanted to call the piece sappy and over sentimental, but he couldn't. Its pure and simple yearning shone through. This lass really wanted to go to Ireland. He felt the tug, the same invisible tug she was describing, that stretched across the Atlantic and pulled at his gut.

No matter where he was, whether in the States or on the Continent, the string that attached him to his land and his roots was there. He could not sever it if he wanted to. He'd heard the same of so many ex-patriots like himself, who for love or money, trekked across and stayed for a year, ten years, a lifetime.

Generations later, from what this woman wrote, the tug was still there. Galen had read about soul mates once. He'd never been in love, not truly, not madly, like in the movies. But the book, written by an American astrologer named Linda something or other, talked about a silver cord that links the souls of those fated to be together. The Irish must have something akin to it that drew them home.

Perhaps it was the manner in which so many left during the famine, exiled not of their own accord, but to escape the crushing hunger, imprisonment, or even death. The Irish often left making light of their leaving, taking with them little more than the clothes on their backs and the songs in their hearts. But Galen knew better. He knew from the heart wrenching stories of those generations left behind, that no Irishman or woman left Ireland without leaving a piece of their heart.

Perhaps that having to but not wanting to go made the difference. Maybe from it grew the invisible glimmering cord that spanned the ocean and kept families, generation after generation, linked.

Galen highlighted the entire entry and pressed print. As he scooped up the hard copy to lay it on Martha's perpetually tidy desk, he noticed the name of the writer. Maggie Carroll, 555 Railroad Street, Greenville, Pennsylvania, USA.

Well, Maggie Carroll, you've made it to the final 10. With a self-satisfied feeling he couldn't explain or shake, Galen carefully put the two page copy of Maggie Carroll's poignant plea on the pile with the neon green stickie marked "CONTEST."

The twilight had already begun to settle over the city when Galen put on his overcoat to head home. In Ireland, the night fires would already have been burning for several hours. His mother and da already settling in to listen to the news. Galen wondered would he ever find anyone to settle alongside him for the nightly news. It must be a peaceful feeling to have that kind of compatibility and comfort with another person.

As he stood huddled in the cold Manhattan night, flagging a taxi and wishing for a hot meal and a pint of Guinness, he thought of Maggie Carroll and what she might look like, what she might be doing tonight. Pennsylvania was far closer than Ballycraig. It was good to know kindred spirits were on both sides of the pond.

As the cab pulled over and Galen slid in, he decided that it might be a good idea to bring a few of the final contestants to New York, just to add some publicity to the mix. After all, the internet, while a wonderful tool for business purposes, could not replace the good old fashioned media for mass exposure.

He'd have Martha begin to make the arrangements tomorrow. Mattie would love it…he and the Heiress would make the front page of the *Times* and possibly the *Today Show*. Perhaps they should fly in the top five…an all expense paid trip to New York for the final decision and announcement of the grand prize winner. Galen felt the taste of success on his tongue and it tasted as fine as the best champagne he'd ever had.

———

"Mommmmm."

"Rosalie, I'm making supper. What?"

"There's an email for you from that tour place."

"Oh, Rosalie, it's probably some junk. Just get rid of it."

"No, Mom. It's from that Irish tour place. The one you entered the contest one. It says…Dear Ms. Carroll…We at O'Carrick Traveling Tours are pleased to announce that you have been selected as one of our top five finalists in our 'Pipes Are Callin'' Win a Trip to Ireland contest. A representative from our company will be calling you…"

"Rosalie…I can't hear you over the microwave." Maggie came into the study, drying her hands on the dish towel. "These blasted advertisements on the internet are worse than telemarketers. Just erase…"

Her daughter looked up. "Didn't you hear me? And you accuse me of not listening."

"Rosalie, get to the point."

"Mom, you are in the top five. Your entry is in the top five!"

Maggie couldn't speak. She stared skeptically at the screen, scrutinizing its contents, brow furrowed in a critic's expression. Rosalie, in her thirteen-year-old zeal, could have misread the email. They probably wanted her to buy some stupid subscription to something and she and a zillion other people were getting this "one-time offer." The internet had become a travesty of commercialism she was sure had never intended by its creators. She was trying her best to not get taken by cyberspace carpetbaggers.

Dear Mrs. Carroll...We at O'Carrick Traveling Tours are pleased to announce that you have been selected as one of our top five finalists in our "Pipes Are Callin'" Win a Trip to Ireland contest. A representative from our company will be calling you...

We assure you of the validity of this communication and request you reply immediately at www.ocarricktours.com. that you have received notification of your finalist status. Mr. Galen Devlin, vice-president of Promotional Operations at O'Carrick Traveling Tours, is personally handling the final details of the "Pipes Are Callin'" competition. Please direct your questions to him when he phones you next week. He will be discussing releases for publicity photos and stories.

Thank you for your interest in O'Carrick Traveling Tours and good luck!

Maggie reread it. Rosalie had made no mistake.

She felt a warm rush of pleasure that her work had received positive notice by others. Then she panicked.

"OhmygodRosaliewhatdoIdo?"

"*Mother...*"

Her daughter's tone was resigned. "Click on the reply box."

Chapter Four

Parted, 1874

Since Danny had arrived in the bustling Port of Philadelphia, he'd been in awe of this new world the Irish called "Amerikay." Off the boat, literally thrust into the street with no belongings and little more than his name, he was still in shock. America. No amount of stories brought home by travelers who'd made the round trip could have prepared him for this. Nor did his shipboard conversations with his newfound friend, Paddy Doolin.

If anything, Doolin spoke in tones as dark as his swarthy complexion, about the need for the good fight to go on here, as it had in Ireland. Danny was torn, for despite the noisy chaos and confusion he saw before him, there was hope in the faces of those around him. He'd listen and learn about his new home. For good or evil, he was stuck here.

And though he missed his family, and burned for Brigid to be in his arms, he knew he must make the best for now. Perhaps his captors had not realized they had given him a ticket to freedom he'd not otherwise have sought. He might not return to Ireland for God only knows how many long years. Those years he would make well spent. The day would come, God willing, that his captors would rue the day they trod on Daniel Charles Carroll.

———

"On your feet, Lad. The barge is off for Schuylkill County."

Danny awoke from a restless sleep where he'd dreamed of Brigid callin' to him, singing to him...pipes were calling. He quickly wiped wet eyes so Paddy Doolin would not see his pain. His back ached from leaning so long against the wooden shack where Doolin had told him to wait until he returned. Paddy had promised to see him to the little mining town in the hills of northeastern Pennsylvania, in the county of Schuylkill.

Doolin offered him a hand up.

"Ye'll see, Danny, it's like Erin herself...well, as close as ye can get on this side of the sea. County Schuylkill is green with trees and rollin' hills. And there's those of us there who have brought as much of Ireland as we could in a home away from home." Doolin paused. "But there's evil there, too."

The older man's voice became bitter and his hard words hushed, so that only Danny could hear the venom.

"The English are not the only ones who wish to keep the working class in their place. There are those, the mine owners and the rich, who will want yer blood, sweat and tears as much and even more than that for a hard day's work. They spit on the Irish as if we were bugs in the dirt, to be stepped on, our blood ground into the earth."

Then, as quickly as it had come, the shadow on Doolin's face passed. The sun came out again.

"Ah, well. Time enough for that, Laddy. The day is young, and life is short."

The pair boarded the barge that was teaming with other Irish, like themselves. The brogues and lilting words of their conversation, interspersed with Gaelic, rose up around Danny and Doolin. Danny thought to himself they could be in Ireland. The smells of unwashed bodies rose up too, however, reminding him of his long voyage over. How many of those around him were escaping the famine that was settling over Ireland like a plague of locusts?

Danny settled in, packed tight against the other Irish on the crowded barge. Doolin spoke of the rich, here in America, who were continuing to oppress the Irish. It was no different, then, here. He remembered well the English snobbery as they shrugged off the hunger of the starving

Irish as if 'twas no more than a melodrama. He'd fought to keep his lands, openly and as a hard-working farmer.

Then, as time passed and it became obvious that would do no good, he'd taken to joining with others, covertly. In the night, they unleashed the anger and pent up hostility towards the aristocratic English landlords, and some of the Irish ones, as well. Blood only ran so deep; greed and contempt ran deeper.

Danny, in desperation, became one of Molly's Sons, as they called themselves. Helpless in the light of day against the tyranny of the landowner, he and his "brothers" carried out retributive justice in the dark of night. Danny drew the line at murder, but he knew those who had willingly stepped over it. It had not been enough to save his farm. Protest didn't put food on the table nor did it pay the rent. His memory clouded.

But he almost had saved the farm...he remembered, almost dreamlike, stumbling home in the dark of the morning on the day he was arrested. He struggled to recall the events. It had been on the way to home...in the wee hours of that Sunday morning. The Sons had set afire the stable of Donegal's chief land holder, Lord George.

Danny smiled...he'd seen the horses freed first...no sense in killing good horseflesh. The Sons had watched from the dark of the forest, silently chuckling as the stocking-footed Lord and his stableboys chased fire-crazed brood mares through the muck and mire.

After it was safe to get away, he walked part way home with Malachi O'Neil, before they separated at Knock's Mount. Atop the knoll, before he'd have hit the cobble path for home, he remembered seeing the small man. It was as if he'd been cuffed about the ears. Danny's head hurt as he fought the desire to leave the stones unturned. It was like pushing through a thick fog trying to recall the specifics.

The little man had been busily counting coins, so many they were spilling through the stumpy fingers of his gnarled hands. Odd...Danny had thought...because even in the night, the man cast off a faint glow that illuminated him against the dark shadows. The glow had risen upwards against the night becoming morning, growing into the faint outline of a rainbow. Danny's headache worsened. Then he remembered.

He'd been bested.

Bloody, wee folk! No wonder he'd been in such a state the day he'd been arrested. He'd not a lick of sense about him, or perhaps he'd have been slick enough to evade his captors. The little man had put a glamour on him. Danny had bested him for his gold and the whiskered weasel had tricked him back!

Danny winced. He had the luxury now to remember everything. Exhilarated in the aftermath of the Mollies' arsonous escapade, Danny had snuck up on the leprechaun. The little man had been so engrossed in his gold, the last thing he'd expected was a stranger to happen by.

"Hallo!"

The four foot tall cobbler elf jumped up, turning around in mid-air. Grabbing at his crushkeen, he wielded the wooden staff at the much bigger man, shouting, "In the name of the Goddess Brigid, and all that's holy!"

Danny had laughed, plopping down on the grass beside the enraged fairy. "Settle down, Little Man, I've just left a great Lord acting like a lunatic...I've no patience left to see yet another!"

The elf had bowed down, introducing himself as Master Thomas Terrance O'Toole, resident of the shire thereabouts. Danny couldn't help but smile...the elf was trying hard to hide the gold coins by shoving them down every open crevice of clothing. The round bulges stood out against his tight weskit and he was sagging with the weight.

"Harrrump...well, glad to have met ye and all Lad, but 'tis off I must be going..."

"Wait one minute..."

Tommy Terrance O'Toole stopped in his tracks. His breath caught and he dared not take another. He thought he been stumbled on to by a dimwit farmer on his way home from a roll in the hay with some lass. Now, he wasn't so sure.

"As I see it, I caught you, fair and square as the cornerstone of St. Patrick's Abbey. You must give me yer gold, Master O'Toole. Lead me there and be quick of it."

The leprechaun had sputtered. His gold! Not his beautiful, shiny, pieces of gold. His brain struggled for a way out.

"You must best me at a riddle."

Danny's tired brain was just about thought out. But not quite. He considered all those riddles he had heard as a child. The fairy was sure to know all those and more. But wait...

There! Aye, he had it. Moistening his lips with his tongue, he waited. The elf's face grew relieved. A human, a clod-headed farmer, no less...beat a leprechaun such as he at a riddle game!

It was preposterous...

"When does the Farmer become the Wife and the Son become the Mother?"

Sweat broke out on the fairy's brow. Tommy was a leprechaun...he knew all the riddles. The farmer was supposed to think of some silly child's riddle...Tommy would answer it quickly before stumping the farmer with a riddle of his own. That was the rule. Finder first, fairy last.

"Come on, Master O'Toole... I'm waiting..."

The leprechaun was now perspiring profusely. He could not think of the answer. His shoulders slumped. He would not embarrass himself by trying to answer. He was bested.

"Do you concede, Sir Leprechaun?"

"I do."

Then, piqued that he did not know the answer, Tommy could no longer contain his curiosity.

"If ye do not mind, Lad...what say you the answer to the riddle?"

Danny laughed. "Why the Farmer becomes the Wife and the Son the Mother when an Irishman takes up the banner as one of the Sons of Molly."

"Ach! A good one! You have me there, Lad." The fairy sighed. "Come along. I'll take you to the rest of the gold."

Astonished by his good fortune, Danny had followed the little man, guided by the faint glow of his body and the iridescense of the rainbow rising into the trees and beyond. The pair had walked and walked. The sky was becoming pink as the sun prepared to rise over the mountain when Danny saw the treasure chest peaking out from under the roots of a large tree.

That was all he remembered until now.

The stinking little fairy had tricked him after all. Danny would have been a rich man. Now he simply felt a fool. A fool far away from his family and his true love. He sighed and cursed the leprechaun. For the want of a horse, the army was lost...groggy as a drunken man from the power of the elf's magic, he'd been an easy mark for the British soldiers that morning.

So, there it was, Danny thought, his attention coming back to his cramped location on the barge as it slowly made its way up the Schuylkill River. It weren't bad enough the English wanted him out of County Donegal...the fairies were even against him. Perhaps life in Pennsylvania was his draw of the cards. Danny stretched his legs and flexed his back.

"Hey, Doolin, tell me more about Silver Creek."

———

Danny squinted against the blackness of the mine. The rustling noises in the corner of the tiny shaft were company in the cold dankness. The sounds of life, rodent though they be, meant the air was good. Danny breathed in. At least he could inhale without charging it to the company store. There was little else a man could get for free. Danny was surprised the Reading Coal and Iron Company hadn't come up with a way to tack oxygen on to the never ending tab he'd run up at McGlintock's.

He'd yet to make enough wages to pay it off. Danny had a sneaky suspicion that was exactly what the Reading Company had in mind for them all. Without the skills of a full fledged miner, he was delegated a nipper, in charge of opening the massive wooden doors across the gangways.

Danny worked in the passageway they called "Mansion Row." All the massive corridors underground had fancy, hoity-toity names given to them by the roughened miners with tongues in cheek. He took his job seriously, for without the doors, there would be little ventilation and the increased risk of death to the entombed miners by the build up of the poisonous gases. The doors left in the fresh air and bad air was forced out.

Nipping was a lad's job, to be sure, not meant for a strapping man like himself. But until he could be "trusted," as the Welsh mine boss put it, there he would stay. Danny still bristled at the discriminatory remarks made to him the day he was hired on. The Irish were treated as dirty heathens by far too many in this new place. Land of the Free. Danny was beginning to wonder if his feet were any less free of British scum than in Ireland.

None the less, child's work or not, the gates were a dangerous place to be. If he did not open the doors in time for the barreling cart full of coal, he risked life and limb. Danny prided himself on his quick wit and nimbleness. A sharp ear didn't hurt either. He craned his neck to listen. The tunnel was quiet. No cars on the way.

In the dark, with only time and the occasional scurry of his rodent mates, Danny wondered what Brigid was doing. Had she forgotten him? He saw the glances of the lasses at church on Sunday at St. Patrick's. He'd been tempted to look back...but he'd made a promise to Brigid and he meant to keep it. He'd find a way home one day.

In the meantime, he thought about Doolin. The man had been a friend to him more than once since their arrival in Schuylkill County. Doolin had been after him to come to a meeting of the Hibernians in Tamaqua. Danny promised to introduce him to a chap by the name of James Carroll...perhaps, Doolin suggested, a distant cousin.

Danny thought about his family back in Ireland. His mother dead of a hunger of mind as well as body, resignation in her eyes long before her heart ceased to beat. His father, wasted in his prime, as much a victim of grog as his mother of starvation. Danny set his jaw in determination. He would never allow himself to be driven into the poverty of spirit to which his parents had succumbed. Danny wondered if his father had sobered up long enough to notice his only son had disappeared without a trace from Ballycraig. He prayed Brigid had not found the need to go to her father for help. She would find none from the town drunkard.

Danny was jarred from his thoughts by the low-pitched grumble of wheels on rail. It grew louder. Jumping to his feet, he threw open the wooden doors. Moments later, the coal-filled car barreled past him on its journey. Its clatter was deafening. Danny covered his ears until the racket began to fade in the distance.

He settled back against the wall, the blackness again taking over. His lantern bravely cast a dim light flickering shadows on the dirt walls. Dear God, he missed his Brigid. Their betrothal date had come and gone. He knew she'd have cried alone into her straw mattress. He would find his way back to her if it was the last thing he ever did. Anger against the injustice that had torn him from his love seared his gut. It was time to eat the meager contents of his pail—a crust of bread, a dipper full of water—but the rage he felt dulled his appetite.

Above the rustling of the rats, he heard another sound, this one louder. This deep in the earth, only humans made noise that loud. He strained to make out the direction the movement came from.

"Danny Carroll, it's Doolin."

A moment after the whisper, Doolin's face appeared in front of Danny, like an apparition. In the flickering kerosene lamp, the older man looked eerily skeletal. "Doolin. Is it scarin' a man you're after or did you smell my pail all the way over there on the other side of the vein?"

"Neither, lad, and I haven't time for chit chat. We're down a man tonight. Are you in?"

"Ah, Doolin, 'twill be a long night tonight. Tamaqua's a long way off. What say you next time?"

"But your man Jimmy Carroll is waitin' to meet you. Himself being the secretary of the order, and all. You two can catch up on long lost family over a pint after the meeting."

"I'm a deported Irish, Doolin. The last thing any cousin of mine needs is to welcome me into the fold!"

"Seriously. Come along, Danny. It'll help to take your mind off of Brigid and the farm."

"Alright, Doolin, but I'm driving the wagon."

———

The dark road made for quiet conversation. The two men spoke in tones hushed not by necessity, but out of respect for the silence. The night was chill already and it was barely past dusk. Danny shivered in his thin jacket. Pennsylvania may resemble the Irish countryside but its climate was a mite colder. The seasons were beginning to change.

"It's not that I do not appreciate the fight, Doolin. For God's sake, oppression by those who think themselves better is nothing new even for an Irishman just off the boat. Does it matter whether it be in Donegal or Schuylkill County? Poor is poor on both sides of the Atlantic."

A trace of bitterness hung on the last of his words. There would always be his betters. Here it was the coal barons and the mine bosses. In Ballycraig, it was his Lordship George and the ever vigilant British presence.

"Danny, your skills are needed."

"Doolin, I said no."

The older man looked at him. It was difficult to see his expression in the lantern light, but a hint of laughter shown in a crinkles at the corner of each eye. "Ah, and if every woman who said no to me meant it, I'd have been one unhappy man all me life."

"Doolin, if you told more lies than truth you'd be a lonely bachelor instead of a happily married man."

"Bested again. God, I'm no match for you. The organization needs a man of yer caliber. Quick wit and a tongue to go with it. Say you'll think about it, Lad."

"I'll think about it."

The wagon rounded a bend in the road between New Philadelphia and Tamaqua. Danny reigned in the horses. Thoughts of Brigid were stronger than ever. His clandestine activities, patriotic though they were, had cost him dearly. Alone, in a strange land, far away from all he knew and loved. Danny fought back the stinging of unshed tears. He would not cry.

"Doolin, it's too much to risk. I want to go home someday. Trouble would only make things worse. Do you understand?"

Patrick Doolin understood only too well. He nodded his head. Fate dealt the cards. It was up to each person to play the hand dealt.

Wordlessly, he reached for the reigns from his younger companion. Danny gave the leather straps over. The rest of the journey was made in silence, weighed down by thoughts too heavy to share and too disturbing to be put to rest.

"Did your mam come from Wicklow?"

The family talk commenced. The tavern owned by his possible cousin James Carroll was bright and warm. The chill of the evening left outside with the horses, Danny felt better. A mug of ale sat half finished. He was not a drinking man, but it was free and he was thirsty. His tongue loosed a peg. Jimmy, who was born in a little place called Packerton of Irish parents, had yet to produce a connection in the Carroll clan that linked the two, but Danny felt more at home than he had since leaving Ballycraig.

The tavern could have been McCormick's back home. Enough Irish graced the stools and long wooden tables to fool the senses into believing it, too. Accents thick with brogues, even the Irish speakers. Danny felt the alcohol relax his shoulders, stiff from the cramped positions he often was forced to assume in the tunnels below Silver Creek.

"Nay, she were from the valley right below us. The bog outside Ballycraig."

"Is she still living, Lad?"

Danny shook his head. He remembered his mam fairly well although she'd been gone five years at least. His mind flashed a picture of her in happier times, before her stomach had swelled with the famine bloat and her eyes darkened with approaching death. She had been a fine woman, ringlets of dark hair against pale, porcelain skin.

There had been one Christmastide…Da had put aside the whiskey and had a job in town at the smithy shop. Danny Carroll had seen his mother smile as his father had given her some trinket, a cheap broach of a jewelled harp. She had sang for them all…in Irish, of the Christ child born in faraway lands. As a boy, Danny had thought her an *angeel,* the gaelic word for angel. Her clear high voice rang out like a bell. Danny believed it must have touched heaven itself. Even though they had but a grouse on the table and only a few potatoes in the pot, Danny felt them rich beyond riches because they were among family. But that was long ago.

"Nay, me mam is gone. Da is alive, or was last I knew. Too pickled on his drink to die. He had a brother or two came over, but he never talked much of them. They were older than Da, I believe."

His cousin went back to bartending, leaving Danny alone again. Doolin was playing poker at a table in the back. No, he was not a drinking man, but companions brought a certain cheer he had not felt since Ireland. It was comforting to know, if God called you home, that someone would remember where you came from and perhaps see it marked on your stone when you were laid to rest.

Doolin had proved a loyal friend. He would see Brigid was sent a packet containing the silver cross Danny wore round his neck and whatever was left in his narrow pay packet once they planted him in a potter's grave.

A chill went up his spine. The spectre of never seeing her again was as frightening as that of his own mortality. Her freckled nose and endearing smile in the blush of youth. The ale loosed his reason. Perhaps he would not return until she was long married to another. Johnny Corrigan had given her more than one look. Fergus O"Rourke as well, as had many a lad he'd not caught in the act. Brigid was a comely lass.

Jealousy replaced fear. He'd have none of it. They'd been promised to each other for near their whole lives. What was left for him to do now? He began to feel anger rear up but something made him stop. Anger was tempting but unsatisfying. Faith. Faith would bring him strength and peace of mind. He needed to be strong of heart and spirit. All he had left to depend on save his own flesh and blood was his soul. Surely he'd been a good enough man to warrant God's blessings…

"Filthy egit…how dare you insult me…I'll rip yer bloody…"

A flash of red hair and arms flailing caught his eye before it flew past him like a banshee escaping daybreak. He was nearly knocked off the barstool. Spinning around, Danny looked straight into the enraged eyes of the saloon's barkeep. Funny, she'd been pleasant enough a few minutes ago. Danny looked about. The card players at Doolin's table were grinning sheepishly. The offensive party must be among them.

"Sorry. Friggin' egit accusin' me of shorting him change. Malachi Mahoney of all people. And himself not having a pot to pee in. Like I'm some common thief…"

Cheeks flushed with anger, Terra O'Donnell was in no mood for nonsense. Wiping her hands on her apron, she hesitated a moment before graciously extending one. Danny considered whether it was safe to return the gesture of friendship.

"Go on. I don' bite unless you deserve it. I'm Terra, short for Theresa, Marie O'Donnell, James' sister-in-law."

Danny grinned and took the girl's hand. It was warm. Terra, short for Theresa, smelled faintly of cinnamon and beer. Danny felt the rush of too many drinks and too many more lonely nights cloud his head. Friends were not easily come by in a place where you worked away the days in a hole as black as night. Brigid was far away. He longed for the touch of a woman. It could not hurt to socialize.

Terra Marie began to laugh, her voice cascading like tinkling bells, as she moved away from him, back to her duties. Danny followed her with his eyes. A session began to the left of the bar, in the common room. A lone fiddler was wordlessly joined by a young lad playing a tin whistle. Terra Marie suddenly threw down her apron and moved to the front of the room.

Positioning her feet at right angles, she paused only a moment to get her composure. Head raised, chin pointed, she rose on the toes of her worn shoes. Despite her drab peasant clothes and beleaguered surroundings, Danny thought she looked as regal as a Princess of Tara surveying her subjects. Only then, with shoulders straight and arms at her sides, did her feet begin to fly in a fast moving reel. Danny smiled and began to tap his foot.

The crowd began to clap wildly.

"She's a looker, cousin, is she not?"

Having made his rounds at the bar, James Carroll returned to the spot where he'd left Danny. No customer was left untended. He was proud of his establishment and skill as an innkeeper. Everyone had a drink in hand who wanted one. Although he was one of the few tavern keepers to have not mined himself, James had known the life underground only too well. Born in Pennsylvania, he'd watched his immigrant father and older brothers blacken their hands and their lungs enough to pay the family's dues.

James shivered with thanks. Ah! To relish the ease of a tavern keeper's life...to stop for a bit of banter with his cronies, or to help out his missus, Annie, now and then. James knew a luxury most of his customers rarely experienced. The mines took so much, sapping those who entered of their heart and soul.

"Aye, she is that, cousin."

Terra Marie's shoes began to clack in rhythm as she followed the musicians into a hard jig. Danny recognized the strains of "The Irish Washerwoman." Batter one...batter two...batter three...batter four, batter batter, hop back and hop back, two, three, four. The easy rhythm lulled him back to Ireland.

His sister, Moire, had stepdanced. Her hours of practice before a hoolie or parish picnic had driven them all crazy. Stepdancing kept the Irish culture going when the English bastards banned Catholic services and any form of ethnic celebration. The English soldiers often looked in the windows of a suspected gathering, only to see the stiff upper bodies of the dancers...never their flying feet.

James leaned in. "She's not taken. My missus' cousin. She's a good girl and a hard worker."

Danny thanked him with a smile but shook his head. "There's someone. Back home. We were to marry except for the objections of the British army." He half-grinned. "They decided I was too valuable an Irishman to waste away on a farm in Donegal. 'Twas off to the Americas for me."

Head down to hide the wetness filling his eyes, Danny was lonely and tempted more than he thought he could be. He allowed himself the luxury to think of Brigid. She would be waiting for him. He knew she would wait. Had they not made a promise?

Danny had another ale. The pleasant numbness rendered him immobile for a bit. His cousin James, taking advantage of a captive audience, was only too happy to supply him with an account of the affairs of the WBA—the Workingmen's Benevolant Asscociation. The AOH must support the mineworkers. And not just those who were Irish. The fight must be for all driven into poverty and destitution by unfair labor practices of the wealthy railmen and coal barons.

Where Doolin had not gotten through, James Carroll succeeded. As the tavern emptied and quieted, the gas lamps flickered long into the night with hushed conversation.

In the small hours of the morning, as he and Doolin made their way back to New Philadelphia, Danny understood. Things were no different here than in Ireland. His fight was not finished because he'd left the British behind. No sir. It was a new country but an old war. The English had torn him away from all he held dear. Danny felt a rage he had not felt in all his days fighting for a free Ireland. And in his rage, he saw an outlet for pain.

Once a Son of Molly, always a Son of Molly. And Molly's Sons always avenged their mother. Regardless of what side of the Atlantic she was calling home these days.

Danny blessed himself. Sweet Jesus, protect us.

———

Ballycraig. Ireland
May 04, 1874

Dearest Danny,
I hope that you get this. Kin of Malichi Malloy are sailing tomorrow and I am desperate to get word to you. I have heard you are settled in Pennsylvania near family of your father's. Bridey Malloy said she would find you when they get to the northeast somewhere near Scranton. I hope that it is somewhere near you.

I miss you so, Danny. We should be married by now. I walk the moors at night and stare out at the ocean. Sometimes in the glen...where we would go on

Sundays, you remember...I swear I can hear pipes in the distance. They say it is the ghosts of the soldiers long passed over, but I do not believe it, Danny. I think it is the echo of my heart crying with loneliness. The bagpipes cry for what should be, Danny. Father said you shan't be back. I hope him wrong though my secret fears tell me he is right.

The Troubles here never seem to cease. Red Shaunessey was badly beaten last Tuesday for setting fire to Lord George's stables again. I saw his mother at Church on Sunday and she said he is black and blue about the face but thinks he'll be alright. He is lucky not to have been shot. In some ways, it is a blessing to have you there. If ye were here, Danny, I fear they would have hung you by now.

Your father is well. He has taken up with the Widow Logan although I hear your sister is not so happy about it. The widow plans to move in...but not until your da has paid his dues. Rumor has it she told him in no uncertain terms that only if he stops the drink, will she marry him. 'Twould be good for him, Danny, I suppose. We're all hungry but she has enough for herself and a bit more. Times are hard here. But no more than there, I think. They say it is not any easier for the Irish in America.

Write me back soon, please. I fear you lost from me forever.

Listen for the pipes in the glen, Danny.

All my love, darling Danny,
Your Brigid

———

September 12, 1874
Ballycraig, Ireland

Dearest Danny,
I thought you would have written me. Prayed you would have written by now. Not even your sister has heard but a word of you. Declan Flannery and his wife, Julia, are sailing from Liverpool next Tuesday and promise to give this to you if they find you. They are not going to Pennsylvania but to the Port of New York. It is not too far from where you may be, I think.

Did not you get my letters? Summer is passing...all the flowers dying. I walk along the cliffs and look out across the sea. I close my eyes, and wish, wish, wish so hard that I feel the sting of the tears against my cheeks where it mixes with the salt spray. I can see your face as if it were yesterday when we walked together. Do you not think of me, Danny? Why have you not written me?

Father is ill, Danny. He cannot keep up the farm. Mother is no good to any of us...she simply cries into her handkerchief. Perhaps if you were here, well, it would be different. You could help me keep things going. But, Danny, I don't know what to do. I still hear the pipes, Danny. Calling you to come home. We need you, dearest Danny. I need you. We are all so hungry. There is nothing to eat except roots and berries. All the animals have been eaten a long while ago.

It will be a miracle if we get through the winter.

Please, Dear God, let this reach you. I know you are not dead. I would know. But Danny...Fergus O'Rourke has asked Father for my hand. Dear God, Danny...if you do not come home soon, Father swears he will tell Fergus yes. But come ye back by summer, Danny...aye, and it shall be us wed in the meadow. All would be well...

The roses are fallen at the far end of the garden, Danny. Winter is coming early. I am cold inside and out. I thought I could be strong and accept Fate but I am not strong. I swore to God if he sent you back, I would do anything. Anything...but he has listened not to my pleas.

I shall bide my time as long as I can.

All my love,
Your Brigid

———

January 19, 1875
Ballycraig, Ireland

My dear brother Daniel,
Oh, Danny! We do so long for you here in Ballycraig! The Widow Logan has married Father. You would not believe it, Danny, but he is sober as a judge. Funny, it is, how money changes a person. He is no different in temperament, but methinks he has met his match in the widow. Ma just smiled and let him have his head. The widow will have his head alright...on a silver platter...and Da knows it.

Perhaps you will get this letter for I know poor Brigid's have gone unanswered. Are you alive or dead? Brigid says, nay, not dead...for she fancies herself with the Sight, and knowing the Devlins, who am I to argue? But, Danny, why have you not written us to let us know where you are?

Now that Da and the widow are all legally married and that, well, honestly, we are a little better off. 'Tis only for her generosity that we have a bit more than others. I lost the wee bairn I was carrying when you left. There was no food for the longest time...

Gerald was shot in a skirmish with the English two months after the bloody soldiers took you. He could hunt not nor go out on the boats so he was for England to work in the factories. He sends what money he can, but the girls and I have so little. We get by.

Brigid's family is worse off than us, by a long shot. Her pa is ill and her ma worthless for the grief of it. She does not seem to get over the fact that Mr. Devlin is not himself. Brigid has been by as often as she can, Danny. Mayhaps it not my place to say, being your sister and all, but 'tis just this...

Her father has sworn he will give her hand to that blockhead, Fergus O'Rourke. Brigid is beside herself but her brothers have all gone to England. Her family cannot go on without the help of a strong man about the place.

Brigid loves you, Danny, but her heart has broken for you. Why do you not send for her? She thinks you have forgotten her. She swears you will never come back and she is lost. The bloody Sight again.

Where are you, Danny? Can you not find a way to come home? At least to let us know if you are living or dead. Come ye back, Danny! I fear if you do not return soon, Brigid will be forced to marry Fergus.

Dear brother...for the love of God will you not send word of yourself to us soon? May God bless you, wherever you are, be it on this side of heaven or the other. I post this at Noon from the docks of the frigate Brittania *on this 19th of January in the Year of Our Lord, 1875.*

Your loving Sister,
Moire

———

Danny often watched others leave the post with a parcel or a packet of letters. He received no communication from anyone. He sent none either. He must use a care these days. Brigid nor his family were never far from his thoughts but he could not think of home now. Danny Carroll remained a man existing outside his own country yet inside another. A man without much to lose had everything to gain.

It was hard to say at what point he had changed his mind about what freedom was. When he was in Ireland, he thought freedom was simply the ability to work one's land and provide for his family without fear of retribution or reprisal.

Working next to other Irish in the mines of Pennsylvania, alongside the blood, sweat, and tears of not only his own countryman but that of the sons of other homeland, Danny learned a new definition of the word freedom and new respect for this land called America. It was not enough to be free oneself. Freedom was for everyone. Black, white, red, yellow. Catholic or Protestant. Irish or German or Italian. It mattered not.

It was this realization that made him finally say yes to his cousin and to Doolin as well. Danny would help the fight for freedom in this imposed home away from home. He sensed this fight was as important, if not more important, than the one he had left behind in Ireland. But it was not for altruism alone, though he admittedly felt rather lofty in his newfound philosophy of enlightened thought.

Danny, in exchange for his "cooperation and participation in the assistance of said activities of the Ancient Order of Hibernians and other tasks as delegated by the Body Master" had found a way to earn his passage back to Ireland. Complete with new papers that would throw the British off his scent. Only then could he go home across the ocean to Ballycraig and Brigid.

The thought that he might fail at his task only briefly shadowed his thoughts.

This he knew. He would bring no more trouble on Brigid's family or his own. The price was too dear. He would return to Ireland with a clear name and a clean conscience. He would find a way to fight for the freedom of his countrymen that did not jeopardize his loved ones or the cause.

Or he would not return at all. Until then, it was best no one knew his business or his secrets. Not even those back home. Too much was at stake. He was just Danny Boy, a lad from near County Donegal. No one need know anymore or any less. It was best for all concerned. These were dark times but Danny knew in his heart of hearts that things would get blacker before the light.

Chapter Five

Kindred Spirits

Tommy O'Toole was in a quandary yet again. Downright puzzled as 'twere. In the event he were to live 100 more years he still would have to admit having not a clue about the fairer species…and he wasn't meaning the High Elves, muckety muck that *they* fancied themselves.

Women. It was a wonderment. How could a heart's desire stare one in the face and be denied?

Tommy had taken the utmost care in planning things exactly so. His very future depended on it. He was taking no chances whatsoever. A bit of selfishness really was at the heart of it. Queen Maeve was likely to pull out every whisker of his formidable beard if he botched things up again.

Tommy was rather fond of his beard, having grown it for these many long years. He gave it a little pet and a pat just to make sure it was safe and sound. But alas…even more than his fondness for his chinhairs, it was for love of his Lady. Missus O'Toole. Betsy…the fairest of all the lassies. When they were young…why, he was the envy of every bachelor in the fairy hills surrounding Ballycraig.

Tommy could practically feel his plump wife in his arms again. Tir Nan Og and the Missus were waiting. He had to figure something out.

Modern day American women were nothing like women in the Ireland of Brigid Carroll's day. Even today…why, any Irish woman worth her salt would have leaped on the chance to experience the trip of a lifetime. But nooooo. Not herself. Not Maggie Carroll. She was as thick as her bloody great-great grandfather.

And he was about as thick an Irishman as it got. It vexed Tommy to have made such a grave error of judgment about the lad, but who could have known the farm boy had such promise? Or have foreseen that he and his ladylove would be parted so tragically?

Tommy felt a twang of guilt. True, he and Betsy were apart, but being Immortals, their absence was just a tease to make the heart grow fonder. They would be together again. Tommy knew it in every fiber of his being. But Danny and Brigid…

The wizened old elf had a sudden flash of insight into the devilment he had done by meddling into the lives of two mortal young lovers. A tear worked its way down his face and dripped onto his hand. He would find a way to make it all work out. He couldn't help Danny and Brigid…God rest their souls…but he had a chance to help their descendants. By the Power of the New One God as well as the Old Ones, he would make amends.

But first, he sighed, one must deal with the formidable Maggie Carroll. Imagine…presented with the dream of a lifetime and she turns up her nose. Tommy Terrance O'Toole wasn't sure which he needed more…his magic or a sledge hammer to knock some sense into her feminine but nonetheless thick Irish skull.

———

"Mother! Phone!"

The voice of Maggie's oldest sounded like the shriek of a banshee especially when said banshee was annoyed. The phone not being for her was apparently justification enough for the teenager to be vexed. Maggie liked the word vexed.

It was such a pleasant alternative to the phrase "pissed off."

Come to think of it, she was a little vexed herself these days. As she reached over to pick up the cordless, she stopped to gently but firmly make crop circles with her neck. She felt every ounce of tension she'd been under the past week.

Dear God and at least one major saint…make it not be that annoying secretary from the advertising firm. Over the past week, she'd had just about enough of Mrs. Martha Jones from the offices of O'Carrick Traveling Tours. She barely got out her hello when the voice on the other end began talking.

"Yes, well...see here, Ms. Carroll...this is Galen Devlin from O'Carrick Tours. This is Ms. Maggie Carroll, is it not? My secretary hasn't been having much luck pinning you down, so we thought it best to just let me take a stab. Are you there?"

Maggie was there but momentarily speechless. She did not expect a deep male voice with an Irish accent to be on the other end. Galen Devlin? Her memory kicked in. Oh yeah...the guy who would be personally contacting her except he'd sicced his secretary on her instead. Well, it wouldn't much matter. She'd tell him the same thing she'd tried to tell Mrs. Jones.

"Mr. Devlin. I see. Well, what can I tell you that I haven't already told your secretary?"

"That you'll come to New York for the week leading into St. Patrick's Day. It's all set up for the finalists to appear on the *Today Show*. The winner will be chosen and the runners-up will receive a cash prize and a consolatory dinner at Brannigan's Irish Pub and Restaurant in the heart of Manhattan."

"I can't."

Galen took a deep breathe. Mattie had told him to always breathe in and count to ten before he went for the jugular. It prepared one for the bloodbath to follow. Five, six, seven. Wait a second...she said she couldn't. She was supposed to be *agreeing* with him...

"Did you hear me, Mr. Devlin? I simply cannot get away at this time. I have no one to watch my daughters. Surely, Mrs. Jones passed along that message."

Martha had but Galen didn't think she had been serious. Besides, he was not taking no for an answer. The foolish woman on the other end had gone so far as to tell Martha to just choose another name. Galen was having none of it. Dammit. Hers was the best in the contest. He refused to settle for another one of those ridiculous entries that crooned on and on about leprechauns and fairy hills. Leprechauns for Christ's sake. He bit his tongue again. Tactfulness being a virtue and all that.

"Ms. Carroll, now see here…you can't be serious about turning down the chance at an all expense paid trip to Ireland? I read your letter. It's your dream."

"So is selling off my songs and buying a castle on Erin's shores, but who's counting dreams abandoned?"

"I am, Ms. Carroll. Your entry was superb. It…" Galen hesitated. Was it really necessary to cajole this girl into this? Didn't an executive of his stature have better things to do than sweet talk some female from rural Pennsylvania foolish enough to walk away from something she'd wanted all her life?

"Mr. Devlin?"

Galen cleared his throat. He was suddenly uncomfortable despite the distance of a state between them. There was something too intimate about what she had written and how he had responded to it. He was glad this was a phone conversation and not a face to face one. "It touched me, Ms. Carroll."

The phone wires fell silent. Maggie didn't quite know how to respond to that one.

"Ms. Carroll? Are you there?"

"Yes." Maggie had to say something but her thoughts had gone all fuzzy. She'd lost her edge, dammit. He'd gone and thrown the proverbial curve ball.

"Mr. Devlin?"

"Yes, Ms. Carroll?"

"Why were you touched?"

"You reminded me of how it feels to be homesick. Melancholy. Just the right hint of bittersweetness. Like excellent dark chocolate."

Maggie tried valiantly to regain her composure. This guy was good. Seductive. Pretty words like thick sugar mixed with whiskey. She drank in the sound. Galen Devlin *talked* New York but his voice was 100% Irish. The lilt was there, suppressed by corporate culture and international travel, but there all the same.

If Maggie was a lady, she would have sworn she swooned. She sat down instead. Auditory pheromones. The equivalent of a ton of bricks. This guy had no idea what an Irish accent did to her. Hell, up until now *she* had no idea that an Irish accent would do that to her. Must be the close range.

Ah, hell, Maggie decided. A little swooning never hurt anybody.

Good thing this was a phone call and not a face to face. She was not prone to blushing but her face felt suspiciously warm. Maggie shrugged off the thick Fisherman's sweater she'd tossed on earlier due to a chill. *Okay now, stay focused on that marvelous voice...*

"Ms. Carroll, have I lost you?"

Maggie zoomed back to reality. A sexy voice and a half promise of a trip to Ireland didn't change a thing. Que sera sera.

"No, you haven't lost me." Maggie took a short breath in. "Mr. Devlin, the problem is not that I don't *want* to go to Ireland. The problem is that I can't *get* to New York."

Galen digested this. "It's only a few hours by car."

"That's true."

Licking his lips, Galen waited for her to buckle. A little Gaelic charm goes a long way. He'd learned that early on with the American tourists. Silence. It was a sure sign he'd won. Never be pushy, that was Galen's motto. Always let them think it's their idea.

"Well, there you go, then. We can move right along with things. Now, Martha, you remember Martha, my secretary? Well, she will..."

Maggie, on the other end, had digested just about enough of the Irishman's words. They were slowly rising in her throat and threatening to choke her. She decided she'd rather choke him instead.

He didn't get it. Conceited bastard. Charming, alas, but conceited. Maggie's intoxication with the man's voice was sobered by a hot flash of feminism. How *dare* he minimize this into the triviality of a transportation problem. Wasn't he listening?

She cleared her throat.

Galen already had his planner out, absentmindedly paging. He needed to schedule a meeting with the five semi-finalists no later than Thursday. There was publicity to arrange, a press conference, of course. Ms. Maggie Carroll had been the fly in the ointment. Mentally, he patted himself on the back for winning her over. God, he was good, wasn't he?

"Mr. Devlin, is it?"

"Yes, that's right."

"Mr. Devlin, I don't know any other way than to state this plainly. You have a lot of nerve. It is conceivable you are singlehandedly the most arrogant, condescending male I have yet to run into today." Maggie paused, her voice dripping with sarcasm. "Of course, it's early."

"But..."

"Don't but me. How dare you! Weren't you listening? Do you think for one minute I'd pass up a trip to Ireland for the sake of a two hour drive?" Maggie's voice rose an octave higher in an accusatory challenge. "*Do you?*"

She didn't wait for an answer, slamming down the phone instead.

Maggie felt her mood swing from annoyed to excited to attracted and back to annoyed. She hadn't felt this emotionally unsettled since emerging from the cocoon of adolescence. Except for the divorce, of course.

Her internal seawall was being battered by too many emotions at once. It had held back her tears from the eyes of the outside world but the storm finally took its toll. Maggie threw herself onto the bed and burst into sobs. It was all so unfair. And the worst unfairness of all was that Mr. Galen Devlin was right. She must be crazy to just give up something she'd wanted forever.

"Mommy? Are you ok?"

God, the girls had heard her. Maggie sat up and composed herself. She'd blown her chance to see Ireland but she wasn't going to blow it as a mother. She wiped her eyes. Her kids came first.

A knock followed.

"Mom, it's us, me and Rosalie. What's the matter?"

Drying her tears, Maggie took a second to reapply her smile before opening the door of her bedroom.

"Not a thing, girls. Everything's just fine."

She'd hung up on him. Well, imagine that.

Feeling a tad shell-shocked, Galen was left holding a dead phone in one hand and his Day Timer in the other. It had been a while since a female had hung up on him. He wanted to mumble how dare she and a few well placed swear words, but oddly, he didn't feel like it. Although he'd encountered a wild woman or two in New York City, he had yet to meet an American female whose temper was a match for even her meekest Irish counterpart.

Until today, that was.

In his analytical way, he critiqued the phone call. He'd certainly done something to piss her off. The state of being pissed off, as Mattie had taught him, was part of the mystique of the American woman.

Duh. What an ejit he was. He suddenly remembered what it was that had gotten her ire up and decided he ought to be ashamed of himself. Bingo! The beginning of their conversation. *That's* when she'd said it. She'd said she couldn't come because of her kids. It was the Mama Bear Syndrome. And he'd blown her off. Served him right she'd returned the swipe.

Galen accepted a hasty retreat. He may have lost the battle, but he planned on winning the war. It was only March 4th. He still had a few days before all the plans for the St. Patrick's Day contest finale needed to be completed. He'd arranged for all the contestants—except Maggie Carroll—to be in New York for a briefing this Thursday. Today was Monday.

Well, there was only one thing left to do, then, wasn't there?

He had to lasso this one and bring her in. Galen visualized himself roping her in like a feisty young filly. A little risqué for him in the fantasy department...and Maggie Carroll's contest entry made no secret—she was well past the filly stage. But by God, this woman was doing something to his hormones. He was starting to wonder...

Then, for some reason, his thoughts flashed to his dear mother back in Ballycraig. The cowboy fantasy vanished and he laughed out loud.

She reminded him of Ma. Galen smiled. Spitfires both. Leaning into the desk intercom, he decided he may as well take this bull by the horns. He should be annoyed, but he wasn't. For the first time, in a long time,

Galen instead felt a spark of excitement. He pooh-poohed it, blaming it on his enthusiasm for the project. Now that he knew what he was dealing with, Galen felt much better.

"Yes, Mr. Devlin."

"Martha, always the height of efficiency. I would like you to rent me a car, unlimited mileage."

"*Humph.* A car. You want *me* to rent *you* a car?"

"Martha, that's what I asked for."

"Going to drive down to Pennsylvania, aren't you? My, my, my, but she's got you sniffing around now, doesn't she?"

"Sniffing around? Martha, you have a filthy, dirty mind."

"You bet I do, Honey, and that's why you keep *me* around."

"Well, that and your phone skills."

"Smart ass white potato boy. Flattery will get you everywhere. Your car will be ready for tomorrow."

"Oh, and Martha... make it an SUV, won't you? I hear Pennsylvania has some bloody awful winter weather."

"Shazam! I was right...but it's a little short notice to be picayune, boss man. Could you have waited any longer to let me know?"

"I have every faith in your phone skills, Martha."

———

The little stooped over old man who was sitting in the waiting area of O'Carrick Traveling Tours, Manhattan Offices, had sat so quietly that even the big black woman who was presiding over the office like a Doberman hadn't seen him. Of course, it was partially because he was only 4 feet tall but also, as Tommy liked to think, because of his soft and stealthy step.

Despite his lofty age, Tommy prided himself on his balance and agility. He rarely had to dash away anymore. There was little need to escape the occasional human who chanced upon his gold treasure because Americans did not believe in Fairies. They liked to read of them and talk of them, but they did not believe well enough to make themselves rationally accept one could be right under their noses.

Even when one *was* right under their nose.

Americans seemed to be in a state of chronic cognitive disbelief. About pretty much everything. What a shame. Perhaps because nothing was a marvel to them anymore. Tsk, tsk.

"O'Carrick's Traveling Tours...exclusively Ireland. Martha here. How can I help you?"

Tommy heard the greeting again, and saw his opportunity. The Doberman was occupied with the phone. Slowly rising from his leather-cushioned seat, Tommy jauntily made his way past the front desk and down the hall. He was short enough to walk right past, so he did. The offices were not extraordinarily large. He peered into the first office on his right. Empty. Wrong door plate.

Tommy kept going. The next office was lit. Tommy saw he'd hit pay dirt.

Mr. Galen Devlin.

Brigid Devlin's great-great grandson. Tommy took a deep breath. Well, no time like the present. It was time he and young Galen Devlin had a little sit down.

Chapter Six

Fateful Encounters

Danny had fallen into regular habits living in the boarding house belonging to the O'Learys. Mrs. O'Leary was a good cook, and the company house kept up. As a bachelor, he required little. Wryly, he decided that was a damn good thing, since he had nothing. An immigrant Irish coal miner with naught more than the shirt on his back, and a good one for Sunday.

He should not have been surprised, yet he was, when he arrived at the house that last Thursday in May, 1875, covered in coal dust and found Mrs. O'Leary weeping on the side of the road. Her four-year-old daughter was clinging to her skirts and young Thomas, a ten-year-old breaker boy at the Colliery, was crying as well.

"Missus, where's Tom?" Danny bent down, and put a hand on the older woman's shoulder. She shook her head, never looking up.

Danny knew immediately what had happened. It was an all-too common occurrence these days since Captain Robert Linden had taken control of the Coal and Iron Police. They'd talked of it at meetings. The AOH was becoming more and more angered by the coal company's treatment of the miners and their families.

Jack Kehoe continued to urge the miners to fight back by supporting plans for a strike. But the poor immigrant miner, who'd come here for a better way, a better life was in some ways worse off than in the Old Country. At least family was there to fall back on...

But here, where there was no family, they had each other. They had the Ancient Order of Hibernians to stand for them. Brother for brother.

It was the code they followed. Never to let a brother in need…it was the oath by which they swore to abide.

The O'Learys were one of many who could not pay the rent. The family's belonging were strewn on the dusty street. Danny's own meager possessions were among them. Danny looked around. There it was—nailed to the front door. Indeed, the C & I's had paid a visit. The bastards left their calling card—an eviction notice. There was no sign of the police themselves.

"Ah, Danny, and Tom doesn't know yet…" The woman resumed weeping.

Tom O'Leary would be by soon enough. Danny had not seen him come up at the whistle, but then men often stopped by the tavern to wash down the coal dust before heading home. Danny hadn't foreseen this one.

He'd thought the couple safe, at least having enough room to take on a boarder. Danny paid little—$3 a week for bed and board—but on a paycheck of no more than $5 a week, it was a sizable chunk.

The minutes dragged on. Neighbors from the row of gray company housing began to gather and offer support. Danny knew the family would find a roof tonight, for they were well liked. But what of tomorrow, and the next day?

Danny, his now grubby Sunday shirt trailing from his back pocket, headed straight to Mike Madigan's to find Tom. His wife needed him. Besides, as Tom was a member of the AOH, Danny felt an obligation to alert the brothers to offer their aid and assistance. His heart went out to the family. Tom liked his beer, but he was a good lad. He didn't deserve this.

Danny walked quickly, in long strides, back up the dirt road, turning right onto an alley where Madigan's Dublin House was located. He found Tom O'Leary at the bar, draining the last of his ale. When Tom saw Danny's face, he knew instantly something was wrong.

The older man's face paled. "Dear God, man, what's wrong? Is it Peggy? Young Tom? Little Mary Ann?" Tom gripped the edge of the bar awaiting an answer.

":No, no, not that. But…"

Danny did not want to be the ill-bearing messenger, but had no choice. The man had to know. His family needed him. "The flying squadron, Tom."

Tom O'Leary's knees almost buckled then he closed his eyes, for a moment only, before making the sign of the cross. Danny steadied him.

"Dear Jesus, are Peggy and the children alright?"

"Aye. Shook up, crying, but not a hair on their heads out of place. The good Captain Linden must not have been riding with his gang of ghouls today. They were gone by the time I got there."

"The bastards come when we're still in the hole, when our women and children are defenseless." Tom's eyes were beginning to fire up and his voice become shrill. He looked around at the others. The quitting time crowd was in, beginning to rouse to the news of the O'Learys' eviction. Blackened faces began to show their angry reaction to the incident.

A voice rang out from a rear table. "*I* say we find the sons of bitches and show them what the Irish do to cowards who prey on women."

"Aye!" Another enraged voice joined in. "Haven't they done enough to us? We slave in the blackness and muck so Gowen and his like can live in luxury and leisure." A few jeers were heard in support. "Christ, then…why *then* they take back every penny and more they pay us for rent and tick at the company store."

Danny knew he had to do something before things got out of hand. Jack Kehoe never let those in the AOH's central core forget how important it was to fight the good fight. The Irish had a role to fill in this new country and the labor movement was a key item on the agenda. But Jack also reminded the men that violence begat violence.

"We must empower ourselves not only for the good of ourselves, but for all workers. Tyranny and oppression can only exist if they are supported and encouraged by the politicians and their backscratchers. If we allow ourselves to resort to violence it will weaken our forces not strengthen them."

Kehoe often spoke to his followers with wisdom and a quiet passion. He knew the Irish were a force to be reckoned with but they needed leadership. They needed to become a political force. "Black

Jack," as he was called due to his thick black beard and swarthy complexion, was destined for great things.

Danny knew he would make a fine leader at the state capitol. Currently magistrate in Girardville, Kehoe ran the Hibernian House. The tavern was a popular meeting place for the town's AOH society. Kehoe was well liked by neither the coal barons or the local gentry in Pottsville and its surroundings.

Ah, but he was adored by the working men. Ben O'Bannon, editor of the *Pottsville Standard*, lambasted Kehoe in his rag often. The joke at the bar was the politicians in the area knew if Kehoe ran, he'd win. The Irish vote in Schuylkill County was strong. It would not do to give it too much power.

It was well known among them that there were those who wanted to take Jack Kehoe down. Those in the Ancient Order had sworn to protect their political hopeful as best they could, but the men knew it was only a matter of time.

Danny knew Jack would not approve of a lynching or vigilante justice. The O'Learys' eviction was a travesty but had it not happened all over Ireland, to not one nor twenty, but hundreds of families? The difference here was that there was hope for a better tomorrow. Danny didn't know what to do, but he had to calm these men down before they did something foolish enough to jeopardize all their heads.

"Lads, listen up…Aye, Michael, 'tis the same sentiment that echos in me own heart…but we must think with our heads now, not our hearts. Tom, go to Peggy and the wee ones. The rest of us must help the O'Learys find a place to store their belongin's until they've found somewhere else to go. Peter, Cletus, and Andrew…won't ye go with Tom now, in case he runs into trouble?"

Danny barked out directives until he was hoarse but his take-charge attitude finally dispersed the crowd and gave them a productive outlet for their outrage. As things quieted, his own breathing began to slow…his anxiety lessened. He began the walk back home when he remembered… he had no home to go to anymore.

Being homeless, countryless even, made a man grateful for what he had. 'Twas a good thing the night was warm for May. Rolling up his good shirt into a pillow, he located a fine tree growing outside the widow Brennan's front door.

Propping himself up against the trunk, he cushioned his head with his makeshift pillow and slept until morning. He was so tired he didn't even dream of Brigid. He didn't wake until the sun was high in the sky.

The colliery whistle was blowing loud when Danny jarred himself awake. Disoriented at first, he remembered last night's events and realized where he was. His neck ached from his awkward sleep position. It was late. He began to feel anxious again. Had things remained calm during the night?

Jumping up, he ran breakspeed across town and up the long dirt road to the more populated section of New Philadelphia. Jackson Reed, a fellow miner's butty from the Silver Creek Mine, was walking up Pottsville Street. A meeting was scheduled today at quitting time. Danny figured he was cutting it close.

"Sweet Jesus, am I very late, Jackson? I slept on the ground…"

"Aye…yer not so late, but the first whistle already blew. I heard about the O'Learys…trouble's brewing. Can ye smell it?"

Danny could, and nodded his head. "I dispersed a crowd last night, wantin' the taste of blood. Jack Kehoe is going to need to have a meeting among all the Lodges. This tension is bringing out the worst in all of us. There's talk of a strike."

Jackson nodded. "Aye… and a strike is what we need. The mines can try to operate without us but production'll go down. I say hit 'em where it hurts."

Danny was careful not to agree or disagree. His mind's eye saw both sides of the argument. He knew a strike would mean things would get worse before better, yet without it, nothing would get better at all. The O'Learys were a perfect example. No matter how hard the family tried to improve their lot, they remained in debt. Now their home was lost, as well.

He hoped for all their sakes they'd find some direction at tonight's meeting. Perhaps then, he'd know how to cast his vote, should it come to that. A strike meant more hunger, more evictions. More families on the street. No better than in Ireland.

No… Danny decided…it was wrong to continue living and working in these condition intolerable for any man. Something had to change, or nothing would be any different. Then, it *would* be no better than Ireland.

As he entered the hole that morning, Danny decided he would vote for a strike, if a vote were called. Danny, now having worked his way from door tender to the butty of a miner named Charlie McManus, had seen first hand the atrocities inflicted by the mine owners on the immigrant population. Old men, young men, boys…all put their lives on the line to line somebody else's pockets.

He remembered the eloquent words of Jack Kehoe as he kept trying to rally them to action. *This is not Ireland…it is*, what had Black Jack called it, a *democracy. All those who are willing to become citizens will have the right to vote. And all those who vote have the right to govern.*

He called all of them to become naturalized. *It is through the power of government…the miracle of freedom of speech…that we Irish will break the tyranny that has followed us here from Ireland. We are Irish in America…become a citizen and we will be free Irish in America. Vote with me… together we will have the strength of numbers to make a difference.*

Danny was stirred by his words now and then. Black Jack was right. He missed home, and more so, now than ever, he longed to have Brigid by his side. But, here, not in Ireland. He would go back to Ireland only to bring Brigid back as his wife.

Here, they had a chance to change their lots in life. A strike would delay him returning to her, but unless he could provide her with a life here, she would be better off with her family. Danny longed to see her, hear her voice.

He'd tried to send word to her…in his limited penmanship he childishly printed… *"To Miss Brigid Devlin…Ballycraig, County Donegal, Ireland…I miss you…wait for me…your Daniel Carroll."*

The problem was there were few Irish returning to Ireland to give the letters to for delivery. The slow exodus out of Eire that had begun in the '40s was now a flood of emaciated Irish bodies pouring off the tall ships from Boston to Virginia. Those brave enough to risk a return trip were not of the most wholesome of character. Danny feared his scrawled notes probably ended up swimming in the Atlantic along with their bearers.

Someday Brigid would be among those whose gaunt pale faces survived the voyage and lived to tell of it. Danny said a half prayer that she was safe and well. He'd not heard from her either. Had he the means, he might consider sending over the money to sponsor her passage. At times like this, he wished he had a partner, a loved one to share his fears. But to bring her here, now, when times were so uncertain…

The tunnel darkened. The miners' idle chatter ceased as they eased with caution further into the depths of the caverns beneath the earth. Outside noises grew dim. The only lights were those of the men's lanterns as they marched to their areas in somber silence.

As Danny and Charlie McManus made the turn for their "street," as the miners called the current corridors they were working in, he silently said a prayer to the Blessed Virgin to watch over Brigid. He left it at that. The mines were black enough without sad thoughts and miseries. He jabbed the dark outline of a shoulder belonging to the light to his right before heading in his own direction.

"So, Seamus, Lad, you are going to the meeting tonight, are you not?"

"Aye, Danny Carroll, and 'tis a strike I'm after. The littlest O'Leary, Mary Anne took a fever last night. Poor Peggy is beside herself. Thank God, the widow Brennan took them in."

"Aye." It was all Danny could reply before disappearing into the darkness. He felt his own throat close and tears come to his eyes. For once, he was thankful for the velvety underground world where he could hide from the harsh realities of the daylight.

Chapter Seven

Turbulences and Troubles

The duties of a member of the Ancient Order of Hibernians were neither as arduous nor as extensive as Danny expected. Mostly, his tasks were hindered by the difficulties encountered in trying to organize a group with little else in common except poverty and their dubious status as Irish immigrants.

"What du the likes of ye want to be signin' me up for, Danny Carroll? You bein' from Donegal way and me from Roscommon."

"Boylan, our differences are small ones. But our need to stand united is great…that is what will help us earn a fair wage. We must work together…keep organizing, like John Siney is preachin' with the WBA."

"Danny Boyo, my days in the hole are numbered. For what reason on God's green earth should I be joinin' up with you and the likes of that rebel Doolin?"

"The Irish need a voice. That voice can be strong through us miners. 'Tis important that our bellies are full, O'Brien, but even more important, we must not forget what it means to be Irish. Jack Kehoe can speak for us, but we must hold him high up on our shoulders so the world sees he does it with our blessing."

Those he could not win over were left to another day. Danny believed in the cause. He would not have championed it otherwise. His fellow Irishmen and women needed to be established as equals in this new homeland. It was not hard to convince most that a better life could be had. The difficult part was convincing them that unionizing labor in the mines was the way to go about it.

"Dues to the Ay *Oh* of H, is it now? Danny Carroll, I have little enough to feed the family let alone pay admission to your little tea party. The Coal and Iron's are ready to force me out for back rent. I owe so much to the company store they'll naught extend our tick another day even if the mines do open up. See me, Danny, when the Strike is over."

Danny found that if he listened more than he talked—and talked over a glass of beer—he managed to convert more into the fold of the AOH than not. He was doing his part for recruitment. "Black Jack" Kehoe often said it was up to the Irish to make their way in America, not for America to make way for the Irish. Danny thought that was a masterful quote. Kehoe's eloquence was sure to take him all the way to the capitol, perhaps even to Washington. He was the Irish-American's greatest hope. Jack was the working miner's hero.

Despite their meager resources, the AOH managed to stay organized. The Long Strike seemed to go on forever. Tensions were rising. Thank Jesus, it was April and the winter weather was breaking up. Many were living in hovels and caves, evicted from the one room company houses for back rent.

The strike was a boon to none. The miners and their families were suffering. And the longer it went on, the redder grew the faces of the furious mine owners. Production was slowed. There was talk of alternatives to coal by the urban buyers. This was not to the satisfaction of a great many including Benjamin Bannon, the editor of the *Miner's Journal*. Bannon constantly badmouthed the Irish, especially Black Jack. Every murder committed in the county in the '60s was attributed to the dastardly evil Mollie Maguires.

The Irish, especially the Hibernians, knew better. There was a movement that sought to keep the Irish down and out of politics. Cousin James Carroll cited Gowen and Bannon as perpetrators of the Mollie Maguire myth.

"They are tryin' to turn public opinion against the Irish moving up in the political system. We must continue our work in secret if we are to get Jack Kehoe into office. The dream of a labor union must not fail. Then you'll see, Laddie, the breakers will be back on full time. All will be well."

Danny believed him. He poured whatever remaining energy he had left into the AOH meetings and then found a little more to put into supporting the WBA. Many a long night as he and Doolin rode over the mountain into St. Clair to meet with the South of the Mountain laborers. The strike was successful but solidarity was growing thin.

There were those who felt the laborers should not be organizing with the miners. The wildcatters in the Northern Vein were becoming restless with the idleness of work. The big companies South of the Mountain were becoming hostile. Trying to get the workers from Hazelton up to Scranton to support the strike was only marginally successful.

Siney made it clear that the upper and lower regions had to work together if the strike was to hold. Danny decided it was difficult enough to get the private enterprises in Schuylkill to back off and support a stoppage let alone try to organize Luzerne County. He'd leave it to someone else. He counted the days until he'd be onboard a ship sailing back over the Atlantic to Brigid and home. Perhaps, he'd think to himself, I could sail by August and miss the September gales and hurricanes.

On meeting days, Danny's duties were limited to making sure the back room at the Columbia House was cleared out by meeting time. The night of the Ancient Order meeting, he rode up to Jimmy Carroll's tavern with Doolin' usually. Doolin' was higher in the lodge, more involved with Kehoe and the movement. Doolin' was loathe to talk of it in public, but in private, as they rode, his tongue loosed to the rhythm of the hooves.

"Danny, we have a chance to make our dreams here. To be more than our fathers, to have more for our children. This land is free, Danny, even if Gowen and the railroad control the breakers. We may be poor, but we're free. There is no queen in America, Danny, and no English guard."

"Aye, Doolin', but thare are the Coal and Iron's."

"Bugger them, Lad. We are doing naught a thing except organizing together for a better life. Gowen may not like it…the bosses may not like it…but God willing, Danny, we will see the day when we earn a decent wage or so God help me…"

"God helps those, Doolin."

"Aye. 'Tis true. And 'tis helping ourselves that's what will get us either into heaven or onto the gallows." Doolin lowered his voice to an almost hush.

"I've heard word through James that Kehoe is urging us all tonight to keep striking. Siney feels we are close to breaking the bastards. The *Scranton Republican* and *the Harrisburg Patriot* are supportin' us, Danny! Do you believe it? We're to see no one interferes with the 'preliminary negotiations.' Are you with me, Lad?"

"They say that the C an' I's arrested a few of the lads in Heckscherville for holding a coal train hostage."

"God help us then for if all goes by Siney's plan, we're to continue the strike indefinitely. Kehoe wants us to keep the morale up here in Tamaqua, and New Philly, and Silver Creek and hereabouts. Get them to the meetings. We're to try to stir up the blood of the ranks. So's the coal dust don't settle in their veins," Jack said.

Danny laughed outwardly but inside, he shuttered. When all was said and done, he prayed they still had warm blood coursing through their veins and necks free of the noose. A chill went through him. Someone walking on his grave according to Irish superstition. Danny made the sign of the cross, just in case and mumbled a Hail Mary.

"Aye." Doolin nodded, adding thickly, "Mary, Mother of Mercy, pray for us."

———

They indeed did have four men in custody in Irish Valley for overtaking a railroad car full of coal. Another six lads were in the Ashland hoolie for staging an uprising. Bursts of violence and mayhem were occurring all over the region. And it was all over the newspapers, as well. The editor, O'Bannon, making long winded work of the Irish again.

The editor's pen was busy denouncing the striking miners, accusing them of perpetrating the violence…proclaiming the Mollie Maguires the Scourges of the East. It had not taken long in America for Danny to learn that the Irish were looked down upon. The wealthy coal barons and others in the industry considered the new immigrants arriving daily off the boat to be of little value except for servitude.

Danny vowed that he would help the labor movement survive. For the sake of his countrymen kept in poverty by indecent wages and a mountainous debt to the company store as well as those from other countries in the same situation.

It was bloody irony that neither Schuylkill County paper, the *Miner's Journal* and the *Standard*, had a word of good to say in favor of the cause. It seemed ridiculous that the public might believe the wild accusations of those who so clearly had a conflict of interest.

In fact, Doolin' told him, the entire AOH was being fingered by their own faith. The Bishop of the Dioceses labeled the group as an organization of murderers and thugs. Families were encouraged to disown any suspected of being a dread Mollie Maguire or face excommunication themselves. Danny's blood boiled but he knew better than to lose his head to anger. There was too much at stake. He would not repeat the mistakes of the Old Country in the new.

He decided the key was a low profile. He could not recall back in Ballycraig that he tried very hard to stay out of the English's sights. In fact, he'd almost taunted them at times, for a lark. He'd gotten to know more than a few by face, and one of two by name. Odd, to know your enemy by name...

What 'twere it Ma used to say? He remembered it in the next breath. Keep your friends close, and your enemies closer. Aye, Ma. He would keep them all close, but no one close enough to betray him. Danny would make it through this. Ireland called to him. Brigid was waiting.

But it all left a bad taste in his mouth. Perhaps some of Brigid's Sight had worn off on him. There were troubles ahead and no amount of watchfulness could predict what or when. Deep in his heart of hearts, Danny knew without being told. It was time to start watching his back.

Chapter Eight

Bridges and Crossroads

Maggie had tossed and turned for the last time. Finally, she bolted up and sat on the side of the bed. She hated when she was wrong. Hated admitting it and hated atoning for it.

Bottom line was she was playing the martyr. Unfortunately, the role, classic as it were, was totally wrong for her. No wonder she couldn't sleep. Both her Good and Bad Angel had joined forces and were staging an assault on her conscience. Intense guilt was their calling card.

Served her right, of course. She had been offered a once in a lifetime chance to go on an all-expenses paid trip to Ireland. The trip of her dreams. And, not once, but twice, she'd turned it down.

Turned it down *cold*. Pat, let's recap that Wheel of Fortune blooper of the week. Watch as Maggie Carroll, divorcee and mother of two, singlehandedly blows her once in a lifetime chance to go all expenses paid trip to Ireland. Vanna, spin that Wheel!

She must be insane.

In the cold darkness of the early March morning, Maggie felt every one of her 42 years creep up on her. What were the chances of this ever happening again? Would the girls really suffer even a wink if she were gone for to New York for a few days? It wasn't like her best friend Roxie wouldn't spend a few nights. After all, that's what friends were for, right?

That egotistical Irishman was right. Why *would* she deny herself this?

One half of her alter ego, the Good Angel, answered from deep in her subconscious with his high-pitched Jiminy Cricket's voice…

Maggie…you're scared you'll blow it…scared you'll get all excited and won't win it. So rather than try…you just let it go. Give up. Is that really what you want?

No, you half pint green excuse for a psychoanalyst, it isn't what I want. Maggie waited for the Bad Angel to chime in with her two cents, but Tinkerbell's side of her cerebrum remained quiet. Hmmm. Even the critics were mute on this one.

She must be *way* off base. Maggie decided in about twenty seconds flat that hell or high water not only was she was *going* to New York but she was going *today*. And now, before she caved and changed her mind.

Maggie turned on the lights. Might as well begin to pack. She was up anyway. She'd be on the phone to Mr. Devlin by 10 am. Better yet, why not bypass the boss and deal directly with what was her name? Loose association…oh yeah…Paul McCartney's sheepdog, Martha.

Of course, Martha would be a start. Probably arranges everything anyway, Maggie decided. Including Galen Devlin's appointments. Maggie planned to deliver her news to the fella with the Irish accent in person.

After all this, she had better be the lucky damn contest winner or there'd be hell to play. Ireland or bust.

———

"So, girls, I've decided to have Aunt Roxie stay here for a few days while I go to New York."

"Cool, Mom."

"Aren't you even going to ask me *why* I'm going to New York?"

Rosalie looked up from her *SEVENTEEN* magazine. "You're going to New York?"

"Did you hear a word I said, Ros?"

"No, but New York on the end of that last sentence got my attention."

"Brat faced daughter."

"Wicked biological mother."

"Touche."

Her oldest daughter peered at her intently. "Siobhan and I won't be scarred for life, Mother. This is something you've always wanted. Live a little." Rosalie smiled wickedly. "Dad would. And he wouldn't feel guilty either. Remember that summer he went backpacking with the girlfriend who looked like Barbie's twin sister? We didn't see sight nor light of him for a month."

Rosalie's point was well taken. The girl's father had some role in this as well. It wasn't like she was running away with the circus or abandoning her children to elope with the gardener. Maggie sheepishly admitted to herself that she sometimes was resentful of accepting all the responsibility for raising two children. Her ex-husband was perfectly trusting of *her* ability to take care of Siobhan and Rosalie. The trouble was her reluctance to have that same trust in their father's competency. Stellar parent he was not, but he was the girls' daddy.

Maggie felt a sudden lightness in her heart. Call it intuition, call it a premonition but she *knew* she would win this contest. Even though it was a random drawing, Maggie believed it was meant for her to have this chance. She thought of Galen Devlin and wondered what the man behind the voice was like.

"Call your dad tomorrow and tell him I'll be out of town for a few days this month around Saint Patrick's Day. And from tomorrow until Friday sometime. Hey, maybe you guys can hook up and see a movie or something while I'm gone."

"Forget it, Mom. His house is a drag anyway. The new girlfriend, Ginger, you know…Siobhan said she looked like the chick on Gilligan's Island…doesn't like it when Siobhan and I go on the Internet because she can't get on some goofy country music chatline she's on all the time. Daddy told her to get over it and they had a fight."

"Rosalie, if your father ever tries to bribe you into defecting over to his side, I'll double his offer."

"It's a deal."

———

Galen set off late for Pennsylvania and therefore was annoyed with himself. Having very little for breakfast except caffeine and some orange juice, he winced as his stomach growled in protest. He fancied it would be a bit until he could stop for dinner. Perhaps near the Poconos...he'd watch for signs. The Mom and Pop places were the best.

Strange how the last day and a half had just sped along. He'd been caught in its propulsion. The argument with Maggie Carroll, the impulse to go to Pennsylvania to the little hole in the wall town of Greenville. It had been a while since he'd felt this excited. He told himself he was a big boy, not prone to snap decisions made on impulse. Galen rationalized that it was the excitement of a new ad campaign...the thrill of a ride to a place he'd never been...

But there was a piece of him consciously that knew he couldn't wait to get his eyes on Maggie Carroll. He realized it was hopelessly male of him, but oh well. It would be strictly business and all that, but...he knew she would be beautiful. He didn't know how he knew that, but Galen Devlin was as sure of it as he was his mother's maiden name.

He'd been giving Maggie Carroll a lot of thought since yesterday. Funny thing, that little old man coming in at the end of the day, joking on with him about trying to book passage on the fairy ship!

"The ship to Tin Nan Og. One way," the wizened old lad had quipped to him. Galen recognized the accent Irish, the build short in stature, bent a bit with age. Galen had laughed, saying don't we all want a ride on that ship to dance with the fairies. And Mr. O'Toole, Galen believed it had been Thomas O'Toole to be exact...had booked first class into Shannon.

How had he put it? Yes...that was it..."time to go back to the Sod." Bit wistful he'd looked, too, Galen reflected. Homesickness of sorts. He supposed all Irish had it...the yen for the land. Even in his Manhattan loft, Galen had urns of fresh parsley and garden lettuce lining his small but sunny balcony. The warmth of the morning rays baking the rich earth reminded him of his family's farm in Ballycraig.

An ocean separated him from home but a day rarely passed without his thoughts traveling there.

He was not much different than Mr.O'Toole, he supposed. Longing to get back. But first he had business, here and now. He stopped at the next rest stop. Amazingly, he had passed the time deep in thought. His stomach was still growling. No wonder. He'd overshot the Poconos. He needed to end up in a little town called Frackville—the next exit on the interstate.

Ah, well. The dot com directions had been useful while they lasted. Now he'd be at the mercy of the locals. He hoped people were better at giving directions here than New York. People in the city were likely to shrug, laugh and throw up their hands. In learning his way around the Apple, Galen had heard more than his share of "How would I know? I don't drive."

Well, he'd made it across the Atlantic several times and back again. He'd mastered the cabs and subways of New York. How difficult could it be to find Greenville?

Two hours later, he was sorry he'd tempted Fate with that rhetorical question. The directions on *GoAnyWhere.com* had been a bit misleading. In fact, he was uttering sporadic words of profanity after he realized that he'd passed that old sign for a Texaco for the third time. He'd made his first mistake in deciding to drift off the Interstate to feed his hungry stomach.

It was true that he'd gone in circles before in his life, but he'd not planned on this trip being one of those tail eating sojourns. Although he'd started out in daylight, it was beginning to dusk "all purpley and pink" as his mother would put it. Visibility was dwindling. Galen was beginning to long for hearth, home, and a mug of something with spirit.

He knew that Mistress Fate was surely against him when he felt the rental car swerve slightly and the thump, thump, thump of the rear tire. Pulling to the side of the rural road, he swore silently that he ought to have known better. Night was settling. Then, an idea glimmered in his thoughts. His cell phone! Duh! He mentally gave himself a kick in the rear just as dear Martha would have done to chastise him, had she been there.

He could hear her voice, with just a slight touch of mockery for good measure. "Oooh, but aren't we the Urban Cowboy, Mr. D! Do you think the rest of the world outside NYC is a third world country or what?" And he had to admit, although a country bumpkin at birth himself, he was a bit of a Big Apple snob. He couldn't be far from civilization. He'd seen a sign for "Mahanoy City" before he'd left the Interstate in Hazelton.

In the dark car, he deliberated whether to call AAA or Martha. His fingers dialed the area code for New York City, and stopped. Why do that? Martha was good, but at this time of day, she'd have to be a miracle worker from one hundred and fifty miles away. Besides, he'd never live it down if he called her. Some things a man just had to do on his own.

The motel he'd booked in that little one horse town called Frackville couldn't be far. There had been no hotels in Greenville. It must be no more than a village. Carefully, reading off the little window sticker, Galen pushed in the numbers for Triple A carefully. He cussed as the rental car hit the berm.

For all his years in America, he still couldn't get used to driving on the wrong side. Galen decided he'd better use a little caution. A stranger in a strange car in a strange place armed with a cellular weapon. Dozens of little red flags waved frantically in his brain.

"We're Sorry…all our operators are busy helping other customers. Please stay on the line or try back your call at a later time…"

Right. Galen figured as much. If it weren't for bad luck today, he'd have none at all. If only…

What to do? His brain kicked into problem-solving mode. If he just knew someone in the area, but who? A local would know who'd still be open. His mind quickly flew through the *A's*, the *B's*, the *C's*…

But even he had to admit…he was far from his usual business contacts and normal stomping grounds. Suddenly he had it.

Brilliant! Silly he hadn't thought of it earlier. He would call Maggie Carroll. Surely, she couldn't turn down a weary traveler in distress. He'd heard of the hospitality of the anthracite coal region, almost legendary in Ireland as so many immigrants from Eire settled there to work in the mines during the famine years of the mid-1800s.

The idea sounded better and better as the minutes ticked by. Had he been an observer of himself, Galen Devlin would have noticed how his eyes shone and his face brightened while he looked for the number in his palm pilot.

But being relatively short on insight, he thought his quickening pulse was simply excitement over the unexpected flat tire. Galen certainly would have never attributed his heightened physical awareness to the sheer thought of Maggie Carroll. And even when the quickening turned to pounding as he dialed her number, Galen still didn't get it.

Tommy O'Toole, on the other hand, wasn't surprised in the least. It would probably take a large mallet and perhaps his blackthorne walking stick. Galen Devlin was no easy task but immortal beings, even the smallest, have their ways.

Of course, Tommy already knew about the nail in Galen's rear tire and the directions to Greenville that ran off the bottom of the page. In fact, just about the time Galen was bumping off the side of the road, Tommy was patting himself on the back for his efforts. Just a few little thank you gifts for that nice young Mr. Devlin in appreciation for all his help in setting up his flight back to the Old Sod. And the lad had even insisted on First Class, no less!

'Twas just the right touch of irony, was it not?

The Leprechaun, seeing young Galen's adventures in the magic crystal given to him long ago by Queen Mauve, breathed in a sigh of relief. Galen was punching in Maggie Carroll's cell phone number. Praise Patrick and the Goddess Brigid! True, Master Galen was in for yet another surprise, but as far as Tommy was concerned, everything was right on schedule.

Kicking off his soft leather boots, the little man propped up his feet on the desk in the office of Mr. Galen Devlin at O'Carrick Traveling Tours. Cheeky of him, he supposed, but Galen wouldn't be back for a day or two at least. And if that female War Hound named Martha happened to snoop in her boss's office while he was out, he'd zap her with a glamour illusion.

Tir Na Nog! Tommy wiggled his toes. Finally. A wee bit of peace in this maddening place called New York City. But Tir Na Nog! Ah, he heard such wonderful stories of the place beyond the Great Sea. He breathed deep. Tommy imagined he smelled the scent of the ocean. Wishful thinking. He knew Galen's office was far too distant from the city's docks to have it be more. Wishful now…but not for long.

Eyes closed, loneliness caught up with the old Elf. A single unexpected tear rolled down his cheek. A long life he'd lived to regret his foolishness in cheatin' Danny Carroll. It was not often that he let his guard down.

Had he atoned for his sins? Queen Meave told him once that he would repent long after his indignation over his sentence died away. She had been right. Tommy had been an irresponsible being. In the Old Ones, it was not fitting. He was so ashamed of what he had done.

Shame. He felt it in the depths of his immortal soul.

There! He'd said it. Tommy felt relief wash over him like the Atlantic waves over the ragged coastlines of the Aryan Islands. For years he'd been denying that he'd cheated Danny Carroll out of that what was rightfully his. Leprechauns can be as thick as the shoe leather they hammer endlessly. Gingerly, Tommy pulled back the curtains shrouding those memories of that early morning in the mists surrounding Ballycraig when a brash young rebel had outsmarted him at his own game.

Sniffling, Tommy realized he had never, before today, taken full responsibility for his action in his heart of hearts. No longer would that be the case.

Tommy Terrance O'Toole was ready to own up to his misdeeds to the one to whom he'd been deceitful the longest and to whom he most needed to be truthful. Himself. Genuine shame hit him low in the belly, but years of wisdom softened the blow. He pulled out his handkerchief and blew his nose. Bless the Queen for giving him a second chance. He would be a better Immortal for it.

A true darlin' that Queen Maeve, after all. What with Tommy seeing the light at the end of the tunnel, he began to feel a wee bit better. Enough in fact, to wander over to the small office kitchen and make himself a light snack of peanut butter crackers and vanilla yogurt.

A wee cry, a bite to eat, a comfortable seat. In no time, Tommy was feeling on top of the world. He even felt ready to wreak a little havoc on it. Grabbing Galen's phone, he began punching in numbers. Oh, 'twas wonderful to be alive! Why today's technology, or so the mortals called it, was almost like magic. Tommy heard the wondrous device ring in response to his manipulations.

Queen Maeve would be proud of him. For once, he was doing something just for the good of it. No gold involved. In a sense, making up for the harm he had done. Retribution. And when it was done? Perhaps then he could hold his head up high when he walked up that gangplank to board *The Celestial.*

"Hello?"

"Yes, well then, hello…yes, hello! Ah, yes, Lassie and sure you must be wondering who *this* is…what with me sportin' a brogue as thick as pea soup and what's more…knowing your cell phone number. What's that? Er…yes, yes, I suppose you do. 'Tis a perfectly respectable call, none the less."

The little man listened for a moment before continuing. Temper to go with the red hair. Couldn't be helped. Curse of the mixing in those hot-headed Norseman with the already half-crazed Gaels. Tommy figured it time to pull out the kid gloves and turn on the Irish charm. He cleared his throat, interrupting her barrage of questions on how he'd gotten her private phone number.

"Now, there, there…*tsk, tsk*…don't you go gettin' yer Irish up and be hangin' up on me, *Miss* Maggie Carroll…yes…well…er, now you have a point there. But, I'm not just anyone, Missy. The difference? Well, for one, what I have to say will influence the future of your family for the rest of time. Now…would ye be carin' to argue with *that*, Lassie?"

Chapter Nine

Travels and Revelations
Now

"Who the *hell* is this anyway?"

Maggie was on the Interstate, headed for New York. She'd filled the jalopy up with petrol and trunk with two small suitcases. The last thing she'd expected was a phone call. For Pete's sake, even Rosalie wouldn't have the audacity to ring her so soon after she'd departed home. Talk about annoying.

Wouldn't you think you'd be free from overzealous telemarketers tracing you to a cell phone number? Probably somebody who knew she had a subscription to *erinmusic.com*. But she was so careful not to give out this number to anyone...

"Now, now, little Lassie. I already told you I'm not just anybody. Let's just say for now, I'm a friend of the family. Now, I understand you are on your way to the Big Apple. What a coincidence! How's the weather for travelin' so far?"

Maggie's hands began to shake. Dear God, was the man some sort of axe murder? What if he was at her house right now holding Roxie and the kids hostage at gunpoint? No, make that axe point. Oh God!

Heart racing, she pulled off the road onto the exit for an upcoming rest stop. Free from the strain of trying to concentrate on the road, she blasted the voice on the other end.

"Now, listen up, you sicko. If you hurt my family in *any way*, any way at all, I'll personally see you and your phony Irish accent strung so high the birds will be nesting in your..."

The voice on the other end began to laugh. Maggie's blood ran cold.

"Lassie, lassie…oh, this *is* priceless. Oh, how the Missus would get a rise out of that! No pun intended!" The maniacal laugh bubbled up again. "Now, I suppose you've got that bountiful Irish imagination thinkin' up all sorts of horrendous acts that I must be capable of doin'."

There was a pause. Maggie wasn't sure what to do now. Her face was burning red. The caller's admonishment was actually making her blush. She began to feel a bit foolish.

"Who *are* you?"

"Ah, well, now. I'll be explaining all that and more when we meet face to face. Now, by my calculations, you should be nearing the Poconos on that highway you're traveling. That should put you in New York in say, two hours? Tell me where you're staying, and I'll…"

"Like hell, I'll tell you where I'm staying."

"Now, Miss Maggie. Stubborn as the rest of the Carroll clan, I see."

"Stubborn is the tip of the iceberg. And if you knew my family, you'd know our bite is worse than our bark."

"Aye, veritable wolfhounds one and all. I shudder at the mere thought."

"Why don't you just tell me what you want from me?"

"Ah, Miss Maggie, so skeptical! It's less about what I want from you, and more about what you'll be wantin' from me."

"You're calling me. It's your dime—I mean, quarter…oh, just forget it."

"Well, actually, 'tis not my dime or quarter, but that, my dear Maggie, is another story. Methinks since you won't share the destination you plan to lodge at with me, perhaps you'll consent to meet me at Hoolie's Pub and Alehouse on 53rd and Winston."

"I have no clue where 53rd and Winston is. I have no clue where New York is at this point. I don't travel a whole lot. And besides, why should I? You're probably some internet stalker or something. How do you know my business, anyway?"

"All in due time, my dear, all in due time. Find your way to the city. Tomorrow meet me at Hoolie's about 4 pm. Aye, that's right, Hoolie's. Wonderful place. 'Twill still be daylight. And crowded. In the event you still think I may be armed and dangerous. It's on the unofficial Irish Pub Tour. They'll be at least one or two busloads at the bar."

"Well, don't drown in your Killian's waiting for me to show."

"Ah, Lassie, 'tis right quick of tongue you are. A true Irishman—er, *woman*. Well, 'tis your choice, of course. But, if you do not come to me…" the sing-song voice stopped dramatically mid-sentence before resuming in a conspiratorial tone, "why, then I cannot tell you the story."

"What story?"

"Dear Girl, weren't you listening? The one I'll tell you when you meet me at Hoolie's."

Maggie fell silent. This was too much. The guy was obviously deranged. Good grief, how *did* he get her number? My God, what if he was some internet stalker who'd been following her trail of Irish bookmarks. She hardened her voice. "Look, Mister…"

And heard a soft sigh.

"Lassie, I may be many things, but I wouldna' harm a hair on you or any other's head." There was a pause and an indignant sniff. "'Tis not my nature."

Something in Maggie softened. "Then, what do you want with me?"

"I want to make wrong a right."

"Alright, but this story *better* be good…*damn* good…and this bar better be what you say it is."

"Oh, 'twill, 'twill! Look for me when the clock tolls four."

She was about to ask him just what exactly she was to be looking for when Maggie heard the phone at the other end go dead. To quote Lewis Carroll's Alice…things *were* getting curiouser and curiouser. Dear Lord, what had she gone and gotten herself into now? She'd agreed to meet a raving Irish lunatic with a perversion for Irish American females seeking their roots. Smooth move, Maggie.

Sliding the cell phone back into her purse, she rested her head on the steering wheel for a moment. Reaching for her CD's, she slid the Chieftains' *The Long Black Veil* into the player. She was in the mood for *Rocky Road to Dublin*. Nothing else would do.

Seatbelt in place, window cracked for air, red curls flying behind her, Maggie pushed at the volume button until music flooded the car.

Too bad Paddy and the boys weren't playing in New York. She was foot loose and fancy free, as her grandmother would say.

Wouldn't it be grand to take in a show while she was there? Or maybe hear a band. Maggie loved music. Had she more talent, perhaps she would have gone to school for that instead of nursing. Nursing paid the bills and she was a good nurse but it was not enough. Her music was for love, not money. Maggie needed it to fill in the blanks in her life. Sometimes her songs were the only way she could say what was really inside of her.

Responsible and caring, her annual evaluations usually read. Maggie was no different at home. She rarely complained and never asked for help. It was rare for her to delegate her responsibilities for the kids, the house, her job. But it worked out okay to her surprise. A quick phone call to work cleared her schedule for a week and put her on vacation time. Her best friend Roxie was more than glad to visit with her favorite "nieces" for a few days. Much to her surprise, things were going okay.

Reflecting on her impulsivity, she was glad she had followed her instincts. Her heart felt lighter. Bizarre phone call and all.

Boy, and what a strange phone call! She grinned. Almost as weird as Mick singing lead with the Chieftains, but look how dandy that turned out. Oddly, she wasn't really scared. Her good mood returned along with her sense of adventure. The caller wasn't threatening or pornographic. No, just a little odd. Some eccentric gone cellular perhaps?

But…what if…what if the guy was legit and not some prank caller? Maybe she was crazy to even consider meeting the guy, but what if he did have some family trivia or a long lost relative's name to cough up? It was possible. She had searched so long, so hard for some trace of her family's trail back into Ireland. Nothing. The story of her grandfather's past ended abruptly with his entry into this country. Or so it seemed.

But the chance existed that there was a person who still lived who knew some trace of information about Daniel Carroll. That chance *had* to exist. The man had a past before he set food on American soil so he had to leave footprints leading back there. There had to be.

And so, all practicality aside, maybe her anonymous caller did know something? If by some miracle something she, Maggie Carroll, had written could possibly get her a trip to Ireland, then by some miracle maybe she'd luck out and dig up her roots. It could happen. Excitement flooded her. The contest, the phone call from that Devlin guy with the sexy voice, now this.

Her mind wandered as she drove. What story could this character possibly know? And why did he think it had anything at all to do with Maggie's Irish ancestors? Her search into the old records at the county courthouse and in the public library in Pottsville had turned up a few dead ends. An old deed, her grandfather's Last Will and Testament. But no birth record, no marker that pointed to where he'd sprung from in old Eire.

The call today would probably lead nowhere. Common sense told her to blow it off. But something, and she didn't have a clue what that something was, told her to go out on a limb. Just this once. Her Irish intuition perhaps? Who knew? For that matter, who cared?

At that moment, Maggie made a conscious decision to push aside the notion that age 42 she was way too old to have this much fun. She so rarely took risks anymore as a parent, she'd forgotten how much she'd missed taking them as a person.

Maggie Carroll, footloose and fancy free if only for a few mad days, made another conscious decision. For some reason, Fate was leading her on one hell of an excursion. To New York of all places. To maybe win a contest that would fly her to Ireland. All expenses paid. Spending money beside. The little girl inside jumped with Christmas morning joy even though it was practically St. Patrick's Day.

"Apples, peaches, pumpkin pie, who's not ready, holler I! Big Apple, look out. Ready or not, here I come!" She half sang, half shouted out loud, to no one in particular. Her neighbors already thought she was certifiable. She may as well extend that image into the public domain at large. Turning her head in the direction of the motorist passing her on the left, she cast him a huge smile.

Then, as an afterthought, she blew him a kiss. The driver, who looked like somebody's eighty-year-old grandfather, smiled and blew her one back. It was to be taken as a good omen. A kiss for luck.

She cried out happily in her own version of a Celtic war cry while fishing for her worn copy of "Lord of the Dance" to indulge in the real thing. Nothing this exciting ever happened to her.

"New York City, you had better batten down the hatches. And warn Mother Ireland on the other side of the Atlantic to get ready...she'll not be safe either! There's a northeaster blowing in by the name of Maggie Carroll."

She thought of Galen Devlin and his mesmerizing voice. He was probably bald and paunchy with a wife who didn't understand him. To waste that voice on less than a perfect 10 specimen would be a felony. Still, baldy or not, he'd better watch out as well. Maggie Carroll was a force to be reckoned with on a bad day, but when she was on a roll?

Hot damn. Those other contestants didn't have a chance. This contest could be hers for the taking. For that matter, Galen Devlin didn't have a hope in hell, either. What the man *did* have was one gloriously sexy voice.

Smug, lost in a brave cloud of her own self-confidence, Maggie made her way merrily towards her destination.

———

"Hello...*hello*..."

"Rosaleen...there's somebody on the phone with a funny voice. He sounds like Mommy when she talks Irish. Well, except he's a boy and Mommy's a..."

"Siobhan...you're not supposed to let on Mommy's not here, you Goose. Give me the phone..."

"Noooo! You're mean, Rosaleen. Ha! That rhymes! You're mean, Rosaleen...na, na, na, na, na, na..."

Annoyed as only a 13-year-old can be at a 4-year-old, Rosaleen whispered harshly as she grabbed the cordless phone from her sister.

"Mommy will murder us both. It could be some child molester. Aunt Roxy said to not tell anybody we're here by ourselves. She'll be right back from the store."

Sitting alongside Granny's Restaurant next to a gigantic bonneted female statue he guessed was undoubtedly Granny, Galen was getting an education on kids saying the darndest things. From the earful he'd gotten so far, he assumed that every hair on Ms. Maggie Carroll's motherly head would curl listening to her two worldly daughters totally blow their lesson on what not to do when the phone rings and Mom's out.

"Hello?"

Galen cleared his throat at hearing the teenage girl finally decide to address his call. He wasn't sure if he should be amused, but he was.

"Yes, why, is this the Carroll…no, er. Perhaps, it would be easier to let me tell you. This is Galen Devlin. I am from O'Carrick Traveling Tours, out of Ireland. Is your mother there? She's won a spot in one of our contests."

Rosaleen's heart began racing. Mommy's trip to Ireland. She gulped air excitedly.

"Oh, my God! She's already, er…I mean…Mr. Devlin is it? She's ah, humm… unable to come to the phone right now." Rosaleen thought she'd heard it put to someone like that in a movie she'd seen on HBO. Still, it didn't seem right to not tell him she'd gone to New York. After all, wasn't he the person Mommy was going to meet?

Rosaleen tried very hard to think like a grown up, but she was having second thoughts. Maybe she should be honest with this Mr. Devlin. He seemed a nice enough man. Mommy was probably close to New York by now and wasn't that where the tour place was? Rosaleen stalled. She wished her aunt had not run out for milk. She wished…

Galen's fatherly instincts, while never put to the test with children of his own, came to the rescue.

"Miss, I know that your mother has probably told you not to talk to strangers. I understand. My own mother told me the same. So, Lassie, how would it be then for you to just give your mother my cell number and she can call me right back?"

Rosaleen thought it made absolute sense. She copied down the number on the white board next to the phone. "O.K., got it. Mr. Devlin?"

"Aye, Lass."

"Are there palm trees in Ireland? My mother says it's so, but it doesn't seem to make sense. Ireland's damp and cold, right?"

Galen, though caught off guard by the child's question, was frankly charmed. What a strange question!

"It's rather surprising, then, isn't it? But she's right, your mother. Though high in latitude and surrounded by the cold North Atlantic waters, there is a bit of Ireland that lies in the path of the warm Gulf Stream. So, yes, lassie, there are palm trees. Few people know it."

Galen paused. So Maggie Carroll taught her daughters of Ireland even though she'd never traveled there. No wonder the trip meant so much to her. "Good-bye, then. And thank you. You've been a big help"

Rosaleen was relieved. Proud of herself for choosing such a brilliant solution, and feeling bolstered by the adult male's approval, Rosaleen dialed her mother's cell phone. That Mr. Devlin was kinda nice in a speaks-a-different-language sort of way. No wonder her mother was a sucker for an Irish accent. She wondered if Mr. Devlin had a son...or maybe a sixteen-year-old brother.

"Mom, it's me. No, nothing's wrong. Some guy, named Mr. Devlin, called and wanted me to give you this cell phone number. What? I can't hear you. Where are you? New York? Listen, Mom. The signal's getting bad. The number is 362-4152. Can you hear me? Mom?"

The fading signal crackled into silence. Rosaleen shrugged and turned back to her younger sister. "Hey, Siobhan, wanna watch *Wheel of Fortune*?

———

Maggie scribbled down the number just in time. Her cell phone went dead as she began to see signs for the city. Traffic was intense. Odd that Galen Devlin had called. Perhaps it was a good thing. He had no idea she was arriving early. She planned on going straight to his office in the morning, but it was handy to have a cell number just in case.

Tucking the number into her wallet, Maggie concentrated on the road. She hated city traffic worse than country music...no, worse than disco. Turning up the music, Maggie sang along with the Chieftains. Imagine being on stage with that caliber of seasoned musicians, improvising the old traditional tunes and making them young again. Maggie loved to sing and traditional tunes were her favorite.

"O kind friends and companions come join me in rhyme and lift up your voices in chorus with mine…"

She wondered about the strange phone call earlier. What the devil had that been about? Should she meet the strange Irishman at where was it, Hoolie's? *Hoolie's*, for God's sake. What did *he* know about her family? Grammy Carroll always said be careful not to dig too deep in the ground or the past…in either case, you may unearth a few unexpected skeletons.

Dear Lord, if a few skeletons were all he'd dug up, she supposed she'd consider it an honor. Or a blessing. Maggie had been searching for her family roots for longer than she'd care to remember. A skeleton would be more than welcome.

If the anonymous caller had genealogy to share, good or bad, she was in. Good thing Hoolie's was a public place. Now all she had to do is find an Irishman in New York. In a bar that was on the city's unofficial Irish Pub Tour.

Right. As in finding the probverbial needle. Maggie grinned wickedly. Ah, but wouldn't it be fun? New York was looking magical with its lights twinkling like stars against the night. Maggie felt entranced by it. She pulled out another Chieftains CD, *Tears of Stone*. Perfect. Brenda Fricky and Anin' joined the band in the beautiful ballad "Never Give All the Heart."

By the time Maggie was pulling into the front of the small hotel on Lincoln Park and Broadway, Diana Knall's version of "Danny Boy" was playing. Maggie's mood went melancholy, but it felt right. There was no place in the United States more Irish than New York, especially in the weeks leading up to St. Patrick's Day.

She wasn't sure why, but leaving home on the spur of the moment had seemed exactly the right thing to do. This morning. Now Maggie wasn't so sure. Her eyes filled with tears.

Here she was. Money being hard to come by, she'd better enjoy it. It would be a serious bummer paying off the credit card debt for a trip gone disastrous.

But it wasn't going to be a problem. Maggie would make absolutely sure of it. She'd come this far. Taking a deep breath, she dried her eyes. Looking up at the sign for the Emerald, Maggie made a promise to herself. Life was short. Grabbing her keys and purse, Maggie decided not to waste even one minute more of it.

———

Galen was quietly becoming furious. With himself. With his situation. With the service station that had yet to show itself. And dammit, most of all, with the growing realization that Maggie Carroll wasn't going to return his phone call now or anytime soon. How now, hot shot, he admonished himself. It had been more than a little foolish to imagine she didn't have anything better to do than jump on the phone and get right on back to him.

But he had been parked in the same spot now for four hours. His patience was thinning and he felt like a caged cat. When Maggie Carroll hadn't returned his call in fifteen minutes, he began to see the ludicrousness of delaying the inevitable. After the twentieth dial, he finally got through to the rental company. They said they would dispatch roadside assistance as soon as possible. They hadn't bloody well said it would be hours.

By the time the garage mechanic from hell showed up, Galen was ready to walk back to New York. The other man's attitude was just as surly as Galen's. Having been called out at 9 o'clock at night to fix a flat, he was a perfect match for Galen's own impatience. The two men glared at each other until it became rather ridiculous.

In desperation, Galen tried conversation. A few grunts and continued silence, he gave up. He wasn't sure what he was most angry about—at his own stupidity in impulsively taking off for parts unknown on the spur of the moment or that Maggie Carroll had basically ignored his call.

Eventually, the tire repaired, his anger began to fizzle. By then, the night had cleared and the moon was high in the sky. Too tired to drive further and risk an accident, Galen flicked the locks on the rental car and made his way to the Motel Six not far from the Granny's Restaurant parking lot. He was so happy for a bed, he didn't even take off his clothes before falling into it.

He'd deal with Maggie Carroll and Schuylkill County roadways tomorrow in the light of day. Right now, he yawned and felt as if he could sleep upright in a hole. Good thing the lads at Motel Six had kept the light on for him.

Damn her, he thought, as he drifted off to sleep in the comfortable, but unfamiliar bed. Maggie Carroll was an irritant he had not planned on. Annoyed, he willed himself to rest.

And yet, he spent a restless night, dreaming of the harsh Irish coastline where the waves of the Atlantic beat the rocky shore. He was on the dock, watching the great ships as they returned from America. He felt his heart would break, straining to look for a familiar face in the crowd. It was not hard. More left than came so it was easy to pick out a loved one coming ashore. Why couldn't he see her? Her face, so dear to him, and yet, he could not recall it... He peered into the early morning fog, its tendrils rising from the waters in great puffs.

The ringing woke him. Galen considered shutting the phone off, but reconsidered. He groped in the direction of the sound. It was likely to be Maggie Carroll finally returning his call. About time. Without breakfast and a cup of very strong tea, he could not be held accountable for his behavior. Galen Devlin wasn't impossible, but one of his pet peeves was returning calls.

"Yes, Galen Devlin here."

"Hummph. That's nice, boss. And where would there be?"

"Martha! You have the voice of an angel. I'm in Frackville, Pennsylvania. At the local Motel Six. They kept the light on for me."

"Ha Ha. Very funny. You telling me something I don't know or are you just making small talk?" Martha's flat tone didn't give him much to go on. Still groggy, he remained uncharacteristically silent, mentally checking off his most recent contacts.

"Little slow on the uptake this a.m., boss, are we? O.K. Let me make this easy for you...you haven't hooked up with Maggie Carroll yet, have you?"

Galen bristled but bit his tongue. Martha was one of the few people he respected enough to put up with her razor sharp tongue. It went arm in arm with her infernally sharp mind.

"Well, no, but get to the point, Martha, my dear. I haven't had me tea yet."

"Well, then you'll love this. You're there. Guess who's here?"

Galen continued to focus on his most recent business contacts. The editor of *Ireland of the Welcomes* had yet to get back to him on the new ad layout. *The Times* had promised him an article on the contest and the contestants. The O'Carrick was vacationing in Aruba with the Missus but wanted an update on the January numbers for the New York office.

"Can't guess, huh? You do need your tea. And you better sit down."

"Give me a minute. Oh Gawd! Ma didn't fly over did she? She threatened last week that if Da complained one more time about chicken for supper…"

"Maggie Carroll, boss. Stopped in this morning bright and early, looking for you. Said she'd thought things over and decided to take you up on your offer."

Galen woke up. "*Offer.* What the hell bloody offer is she talking about? I told her to be here in two weeks and she told me no."

"Right, well, I told her too, boss. That the promotion was in two weeks."

Galen was livid. How *dare* she go to New York looking for him without at least notifying his office in advance! He was a busy executive. Did she expect him to be available at a moment's notice? "And *what* the hell did she say to *that*?"

In her plush office chair, Martha wiggled with delight. She wished she could see the normally calm, cool, and collected Celt now. This lady *must* be a keeper—anyone who could get Galen to break a sweat this early in the morning must be.

"Woo-ee. She done got you all excited, now hasn't she?"

"Martha, I will personally give you an extra vacation day this month if you stop jerking my chain."

"This is March, boss. Too miserable outside to take a day off. I'd rather bring sunshine into your life. Make it for May so I can take an extra long Memorial Day weekend and it's a deal."

"Are you sure Donald Trump doesn't need a new secretary?"

"He'd jump at the chance to get a hold of these bones. I'm prime real estate. But, alas, Trump Plaza's too hard on these old eyes. All that glitter. Overdone even for a black woman. Besides, I promised your mama I'd keep an eye on you. How could I break a promise to your mama?"

"Smart ass."

"If you keep making this fun, I'll never tell you."

Galen shut up. He was no match for Martha when she was in rare form.

"Oh, alright. You've stopped arguing. Fun's all gone. It's time for my break anyway. While the rat's away, this kitten's *got* to play. There's a shoe sale down at Sak's. I have my eye on a pair of ruby red heels."

"For what I pay you, you could probably buy Donald Trump a pair, too. Get to the point, Martha. She changed her mind. So what in bloody hell does she want?"

Martha could barely hear him breathe. Just as she thought. The girl had him hooked and he hadn't even met her yet. She shook her head. Wait till he got a load of Maggie Carroll in person. All red hair and Irish American attitude wrapped up in a pretty little size-six package. The word spitfire came to mind. Galen Devlin was in for it. Big time.

"To see you."

The silence at the other end was delightful. Martha wiggled in her chair again. This was too good. Wait till his mama hears. Galen Devlin gone all speechless and discombobulated over a woman. Martha would be on speed dial to Ireland as soon as she got rid of Galen.

"Jesus H. Christ, Martha." Galen's tone was pure frustration. It was about time, Martha thought. It just wasn't normal for a boy so handsome to keep flittin' from flower to flower like some damn honeybee. His mama was talking grandkids and Galen was still playing spin the bottle.

"Did you tell her I'm here? Trying to see *her*. Because she said *no*."

More silence. Martha figured he was pouting now. She counted down slowly…five…four…three…two…one.

"Doesn't she *have* bloody long distance? What rational person drives three and a half hours without the courtesy of calling first to make sure the other person is there?"

Martha silently snickered. Timing was everything. She paused before delivering the obvious punch line.

"Gee, boss, I don't know. Why don't you go on in the bathroom they have there at Motel Six and have a little look see in the mirror?"

The blood rushed to his face. Galen Devlin realized he'd walked right into that one.

"And, boss, one more thing. I didn't tell her you're in Pennsylvania looking for her."

"Why the *hell* not?"

"It would have been way too much fun to have at work. Besides, I didn't want her to think she's dealing with some irrational idiot who would drive three and a half hours to see some other irrational idiot who drove three and a half hours in the other direction to see him."

"It's too early, Martha. You're confusing me. I'm getting up, finding tea, and showering. Expect me back by 4 pm."

"Right-o. And what about Maggie Carroll and her red hair?"

"She has red hair?"

"Yeah, and freckles. Not bad lookin' either."

"Make an appointment with her for an early dinner tonight. No better yet, tell her I shall meet her at about 6:30. Casual. Um, now wait. Martha, look. Make reservations at Hoolie's Pub. Wednesday night is their sessions. That should do the trick."

"Are you sure, boss? Maybe I should just call her and tell her to go home and come back in two weeks for the big finale. You could wave to each other on the interstate. Like two passing ships in the night."

"Ha. Ha. Very funny. Don't be silly, Martha. Of course I should meet with her. Make sure she's serious about saying yes. Check her out…er, I mean, check out her motives. Maybe she's flighty and would leave us stranded for a winner at the last minute."

"Sure, boss. Always thinking of the company first, aren't you? I'll bet the big boss would just be so proud. Reservations on the floor or the balcony of Hoolie's?"

Galen paused. "Why, the balcony, I suppose. The main floor will be too noisy. The ceili dancers, the music. Better the privacy of the balcony. To talk of course."

Martha hid her sly smile from her voice. "Oh, well of course to talk, boss. Not like it's a date or anything. Hoolie's balcony. Better make that eight bells…in case traffic's heavy. She's stayin' at The Emerald. See you this afternoon."

The receiver had no sooner clicked before Martha was dialing international long distance. She'd leave the message on Maggie Carroll's cell phone later, but first thing's first.

"Hello, Mrs. D. It's Martha. No, no, nothing's *wrong* with Galen. Well, not exactly wrong. Oh, no, *better* than that. Have I got a newsflash for you…Oh, honey, you have no idea…yeah? Well, then, I guess you do…Oh yeah? He already told you about her?… Mrs. D., he's got it worse than I thought… Well, wait until you hear *this* one…"

Another call was coming through but Martha ignored the ringing phone. "No, don't worry about it. The O'Carrick is sunning himself with the heiress on some beach, your son is showering in a motel in Pennsylvania and *I'm* on break. Now, go on and get yourself a hot cuppa something and we can have ourselves a nice little chat to catch up. No. Not to worry. I'll just flick on that fancy smancy answering service that son of yours insists we have so it can work for its little ol' keep."

Chapter Ten

Unsung Heros
Then

By June, 1875, the long strike was ending. Everyone had suffered and little had changed. Danny felt angry, embittered to the core. He had lost much in wages. There was nothing to put aside, nothing to save to bring Brigid over. Not yet a citizen himself, he would have to find her a sponsor. There would be a fee, he was sure.

It would take forever. They would be old, he thought, and groaned. He hoped he would not miss being Brigid's lover when he was young. It would be all her fault, of course. He'd told her they should more than once in the last year. He grinned, remembering her temper. She told him her sainted mother would make him a daughter-in-law rather than a son-in-law if she found out they'd did it before the wedding.

Danny's mood grew sadder. So many, not just he, suffered. Suffered in hardship through the seemingly endless months of hunger and going without. The eyes of every woman in New Philadelphia, in the little patches of Silver Creek, Tucker Hill and in Cumbola, reflected the gaunt fear of starvation.

They had known its face in Ireland and now it had followed them here. Their children were dying of infection and malnourishment. The women with smiles hardened and faces pinched gave the littlest ones their own portions of whatever meager offering was today's meal. The faces of their men grew harder, too. Their voices were becoming louder.

In the taverns and on darkened street corners, there were faintly whispered hush words of resentment and retaliation. "'Tis time to stand up for ourselves." "Forget the strike! Look what it has got us!"

Matters were growing out of hand. Miners like Eddie Coyle, a well thought of Hibernian, were being murdered. The policemen and the courts looked the other way with not even an arrest made. There was talk of the Pinkertons and the Coal and Iron Police combining forces to restrain the militant miners. Still, Jack Kehoe continued to preach passive resistance. The men listened to Jack, but their anger smoldered like burning coal.

Every day, Danny heard the whispers go from grumbling to shouting. The union members spoke out from everywhere. Voices accused Siney and the WBA of selling out. To your average man, it appeared they had. Danny knew from the troubles in Ireland how slow progress was. One cannot fight an army with a pitchfork.

So much for so little. So much for *nothing*. He could feel a depression of spirit, descending over them all, like the blight had over Ireland. That hole-in-the-stomach, all-the-heart-gone-out-of-it feeling that comes with giving up was bitter in his throat. It was what people like Franklin B. Gowen wanted the Irish to feel.

Defeat. Utter submission.

Danny refused to succumb. He had no choice but to fight it with every fiber of his being. He would not give in. If he gave in, if he didn't keep trying to rally the Hibernians, then what was left? Stuck here, apart of Brigid, he had to have some bright shred of hope. He must cling to it and fight for it until Brigid was in his arms again.

Nor would he give up. He used his own pain to support the others. Everyone had their own Brigid or Mary or Patrick…their *something* or *somebody* that they would fight and die for. That is what he told the men when he met them at the meetings or at Church on Sunday. He struggled to find words the caliber of those Jack Kehoe or Doolin might say to inspire *their* men.

Keep the faith, he encouraged them, when he heard the hushed whispers on the street corners. The union may be cavin' in, but we must stick together for our families. In the dark corners of Malony's Bar in the little patch called Wiggans' where he now resided, he listened to the woes of the family men and offered what little support he could. In private, he thanked God he had no youngsters yet of his own to feed.

Danny prayed for them all. He was not much of a churchgoer but he was a believer and figured God counted that for something.

The mine owners continued to beat the men into the ground. Even though they technically had won the battle. The insufferable bastards. Wages were at a low. The lads joked, "It makes a man feel dirty cheap, you bet, to work a month and come out in debt." The operators and their bands of hired vigilantes policed the towns and mine patches, roughing up the residents and inspiring hate. Aye, the heart had gone of it, for sure.

But the Irish had the heart go out of many things before *and gone on.* Life would not be easy, nor would it be for a long time. They all were in this mess together. It made sense they would stand together to face what came next. The wealthy coal barons and railroad executives hadn't planned on that kind of solidarity.

Danny himself was hit with homelessness. After losing his room at the Sullivans' place, he'd been unable to find anywhere permanent to board. The strike had left him penniless except for the odd coin or two earned helping around the Patch, and the wee bit of compensation he earned through his place within the Order. There was little chance of getting his job back at Silver Creek since he'd been identified as one of the lead strikers.

He'd holed up in his Cousin James Carroll's place in Tamaqua. James had been kind enough to house him in one of the few small rooms above the tavern. For just a few days. He felt guilty, having nothing to pay, but James said no, not to worry. He would kick him out when a paying customer came, and not a day sooner.

James had given him not only lodging, but also an idea. In trying to help Danny secure a room, he also pointed him in a direction to go. Up north, the other end of the county. Past St. Clair, over the mountain to the booming town of Mahanoy City. It was here, James said, that things were growing at a tremendous pace. Lots of wildcat mines. Perhaps Danny could get in on the ground floor with another lad or two.

He knew these things because his wife's aunt, Margaret O'Donnell, had a boarding home up there in patch near the town. Perhaps she might even have a room Danny could board out. At the very least, she could recommend him to someone who might.

And the opportunities, James said, were plenty. "So many more chances to make good, even maybe to get out of the bloody mines! You are a bright and personable lad, too. Better chance of succeeding when a place grows up around you." James paused. "See, Laddie, my parents came from Ireland. I was born here. It's maybe why I have a bit more than others. Had a step up that way, do you see? This could be *your* step up."

More possibilities existed than in New Philadelphia and Pottsville, James assured him. Things were a wee bit more civilized this end of the mountain. More settled. Unfortunately, the big coal barons and railroad men had sewn up all the resources. Limits on the amount of growth the average Muck and Moe like himself could make as a private agent.

It also caused many of the scarce apprentice positions to be quickly snatched up by overachieving lads wishing to escape the mines or avoid them altogether. Families watched out for their young and got them into coveted situations with the local craftsman and merchants as soon as one opened up. Overgrown lump that Danny was, he was long past the apprentice stage.

No, James insisted. Relocatin' "up north," as he put it, would definitely be a good move now that he was both out of work *and* a place to stay. Danny was sure to be able to get a job in the mines until then so as to earn his keep until his ship came in. Once the mines were officially open, of course.

The long strike was not over, but it was taking its last breath.

———

It did not take long. Siney admitted defeat in June, and by July, the strike was officially ended. By then, Danny had already made his way to the widow O'Donnell's boarding house in Wiggan's Patch.

"She's not alone… her sons and daughter…a few riff raff of your sort." James cuffed Danny's arm. He had grown fond of the immigrant cousin and the cousin of he. "Husband was Manus O'Donnell."

James Carroll told him of his wife's aunt who'd emigrated from the Donegal village of Gweedor. So many families separated by not only an ocean of salt water but one of poverty, hunger, and bigotry. Danny wondered what ills of the old world would keep revisiting the Irish in the new.

"Her daughter, Ellen, and husband, Charlie McAllister and their little lad live there, too. Along with the two O'Donnell boys, Charlie and James. And the boarders, of course. Big house. Not far from the Colliery. Last I heard, she had four or five lads living there. Her other daughter, Mary Ann? She's married to Black Jack."

Instantly, Danny made note. He was in awe of Jack Kehoe. Danny fancied himself a leader…someday…but Black Jack Kehoe was a leader for the times. The unforgettable tavern owner had the gift of blarney and good looks to boot. The Widow O'Donnell, his mother-in-law, called him "an altogether charmin' man."

There were those who said Jack Kehoe would soon be rising to more than president of the AOH. It had been drunk to at more than one saloon that if anyone could take the Irish vote, it was Black Jack Kehoe. Jack was not only that well liked, he was respected for his integrity. Throughout the long strike, he'd inspired the miners with words of courage and hope. He believed the immigrant population should seize opportunity in this new land.

He made it seem possible to rise up above it. Jack was now a tavern keeper in Girardville but he had run for councilman and won. An immigrant himself, his charm and ability to talk his way out of a rainstorm gave Danny some hope. Black Jack was destined for greatness Danny was sure. He would be remembered in history. Danny made a point to tell Mrs. O'Donnell of his great respect for her son-in-law.

Although he was sad to leave New Philadelphia, it was only a little sadness. He would miss Doolin and his cousin James Carroll, since he would see them much less. But it was not the kind of sadness that he missed home with, and not the gnawing heart wrenching sadness with which he missed Brigid. Besides, he was poor. Empty pockets poor.

He had to do something or starve.

Doolin and his wife had offered to take him in, but their company row in Tucker Hill was already too small for the couple and their three children. Besides, Danny admitted to himself, he didn't think he could stand watching Doolin's clear and present affection for his pretty raven-haired wife, Kate. It made Danny miss Brigid so much it ached.

No, it was time to move on. Pleased with his decision, he had ridden the train north to Pottsville then on to Mahanoy City. The ride wasn't long, but the differences between "north of the mountain" and "south of the mountain" were becoming evident to him rather quickly. He'd gotten off the train at the depot in Mahanoy City and heard gunshots. It was like the tails of the Wild West the minstrels told.

He was well pleased, though, with his decision once he made his way, with direction secured from the Station Master. "Head west, Lad." He'd been instructed and pointed in the right direction. "You canna miss it." Tucking his few meager belongings under his arm, Danny headed out of town.

The town was bustling, and so were the patches around it. The smells of town life faded as he walked along the dusty road to Wiggan's Patch. The O'Donnell house was huge to him. He'd come from a cottage in Ireland, and patch houses in New Philadelphia. The O'Donnell house was a bit intimidating, but then there was Nanny to greet him at the door, like a long lost nephew. And didn't she know it, that her son-in-law, Jack, was a grand cut of a man. Her Manus, too, she told him, with a dab of the handkerchief to her eye. Gone now, these past few years, passed on to a better life.

He could stay tonight, on the living room settee, but she had no rooms. Tom Murphy, James Purcell, James Blair, and the brother of her son-in-law, James McAllister—they were all there for some time now, she told him with some note of pride. "I suppose they have not much to complain about since they've made no attempt to move out."

Face brightening, smile widening, the widow had a thought. She could send him with a note of reference to her friend, Mrs. Mullins, next door. But tomorrow would be soon enough. "Tonight, why sure, wouldn't you be foolish not to be stayin' here. 'Tis fresh up, be you, from New Philly. You must be tellin' us of the news from down the mountain and entertain us all with a story or two."

Danny could hardly refuse. And the next day, his stomach fuller than it had in months from hot soup made of the widow's truck garden vegetables and the warm bread baked in her ovens, he went next door to the Mullins'. The couple, getting on in age, were glad for the opportunity for an extra bit of income. And until he could get a job at the Colliery, he could work off his room and board helping to repair the house and care for the horses.

Danny could hardly refuse that either. It seemed James was right. Things were looking up. Although no place in this time of unemployment and hunger could be considered prosperous, he saw signs that this wild landscape could someday grow to be so. Once the breaker was back on full time anything was possible.

He decided to call north of the mountain home. At least until he could go back to Ireland for Brigid. For it was Brigid, he realized who symbolized all that was his home. Not a dwelling, or a town, or a country, but she who held his heart. He whispered it, almost prayer like in his reverence. He was yet a boy and believed in what magic there was in a world where starvation and poverty were a daily reality.

"Hold on, Brigid. Hold on until I come. I swear I will come."

———

July 2, 1875

My dearest Brigid,
I have learned to write! Read better as well. The lady of the house where I board has taught me. Well, I could afore, but not so well, and not so that I would try to send out a letter to you since it would look like chicken scratch and you would laugh at me. But that would be good too, to hear you laugh. I remember your laugh was like church bells in the distance on a Sunday in spring. Do you remember the morning I was taken? I pray you have not forgotten me.
I am sending this with Patrick O'Donnell, one of the cousins of my neighbor here. He has been here and back again more than once and he tells me he knows of

Ballycraig. He swears he will get this to ye if he can and I believe him. He's a rebel like so many. Left in exile but he has friends to help him to go back to West Donegal to his kin. I live next door to his auntie Margaret and her brood. He and his brother Michael live here in this little village of Wiggan's Patch on the outskirts of the town of Mahanoy City. Patrick says he must go back to Donegal now to help the fight. If only I had the money to go along! But I do not yet. The passage would eat up all I have left. There has been no work for so long.

'Tis worse at times than Ireland was with our lands being thieved from us. The operators take our labor for free, charge rent on houses we shall never own, and demand top price for goods at the company stores. We are making less now than the miners did in 1968. And the owners all lead back to England. They could not kill enough of us in the Old Country…they hunt us down in the New World.

Tensions are high here. It is much like there, but instead of the English army, there are the mine owners and the Coal and Iron Police who belittle the Irish and beat us into the ground. The Welsh and the English are here as well. Not all are bad but they treat us worse than any slave. They forget. We are free. It may not always seem so but we are free men. We shall overcome. Myself and others belong to the Ancient Order of Hibernians. We are fighting for the rights of the working men.

There are those who are trying to say we are doing so with lawlessness and criminal means. The papers blame a secret organization called the Molly Maguires. Can you imagine that? It's like Lord George, ranting and raving about the White Boys!

But you know me, Brigid. I would not hurt even a coney rabbit if the stew pot were not awaiting. The owners, the deep pockets in London...there are others, Brigid...who are evil at heart and would squash us like bugs. These are strange times here, as I know they must still be there.

This place called Pennsylvania looks a lot like Ireland. Much greenery and soft rolling mountains. The mines have finally opened up again after a long strike. I am working at the colliery next to the Patch since moving here from a place called New Philadelphia.

I have met a cousin of mine, James Carroll, who told me to come here to better things. He knows of you and my longing to save enough to bring you here. Would you come? Leave your ma and Ballycraig?

I shall come home, when the summer is nigh and the valleys there are green. We shall marry and you will wear the gown you've been making since long we betrothed each other. I swear it. My heart will never belong to another, Brigid. Never. Though the mountains wear away and the seas become dry land, I shall love you as long as that and more.

Wait for me. It shall not be long, I swear. The breakers are back to work and I am saving every cent that I can.

Your Danny

Chapter Eleven

Fate and Destiny

The evening of July 5th was warm. The doors of Jim Carroll's Washington House Tavern were thrown open. The miners, hot from their day's work, continued to wash down their dust with cold ale despite the occasional soldier lost to a barefoot son or daughter sent by the missus to order their Pappy home to supper.

Jim Carroll ran a tight ship with a simple rule: there was to be no more served to any man being hunted down by his wife. It was just one reason why he was well liked in Tamaqua. Danny, seated at the bar, watched his cousin draw a perfect head on a pitcher of ale. The bartender smiled.

"It's an art form, Lad."

"Aye, as are you listenin' to every Tom and Dick telling you his tale of woe and deep despair. How do ye stand it, cousin?"

"It's me or the confessional, Danny. There's those who have not set foot in Church lately with the Bishop down the Order's back, accusin' us all of conspirin' in corners. It's me or perhaps even the gallows, I suppose."

James winked and nudged Danny's arm, nodding his head in the direction of two men at a table in the dim common room. "Like those two."

"Who are they?"

"A ruffian named Kerrigan and one of his sidekicks. Up to no good, methinks. I just told him his drinks are cut, but he continued to badger Mary Theresa. He started givin' me a bit of guff about it and I showed him where the door was. Two whiskeys and he plans to take on the world."

The pair at the table got loud once or twice but made no more attempts to get the barmaid's attention for another round. The evening passed pleasantly. Danny managed to fill James in on life in Wiggan's Patch. James promised to pass the news sent by Nannie O'Donnell, to his wife, Nannie's neice, Annie.

The gossip was of little significance to either man, but neither would even think of not completing their messenger duties. This cousin had a boy, Nora Brennan married a Sweeney, a new recipe for soda bread. The hour grew late as the tavern slowly emptied. Danny noticed that Kerrigan and his friend had left. James had begun preparations to put the bar to bed.

"Those two were up to no good. Kerrigan was still bristlin' like a caged cat when he staggered out. Mumbled under his breath while his buddy kept nudgin' him to shut his mouth."

"It's men like them that gives drinkin' a bad name, now isn't it, cousin Danny?"

As Danny rode home that night, his smell of honeysuckle filling his nose, and ale his belly, he was lulled into forgetting he was poor, an ocean apart from his true love, and had to rise for Mass in the morning. It was no hop and a skip to St. Canicus. He had promised Mrs. Mullins to drive her in the buggy because the Mister had a touch of gout.

It was after mass that next day that he heard the news. A policeman by the name of Benjamin Yost had been killed in Tamaqua sometime during the wee hours of early morning. Two Irish, one short, were being blamed. Danny breathed a sigh of relief that he had left for home when he had.

He only prayed no one would think he had anything to do with it. Besides, he had arrived back at the Mullins' by 1 o'clock in the morning, had stabled the horse in back and hollered up to the Missus Mullins that he'd gone and locked up the house. She'd be certain to give him an alibi.

Two weeks later, in a note scrawled quickly and delivered by Jack Kehoe himself on his way through Wiggan's from Tamaqua to

Girardville, his cousin James told him to lay low and have a care. It was best, the note said, that Danny had moved north because the troubles were worsening in Tamaqua.

The two fellows who'd been drunk and unruly in the tavern that night were rumored to be suspect in the Yost killing. There were, James finished, talk of arrests.

Black Jack himself put a hand on Danny's shoulder and looked at him with kindness. Black Jack was known for his honesty and ability to look a man straight in the eyes. It was perhaps then that Danny began to understand that something sinister was at play.

Kehoe echoed James' sentiment to use a care but added a grave warning. There was a still a twinkle in his dark eyes, but it was not a merry one. Danny imagined Jack Kehoe often resorted to that look when he had to get his point across in a hurry.

"'Tis like a witch hunt in Salem, Laddie. You must take care not to draw attention to your warts. Too many questions asked and backgrounds checked into." The older man sighed and the twinkle disappeared.

"In Salem, it was the stocks and trial by fire. Here, Danny Carroll, it'll be the gallows."

He turned and walked out. Danny Carroll never forgot the great man's parting words that day, still ominous on the tongue when recalled even many years later.

"Here, Danny Carroll, it'll be the gallows."

Through the heat of the summer, things continue to worsen. The conflicts between workers and mine owners escalated. Wages had dropped to all time lows. Miners tried to joke, but operators took even more revenge out on the beaten workers by imposing worse conditions on them than ever before. The August newspapers reported around the country that conditions in Pennsylvania had reached the point where families were existing on horse and cow flesh.

And the fight continued. It had to. The militant workers had no other way to try to improve their lot. Their families were slowly starving, their own bodies weakening, often to the point of exhaustion and injury. Men died or were horribly injured in accident after accident. Already destitute families were left fatherless.

Summer was leaving...soon, the winter ice and chill would come. So many children left without a roof over their heads. Come winter, they would have no coat either. Danny did not know how much longer any of them could survive. Even he, without a family, had so little. Except for his secret pouch, that is. That was kept hidden well. Danny added a few coins now and then from occasional odd jobs he found about the town.

It was early September. The Patch was enveloped in a canopy of trees. They blocked out the breaker so that it looked as though the small neighborhood of houses were alongside a forest road. As he groomed his horse, one of the few purchases he had managed to make since living at the Mullins', he overheard voices next door at the O'Donnells'. Their stables shared a back row against the coal banks. Danny recognized the voice of Charlie O'Donnell and ducked over to the neighbor's yard for a bit of talk.

Charlie was leaning against the back of the house, talking to his brother Friday. Danny had asked why they called him Friday, but his brother and sister, Ellen McAllister who lived there with her husband, only giggled and said that whenever Friday borrowed money from anyone, he always promised to get it back to them by Friday. Danny accepted this, and having been hit up more than once by his friend, could understand why the nickname stuck.

"Hey, Danny, how goes it, Lad?"

"Alright, nice evening, isn't it?"

"Aye, have you heard what happened at Raven Run yet?"

Danny had not and told the brothers so. They exchanged glances.

Charles spoke first. "Perhaps it best if you know as little as possible. Remember what Jack told you. You came a bit close to the Yost murder. Being a stranger, you could have been implicated."

James, his brother, interrupted. "Charlie, it's best he know. Nobody's safe. He's in the Order. It makes him suspect as any of us."

"Friday, you know that what we heard is hearsay anyway. He couldn't be held accountable for that, could he?"

"Look, boys…" Danny interjected. "No insult intended. Maybe I would rather not know."

Danny held up both hands in front of him. "I can turn back around and finish brushing down Banshee. 'Tis not a problem."

"Sorry. We're all Brothers in the Order. It's just there is reason to use care. The faithful are being told to watch out for a possible infiltration into the organization. We have been told for now just to watch. I know you to be true, for you are kin to Jim Carroll and he kin enough to us through our cousin Annie."

Charles stopped, before adding a solemn afterthought. "Our Mary Ann's Jack spoke well of ye, too."

Friday lowered his voice. "There has been another murder. Two days ago, at Raven Run. Tommy Sanger and some other fellow I don't know. A mate of his named Uren."

Danny lowered his head for a moment and closed his eyes. In his heart, he made the sign of the cross.

"Go on."

"We were at Muff Lawlor's place in Shenny last night. He was in there bragging that he knew all about it. Sittin' at the end of the bar snookered up with some dark featured lad named Harley and that slick fellow McParland that we've been keeping at arm's length. They were listening mighty close to each other. A tad *too* cozy if you ask me."

"Friday and I stayed awhile, over to the other end of the bar. The short one, Harley, wanted to pick a fight with anyone who'd take him on but neither of us took the bait. A trip to Shenandoah is usually good for a brawl or two on the way home. We don't often go to Muff's Saloon but this eigit here…" Charlie nudged his brother with a shoulder, "couldn't wait to get back to town to have a drink. I told him his thirst will be the death of him someday."

Danny nodded. He knew that the brothers meant well to warn him. He also knew it mattered little how carefully a fellow covered his tracks or even how innocent he was should the hangman came to call. He'd seen enough of hangings in Ireland to know that the newest neck in the noose belonged to the biggest and most vocal rebel rouser.

"I appreciate your warning, boys. A tip of me hat and many the thanks for watchin' out for a fellow countryman."

"Many times the welcome, Danny Carroll. Have a care, Lad. Ma promised that Charlie and I should keep an eye on ye, bein' all alone in a strange place and yer only kin our Annie's James. Ma would kick our arses into next week if you went and got yerself killed or locked up."

A woman's voice hollered from within the O'Donnell house. "Supper!"

"Ah, 'tis good to have a ma that cooks. She's made dumplin's to go with the chicken that Tom Murphy brought home from his new ladylove's house. One too many her ma said, 'twould go to waste. It's like Sunday dinner early."

The men laughed. Charlie went inside but Friday turned to Danny.

"Would you like to come in for supper? Ma would be happy to have ye at the table…"

Danny considered the offer. The widow was a renowned cook. But then so was Mrs. Mullins.

"No, tempting as it sounds…and thank your darlin' mother from the bottom of my heart, Friday O'Donnell…but see now, at *my* adopted ma's next door, Mrs. Mullins is making homemade biscuits. I expect she would not take so kindly to me not waitin' to eat whatever she has to go with them."

"Suit yourself."

Danny went back to grooming Banshee. Another murder. They were getting closer and closer to home, no matter where he was living these days. He shivered, with an almost premonitory chill. What was his role in all this? He had come too near both killings here in America. Linden's hound dogs and the local police needed little provocation to bully club an Irishman into paying for someone else's crimes.

Soon, Captain Linden might be snooping into his own past, digging up records from Ireland on his alleged crimes. Danny was getting close to having enough money to go to Ireland to collect Brigid. He refused to jeopardize his dreams by getting arrested now. The innocent were executed while the guilty went free.

Danny slept fitfully that night. He dreamed of Brigid, but she was no longer young. Her face had aged and she was crying. And though he tried to reach her, his hands could not stretch across the wide ocean. He could not swim to her. That old folk song…how did it go?

...and neither have I the wings for to fly...

His voice was silent. It lay thick in his throat and though he wanted to do so he could not call out to her. He woke up into darkness, heart palpitating, with tears streaming down his face.

Alone in his cot in the upstairs room of the Mullins house, Danny lay staring at the ceiling. He would not sleep this night. Tomorrow was a work day but his mind kept churning. He prayed to Our Lady of Mercies to help him have hope. Clutching his rosary, Danny quietly chanted Aves and Our Fathers until dawn broke.

Finally, in the early morning grayness, he rose silently. Danny dressed and made his way to the kitchen. There he grabbed one of the seven lunch pails—one for each working man—that Mrs. Mullins had set out the night before. On his silent pilgrimage to the colliery and then once well into the blackness of the mine, he prayed some more. Here, in the solitude of caverns never penetrated by the sun, things were clearer than in the light of day. Danny knew if God didn't hear him, here deep in the bowels of the world He'd created, He never would.

Summer turned into fall, then fall to winter. The leaves finally left the trees. Danny continued to use caution and tried to lay low. The collieries were back on for several months now. When he made the rounds to the mine bosses, he had put down his name as D. Carroll. He continued to do so on the work roster. There were no questions as to his full name. Danny decided to let sleeping dogs lie undisturbed.

In his last job at the Silver Creek Colliery at New Philadelphia, he was labeled as trouble. The "union lovers" were the first let go after the long strike, Danny along with them. It was clear punishment for the upstarts attempting to better their situation. They all knew it. The mine owners now routinely blacklisted anyone who'd belonged to the WBA. This time Danny could not risk the loss of his job. Better to keep his business private.

The only talk of reorganizing these days was at the AOH meetings. The word had come down from Black Jack himself. Discretion was to be the key now and in the future. It weren't only the loss of income, pitiful as that was. A member of the AOH, Danny was an instant target to finger for any crime the Coal and Iron Police choose to accuse him of doing. To be Irish and in Schuylkill County was to be suspect. It was best to keep his nose clear and his record spotless. He needed his wages, paltry as they were, to put towards Brigid's passage.

The nagging feeling that he needed to be doing more for the cause never left him. The unrest continued to grow around him. There was daily talk of Captain Linden's band of thugs making trouble in Mahanoy City and Shenandoah. In the alehouses and taverns, the Irish sang, as they always had. Now their brogues were joined by the Polish and others...

> If in exchange for the labor of a day
> You wish to have an honest, fair day's pay
> In short, if you wish to enjoy God's bounty,
> Go anywhere else but Schuylkill County.

Worst of all, Danny was haunted by Jack Kehoe's parting comment to him last summer. A dark specter lurked in the shadows of the painted corner room on the third floor attic room where he stayed at the Mullins and Danny couldn't seem to will it away. It was there sometimes when he awoke in the early morning darkness to head for the mines. It was there sometimes in the shadows on the sunniest day.

Sometimes, Danny almost heard the specter echo BlackJack Kehoe's words. He fought with the image of despair those words made him feel. Brigid's blasted sight wearing off on him again. He felt death but refused to believe it. Not about himself or Brigid. He shooed the specter away then, forcing himself to have hope.

And yet, despite all that, he could not escape the slowly dawning sense that something evil had crept into all that he knew and loved. The winter cold, despite the warmth of the Mullins' house, never seemed to leave him. And worst yet, Danny could not shake the words that now seemed etched even in his waking consciousness.

"Here, Danny Carroll, it'll be the gallows..."

Chapter Twelve

Murder and Mayhem

On the night of December 9th, Danny had gone to bed early. The skies promised snow. He knew he must be up early to clear a path for Mrs. Mullins out to the stable and then on out to the road. Daily mass came early and was not to be missed by the matriarch of the house. For all the place looked like Ireland in the summertime, Northeast Pennsylvania in the winter was a bloody twenty degrees colder. There was entirely too much snow for Danny's liking..

His feet, in his thin-soled boots, were numb as he trudged through the thick white layers to work in the predawn cold each morning. There would be no thick leather boots for him this winter. Perhaps next, he daydreamed, when Brigid was here with him…and they had a place of their own. Perhaps they might make a little extra money by letting out rooms. Aye, there'd be new boots, perhaps a pair of warm gloves but best of all, Brigid to keep him warm.

Danny drifted off. For now, he was warm and content under the handmade goose down comforter kindly provided by Mrs. Mullins. Tomorrow was another day. He dreamed of Brigid, but this time, it was a softer and more pleasant vision.

They were walking in the meadow, outside Ballycraig. The roses were in bloom and summer filled the air. Brigid was in her white wedding dress. Danny held her hand and was glad for it. He thought it would be forever until he saw her again, yet here she was…

His dreams were jarred into wakefulness by a loud bang, a shot it sounded like, coming from outside. His heart pounding, Danny shook his head to rid it of sleep. Jesus, Mary, and Joseph…what the hell was going on? Fumbling for his pants and shirt, Danny heard shouts and commotion from the back of the house. Then more shots…*two…three…four*…sweet Jesus…*would they not stop!*

It seemed forever until Danny reached the window. Just as he did, the gunfire ceased. He hesitated then peered outside. Snow had fallen, an inch or two. In the blackness, eerily illuminated by the snow and outlined by torches, were men swarming like ants. Some on horses, some on foot, but all scattered out back of the O'Donnell house. There looked to be ten…maybe twelve…no, Christ, there were more… maybe twenty or more. They wore oilskin coats and were carrying long guns.

A few of the men were holding down someone. Off to the rear of the property, straight back from the cherry tree near the stable, were another two men being restrained with their arms held behind their backs. One had a noose around his neck. Squinting, Danny saw the unruly red hair of James McAllister.

Shocked, he held back the curtain and strained to see farther into the night. The stark snowy landscape and glowing orange torches were a hellish backdrop for the murderous scene. Suddenly, one of the two men being held struggled free of his captors and ran into the blackness behind the stables. More shots rang out. The other man saw his chance and bolted as well. Gun powder smoked in the cold night air. More shouts. Some of the long coats ran into the darkness after the fleeing

The scene played itself out in slow motion before Danny's horrified eyes. After what seemed an eternity, the men in long coats got up, brushing off the snow. But the man they'd been holding down did not. He lay limp as the snow grew darker around him.

The other long-coated men returned without any captives. Their pursuit of their fleeing captives apparently had not been successful. One particularly tall villain walked over to the still body lying there and kicked it. There was no movement. By now, Danny could make out the familiar build of the man on the ground. Sweet Jesus, it was Charlie O'Donnell.

He was about to open the window, to scream stop, when he heard a light scratching at his door. Heart thumping, mind racing…he held his breath as he made his way to the other side of the room. He grabbed his pistol from the bedpost as he passed…

"Danny, Jesus Christ, wake up…it's Charles McAllister. I got in through the wooden slats in the cellar."

Even Charlie's whisper sounded deafening. Danny opened the door to the sight of Charles still clad in his white night shirt and bare feet. His face was terror stricken. Danny felt it mirrored in his own.

"The goddamn bastards…I thought I got a glimpse of Frank Weinrich…but I can't be sure. They've killed one of us, I think. Too many gunshots to have not, and none of us armed in the dead of the night! Jaysus Christ…Danny…they put a noose about Friday's neck and were dragging him outside. I got away through the cellars…but I heard more shots…Jesus Christ, Danny. Ellen and Mrs. O'Donnell…little Hugh…the baby…"

The other man wiped at his tear-stained face. Perspiration dotted his brow. Danny gave him a handkerchief before shutting the door and returning to the window. James clutched it in both hands and took a breath before going on.

"As I ran through the cellar and up the stairs, I heard Ellen's ma shouting out. Jesus Christ, Danny, give me your pistol… Little Charlie's there and Ellen's there, too…what if something happens to her and the wee one she's carrying? Will you not give me your bloody pistol, man? Where the hell is it…?"

Charles McAllister's face was red and now he was crying openly. Danny felt panicked but he refused to let that cause him to do something stupid. To go out there would be instant death for both of them. They had to find a way to get help…but first, he had to make sure Charles didn't do anything foolhardy…

"Look, Charles…stop. You must get a hold of yourself…Charlie O'Donnell is on the ground…"

"Jaysus Christ, me goddam brother-in-law…have they killed him?"

"Be quiet…I don't know any more than you…we've got to get you out of here and get help. It looks as though Friday and maybe one other has run off. Perhaps we can get out of here and reach them…"

Danny beckoned him to the window. By now he heard the shouts of the Mullins, the thuds of them running down the stairs. He had to think quickly. Could they have been vigilantes? After the O'Donnell's? Questions filled his mind. Why? Who the hell put them up to it? It would not be the first or last murder of an Irishman, but to attack a home with innocent women about…

"Charles, listen to me…"

"Look at the bastards…that's Charlie, alright, and he's not moving. What are they doing now? Oh, God, my brother James is out there somewhere. Is that Tom Murphy? And James Blair, too? Those are *nooses*…Mother, Mary of God! Do they plan to lynch them right here and now?"

"Stop it! Just think a moment…what are we to do?"

"We're going to take this pistol…"

"Oh, aye, me and you with one stinkin' pistol and thirty men out there with long rifles. Use your bloody head. It shan't help anyone if you're dead as well, Charles McAllister. Look, Christ…you've got to think of your wife and children. I want you to put on a pair of these pants old Mr. Mullins donated to me since he left the mines."

"Danny, look…they're leaving…"

Charles grabbed for Danny's pistol but he was not quick enough. Danny held it away, put a hand on Charlie's arm.

"Wait. I know. But listen…there is nothing you can do without getting killed yourself."

It was a foreboding sight, almost apocalyptic. Thirty mounted men, dressed hauntingly alike in long coats with faces covered, thundered away into the blackness of what remained of the night, leaving horror in their wake. Everything was silent. But for only a moment.

As the sky began to show signs of pink, and the light sifted through shreds of remnant snow clouds…the sound of a mother's weeping was pierced now and then by her wails of agony. Other sounds emerged from the tall fortress-like O'Donnell house. Shouts of indignation…threats of retaliation…grown men sobbing.

Danny went down the stairs first. The Mullins were still in the kitchen, huddled against the door and away from the windows. He saw the fear on their faces, and the relief that it had not been their home that had been terrorized. But Danny knew better, and so did they.

Next time, it very well could be.

He went out the back door into the snowy yard. Young Charles O'Donnell lay still, face down in the snow. There were no signs of life, but he went over anyway. The snow was blood red. Danny touched the boy's hand.

Charles was as cold as the snow he rested on. His nightshirt was riddled with bullets. He'd been shot in the head so many times that Danny didn't need to check for a heart beat to know his friend was gone. He was just a boy…barely eighteen.

"Danny…Danny Carroll…did you see any of it?"

Danny looked up to see Tom Murphy, followed by James Blair and John Purcell. He nodded. "What the hell happened?"

John Purcell rubbed his wrists. "Four strong arms in long coats burst into the rooms on the third floor where me and the boys bunk. Threw me out of me bed onto the floor and tied me by the wrists on my knees, to the bedpost."

Tom Murphy, who had turned over Charles' body, blessed himself. "Has somebody sent for the priest?"

"Nay," said James Blair. "But 'twill be a safer ride into Mahanoy Plain for Father McDermott than into town. The bastards put a noose around my neck, and Friday's, too. They were silent mostly, then somebody accused Friday and Charlie of being murderers and getting their due. They roughed up Tom pretty bad."

"They did. Gave me a few clouts to the head. Asking who I am, and who they were. Finally, they threw me up against the wall and left. Then I heard the shots. And the screams."

"Danny, they shot Ellen. The dear thing's dead and the Missus O'Donnell, they pistol whipped her something fierce. But she fought back… hit one with her cane and cursed them for all eternity."

Danny turned around in time to see Charles McAllister go back into the O'Donnell home. He could not help him face the pain of his wife's death, but it was clear that he had to get him out of there. Danny found him, cradling Ellen's body at the foot of the stairs. She'd been shot four times, but nowhere near her face. In death, she looked like a beautiful angel, fast asleep.

"Danny Carroll…ohhh, Danny…look what they have done to my poor Ellen…"

Nannie O'Donnell sat at the parlor table, face bloodied, her cane at her side. She had buried a 48-year-old husband, and the baby that was stillborn, but this was unthinkable. No woman should have to bury those she loved, but it was a woman's lot.

The black-hearted bastards who did this would be cursed forever by their own evilness. She could do no more, would do no more, than that. It was the way of the Irish woman. She would leave it to God. 'Twas a sin to wish misfortune on another…

But to pray for nature to take its course, and for fate to repay old debts? Nannie cried out for vengeance, for the loss of her daughter and son so brutally taken from her. For the loss of an unborn grandchild, fresh and full of hope. Dear Jesus, a new life snuffed out before it barely had started.

Danny went to her. She had been kind to him many times since he'd come to Wiggan's Patch. He bent his head to hers, as if she were his own mother, and whispered.

"I swear I will come back to help you. But now, we must get away. Charles must go…you must care for little Hugh."

The widow continued to weep, but more quietly. Her shoulders relaxed. Danny waited a minute. "We can do nothing for Ellen and Charlie but bury them. They have gone from us. But you have one son alive… I suspect Friday and James McAlister are not gone far. We must get to them and quickly. We will all come back as soon as it's safe."

"Danny, Charles…look what we found!"

Tom Murphy and John Blair ran in, breathless, holding a large piece of paper. It read:

"You Are The Murderers of Uren and Sanger"

"Those are the murders that Friday and Charlie were telling me about. Happened up in Raven Run back in September. They heard about it in Muff Lawlor's Saloon."

Danny's blood chilled. Captain Linden and the Pinkertons would stop at nothing. He knew both Friday and Charlie long enough to know

146

they were not the murderers. They were just boys. Now Muff Lawlor was another story. It did not take much to buy off a traitor. What could have brought the O'Donnell boys under the scrutiny of Captain Linden's magnifying glass? Simply being in the wrong place at the wrong time did not seem enough to justify two murders and five assaults.

"Charles, get up. Hurry! Grab whatever you wish to take with you. Nannie will care for little Hugh and bury the dead. Until we know why this has happened and who is being fingered as murderers, you must go. Little Hugh will need you later. Besides, Friday and James may be wounded. We've got to find them and decide what to do."

Danny directed James Boyle to ride to Girardville to tell Jack Kehoe what had happened and ask for assistance. They would ride into the woods and try to find the two James. Tracking them would not be hard. In fact, Danny wondered, given the snowfall that night…why the two men were not pursued further. He hugged Nannie, and the Mullins, who had by then summoned enough courage to come over.

His stomach churning with anger and fear, Danny Carroll went back to his room next door and with very little effort, collected and packed all he had. It was not a large bundle. He met Charles outside and the two rode back over the coal banks and woods behind Wiggan's. A decision had to be made. Would they head over the crest of the mountain to Shenandoah or turn west toward Girardville?

"What do ye think, Charles? Where would your brother go?"

"No question, Danny. He'd go to Jack in Girardville."

"Makes sense. We stay in the woods and out of sight until we hit Girardville, alright? The Hibernian House is down along the Creek. And Charles, watch your back."

"Aye, Danny. You might want to watch yours as well."

———

Covering their faces against the chill, the two men did not speak again until they reached the small, hidden-away tavern nestled next to the Mahanoy Creek. By then it had started to snow again. Both were cold and tired. Danny's feet were soaked and his hands frozen. Charles was in a state of grief-stricken shock at the loss of his wife and unborn child. They stumbled into the bar, two miserable excuses for humanity...

A great voice boomed out and though his ears were stinging, Danny knew it was Jack Kehoe. The light from the lanterns flickered on the walls. Danny shivered and stood there, unable to move.

"Get your arses in here where it's warm."

Danny was collared and shoved into a back room along with Charles McAlister. As his eyes adjusted to the dimness of the candlelight, Danny recognized Friday O'Donnell and James McAllister. Charles had been right. His brother had come straight for Black Jack.

Charles immediately began to cry. "Our Ellen's gone, and the new baby with her...and Charlie dead, shot in the snow."

"What of Ma?" asked Friday.

"Beat up pretty badly. One of the gentlemen callers whipped her with the blunt end of his gun. She put a dandy of a curse on them all, Tom Murphy tells me."

Danny noticed that Friday looked like he was all in one piece. James McAlister, however, had a bandaged right arm. James saw Danny's glance.

"'Twere when we ran. They shot a few times, mostly into the trees. I think I might have been hit by a ricocheting bullet. Funny, don't you think...that they didn't chase us harder?"

"I thought so too. It's almost as if they got what they wanted simply by taking blood. To make us fear."

Friday bowed his head. "They say the Pinkertons' bloodhounds can smell fear."

Danny nodded. "Then we better be brave or get the hell out of here."

―――――――

By the time Jack Kehoe came back into the room, Danny felt warmer. There was a fireplace in the corner. Charles had stopped crying. Friday had fallen asleep, clutching his arm, likely from the three shots of whiskey he'd drunk straight down for the pain. James McAllister sat next to his brother, his face blank, saying little.

"I've found out a few things. The murderers who visited Nannie's last night were hired thugs. Likely recruited by Gowen's men. Linden wasn't there, but he was back at their lair, I'll bet, directing the operation. The killings are to be a lesson to us. Stop fighting for your rights or we shall kill your woman and children."

"The note, 'twas left...Friday and you, Charles, are being named. You've got to get out of the country, at the very least out of the state. Charles O'Donnell is gone, and so is Ellen. You can do them no good by swinging on the gallows."

"I'm going back, Jack. My young lad is there. I can not help Ellen, but I can help young Hugh and Nannie. James, if you are indeed not being mentioned, perhaps we can go back together in a few days. Tom and the other lads will watch out for them. Friday, I agree with Jack...you need to be gone and quickly. Have you connections these days, Jack?

The tall man grumbled good-naturedly. "Have I connections! Where would you like to go, laddie?" Jack looked at Friday, who shrugged. "And what of you, Danny Carroll? You are never far from trouble, are you? Weren't you at Jimmy's in Tamaqua the night Yost was murdered?"

Danny nodded. Black Jack looked him square in the face. "Friday needs a travelin' companion. I hear Ireland's lovely this time of year and the voyage over is even lovelier. What say you, son? Since you are going as a personal favor to me, I will pay your way. With money of course, from the Order's special European touring fund."

Danny could not believe what he was hearing. He was being offered the price of a trip back to Ireland. To Brigid.

"Will it be round trip?"

"If you'd like, I'll make it a round trip for two."

Danny felt every care lift. He didn't worry that it was the dead of winter and an Atlantic voyage sheer jeopardy. He didn't give a thought to the fact that he would be accompanied by a man accused of murder. He did not even care where Jack Kehoe would get the money for such a grand gesture. He didn't care and he would do his best not to worry.

"Mr. Kehoe, I would like that very much. 'Tis in your debt I long shall be."

"Nay, Lad. 'Twill make my Missus happy to know someone with yer common sense is with her brother. Friday may be known for his personality, but not for his brain power." The men all laughed weakly. "I will rest easier knowing he makes it across the ocean to Gweedor in one piece. We have kin there. Get Friday to Gweedor, and that will be your only debt to me and mine."

"That Sir, I shall. Have no care and tell your Missus Mary Ann that she shall hear from her brother when I return."

Charles McAlister gave him a quizzical look. "You would come back, Danny boy? After all this, you really would return?"

"Aye, there is one thing left for me in Ireland." Danny managed a smile. "I shall bring her back with me."

His companions understood. They murmured their good wishes.

"God speed, Danny Carroll," Jack Kehoe said finally. "You have been a good friend to us all. I have heard from many of the men that you've taken the time more than once to encourage them over the last many months. It takes a leader to keep up morale when times are toughest."

The handsome man with the big black handlebar mustache winked conspiratorially at Danny. The twinkle, somehow, despite the tragedy of the day, was there.

"Mind yourself, Danny Carroll. May you find that which you seek. When you come back, Danny boy-o, we shall talk of your future."

Chapter Thirteen

Going Home Again

There was little that could prepare Danny for going back to Ireland. Had he more time to prepare, he might have obsessed and ruminated over the possibility that the passport papers Jack Kehoe had arranged would be discovered to be fraudulent. He might have been apprehensive of the choppy sea journey. Ice chunks floated by the vessel and sometimes could be heard scraping the wooden sides. Still, Danny's spirit couldn't be dampened.

He experienced it all with just one thought. It rallied him and bolstered his mood. When this was all over, he was going home to get Brigid. Home to Ballycraig. At some point, the godforsaken ship he was aboard would come hobbling into some Irish port. All the better if it happened to be the harbour at Galway or Donegal Bay. He'd have to get Friday north and safely home to the O'Donnell clan in Gweedore.

Then, and only then, his debt repaid, he could change course. For Ballycraig and Brigid. He hoped he could surprise her, perhaps as she stood in her mother's kitchen kneading dough for morning biscuits. Or maybe as she came out of 7 o'clock mass. He replayed the scene, changing it each time to amuse himself on the long and grey voyage. Friday slept most of the time. He was not what you would call good company.

It had been difficult to make himself physically not want Brigid. They had been faithful to each other, but she'd made him wait to take her virginity. Her ma would kill her dead, she swore. Danny could have pestered her, made her give in. But he hadn't.

Perhaps he should have. Would it have been better now? Made it easier to be apart from her? This separation that had torn the soul out of him and probably her as well. He would kiss her over and over again, his beautiful Brigid. The months apart seemed endless now. Soon it would be over.

They would visit home for a bit. Not for long. Perhaps they could marry in Ireland, quickly. Danny did not wish to tarry here long. He had made a conscious decision to return to America. There were things happening in Pennsylvania. He wanted to be there to help Doolin, Jack Kehoe, and the others. But he would return with Brigid at his side.

He was not to worry about being gone. Jack Kehoe had reassured him, as he'd handed him the altered passport. A place would be held for him in "County Schuylkill," so help Jack. Danny smiled inwardly at the warmth he felt thinking about the new friends he had made. Doolin, Tom Murphy, James Carroll, the Mullins and the O'Donnells. Sad at his departure, they would be glad for his return.

Until then, all he had to do was to enjoy his visit back to the Old Sod under an assumed name with a fake passport.

"Even if ye choose to stay a year and a day, you have earned your place here. You are a credit to the Hibernian Order and your fellow countrymen on both sides of the Atlantic. Danny Carroll, you shall be greatly missed."

Black Jack Kehoe extended his hand to shake the younger man's hardily before he warmly grasped him by both shoulders. The big man's eyes were moist but he would not cry. They all knew the seriousness of what they were facing in the coming months.

"May the road rise to meet you, Laddie."

"Thank ye, Sir, and until we meet again, have a care, will ye? I shall do my best to see Friday to your kin in Gweedore."

His biggest challenge was to get used to being "Daniel Connors," a young man, traveling back to Ireland with his brother, James, for their auntie's funeral in Gweedore. James would not be returning to America. His story was simple—he was staying behind to help his auntie's children settle her estate. Danny was now free to do whatever he wished.

What if he chose to stay in Erin? He could disappear into the Irish landscape, along with a hundred others hiding out from the British under false pretenses. He would be a free man. The English could not touch him. He and Brigid could marry and raise their children as they had so often dreamed. But this thought nagged him—was one's identity worth the price of freedom?

He decided no. That kind of freedom was a pipe dream. One's life was all there was, really. To deny even a piece of it would be to rip a hole in its tapestry. Danny would never live in Ireland again but it would haunt him until he ceased to breath. Things were not easy in America but it held what Ireland could not...the promise of a future. All left for him and Brigid in Ireland was their ancestors' bones and a life of poverty.

That was it then, wasn't it? That thread to the past was the invisible link that would always tie his heart to that beautiful part of his life. Ireland. The ache was deep in his chest. Memories of growing up in Ballycraig, near the ruins of the Assaroe Abbey. The picturesque little village was slightly inland from Bundoran and north of Lough Melvin.

Despite the poverty that permeated every hovel and hut, Danny's childhood had been almost idyllic in many ways. Family, hard work, daily worship, music. It seemed music had always been an important part of Danny's life. In nearby Ballyshannon, as in many of the other little villages throughout the country, the fiddler and the bodhran joined the tin whistle and the horn pipe in music that could charm the angels. Danny closed his eyes and could almost hear the pipes.

The windswept peninsulas and beaches of idyllic northwestern County Donegal. Donegal...the "fort of the foreigners" built by the Vikings. Danny as a youth had explored all that stretched from the lakes and rivers of Carrick-on-the-Shannon a bit to the south in County Leitrimall to Ballyshannon in the north near Donegal. The ruins of castles, the mounds of the fairy hills, and the massive standing stones...the mountains of nearby County Sligo and flat topped Ben Bulben where it was said the Celtic warrior Queen Maeve of Connaught rests in her grave..

Danny missed the home of his youth. Tears came to his eyes. He had never wished to leave Ireland. But he had, and it had changed him.

Danny did not miss the darker things. The poverty of the huts that sprawled within a mile of Ballyshannon's bourgeois Georgian houses. The hunger that gnawed the pit of his stomach. The trigger happy English who liked nothing more than using the odd Irishman for target practice. The snobbery of the gentry whose souls were corrupted by an insatiable greed for power over those with nothing.

Not the hunger, nor the arrogant gentry landowners…not the English tyranny. He knew these things and had survived them, but what of his children? They deserved a future in a different world. Danny would never break away from his lot in life here. In the snobbery of Irish society, Danny had nothing and would be thought of as nothing. Once a peasant, always a peasant.

Brigid would understand. Even in the face of false accusations and the hangman's noose, Danny knew with certainty he would go back to America. He had tasted true freedom beneath the coal dust and it tasted fine. Gallows or not, he would face what came. Danny swore a silent affirmation. He would take the citizenship oath. His children—his and Brigid's—would be born Americans. Irish Americans, but Americans all the same. American and free.

He prayed Brigid had gotten the letter he'd sent a few months before. At least she would know his thoughts. He hoped they could see eye to eye. Such little time for argument. Life was precious. The O'Donnell murders had taught him a lesson. Value the present and those in it for it can be gone in the blink of an eye.

Only a few more nights onboard ship and they would sight land. America had already given him a feather in his cap. A poor lad from County Donegal like he had crossed the ocean twice already. Who would have thought?

"And not soon after," he reassured himself aloud, "it will be thrice."

Not bad for a poor lad, not bad at all. The cold Atlantic chill set into his bones, but he didn't mind. It was the same winter in Ireland as in America. The difference was that Brigid waited for him there, on the old sod. He would return to Ireland this one time more, to bring her back to a new life in Pennsylvania. They would build a home, not rent a company house.

He would rise above his beginnings, as had Jack Kehoe. He and Brigid's children would get, how had cousin James put it? A "step up," that was it. Perhaps their son would become an apprentice to a doctor or barrister. It was more than a poor lad could aspire to, but he hoped it anyway, if not for himself, then for Brigid.

Chapter Fourteen

All the Roses Falling

Brigid no longer had a choice. Fergus O'Rourke was pursuing her relentlessly, begging her to marry him. Fergus was not one to take no for an answer. He was not a mean man, he told her. And life would be easier for her once they were married and settled into the O'Rourke cottage.

Brigid doubted this. From her perspective, she'd be caring for his aging parents as well as her own family. Ah, but then Fergus argued back, wouldn't the albatross of the Devlin homestead be gone from around her neck? The O'Rourke lands were big enough to build a cottage for her parents and the younger Devlins, as well as themselves. In time.

Easy? Brigid looked for excuses. It sounded to her like she would be tripling her problems. A hundred times, kindly as she could, she answered that Danny would be back someday and indeed wouldn't it be a sin, them betrothed and all, for her to go and be marryin' another. Not, she'd add with deep sentiment in her voice, that Fergus O'Rourke wasn't the catch of the county and all.

No, Brigid insisted, she wished to be free for her Danny's return. And although in her heart, she feared the worst, she still professed her loyalty. If nothing else, it freed her, or so she hoped, from the prospect of her marrying another. Brigid simply would not accept the thought of marriage to pudgy, pig-nosed Fergus. Or anyone else for that matter.

It would not be fair, she informed her critics, including her father who'd had his ear bent by Fergus at Logan's Tavern. Fergus swore he and his strapping brother Michael would move the Devlin's lock, stock, and barrel to the O'Rourke farm. It would no longer matter about saving the Devlin farm. They'd simply give it up to the bank

Brigid was buying none of it. There was no question as to saving the farm through marriage to another. She would die faithful to Danny Carroll, even if it meant eviction. Besides, Brigid had thought of another way to save the farm.

A way to save the farm and herself from a loveless marriage she neither wanted nor felt she should be forced into by her circumstances or her father. His name was Edwin McCarthy. A big shot hereabouts. The well-to-do bank officer traveled to Donegal from his Georgian home in Ballyshannon on a daily basis. Brigid had encountered him often on her road to market in Ballyshannon.

She did not particularly care for him, but she sensed he fancied her. Brigid did not care for people who used others for their own means, but she did not plan to be untruthful or sinister in her behavior. She simply planned to be friendly next time he passed. It would not be hard to do.

Edwin McCarthy often called to Brigid when saw her walking back from an errand. Would she care for a ride? What coincidence that they were going to same way! Couldn't they be friends? Nice weather. Brigid considered his attentions neither flattering or welcome.

As was her standard response to unwanted harassment from passersby, Brigid kept her head down. It was best Ma said to avoid looking them in the eye. Many on the road were friendly, but not all. Too many were men, and lecherous ones at that. Still, what was one to do? The Devlin's horse long since had been sold. They rarely traveled by anything other than foot these days.

No, she would shake her head. Then, murmur a quick "No thank you, Sir." If she knew the Sir, she would say the name rather than just the "Sir." Always respectfully. It made them think she knew her place. She would then pull her shawl tighter and pray whoever they were would go away.

Sometimes Edwin McCarthy went away. Other times, he signaled his driver to slow down. The coach and its occupant paced her as she traveled by foot towards either Donegal or Ballycraig. Last time, he said something that disturbed her. Might she ever consider having dinner with him, he had asked with his thin smile a tad ghoulish. Perhaps, he suggested, sometime even accompany him to an exhibit or dinner party.

She knew he fancied her. These new suggestions that they be seen together on some public level gave her the willies. It would be a cold day in Hell before she'd agree to step out with the likes of Edwin McCarthy. Jesus, he was old enough to be her father! Brigid supposed he thought himself something of a catch. She also knew that even if there were no Danny Carroll and Edwin McCarthy was the last man on Irish soil, she would still find the man repulsive.

The girls of the villages knew him well and whispered as he passed. He was not above offering shiny trinkets or a ha'penny for a bit of pleasant company on his ride home from a long day at the coffers. Females, young or old alike, were generally happy to oblige. Most had never seen a fancy bauble in the whole of their lives.

The pretty ones, the loose ones...often came out with a gold coin instead of a copper. Brigid heard them laugh about it. What was it to them to allow the old fool a quick feel up? They let their own lads do it for free, so what of it? Brigid did not doubt that more than groping went on.

Her buxom cousin Tess, on her mother's Brennan side, had been showing off a small prism eardrop, the size of a coin, claiming it a diamond. Edwin, she bragged, had gifted it to her because he loved her smile.

Brigid snickered at her relative's foolishness. It wasn't hard to figure it was Tessie's ample bosom, not her dazzling teeth, the perpetually leering bank officer found endearing. Wickedly, she asked Tess why had he not given her the *other* earring. As her cousin stammered an excuse, Brigid told her she was fairly sure Edwin's impeccably dressed and bejeweled mother would provide the answer from her jewelry box. The daggers she received were payment enough.

Still...and this was where her plan came in...his bank held the note on the Devlin farm. If she befriended him, maybe was at least polite...perhaps he would agree to extend the lease on the Devlin farm for a few more years. Just until times were better. If she appealed to his better side, his Christian side...

Was this what it felt like to be beaten enough to grovel? Brigid suddenly felt her place. The man was well above her in social class. The only son of a wealthy Irish landowner, McCarthy would sell his own father's soul for English patronage of his family's banking establishment. Here she was, a lowly woman, a peasant. Was she no better than any of the other Ballycraig lasses who gave up their favors for a snippet of lace or a piece of sugar taffy?

It didn't matter. Edwin McCarthy held the power to allow her family to hold on to their homestead for a little longer.

Nothing else was left to be done. She fastened the last hook on the high neck of her good church dress. It was blue, Danny's favorite color. Tying on her bonnet, Brigid pinched her cheeks and bit her lips in hopes of bringing up a touch of color. The Devlin's had no looking glass to check her reflection but she felt as pale as the watery milk she'd coaxed this morning out of Old Susie. The cow, their sole remaining piece of livestock, had seen better days.

Her thoughts went to Danny. She prayed he would forgive her for having to beg. If only he were here to help her. Why couldn't she be wrong? It was not that she didn't pray to the Virgin night and day that there was some way to bring him back to her. Brigid bargained in her prayers to Mary. That the Sight could have been just a premonition, perhaps her nerves gotten the best of her. She beseeched the Mother of God and a long litany of Saints to which daily she added a new name...

She prayed that Danny was at least safe for surely, they would have heard if he were dead. Although many months had passed, the memory of the visions in her dreams still haunted her. Brigid, as much at peace with it as she could be, had little recourse.

She would wait for him, she told her family and his as well. The Devlin family would have starved already but for the generosity of the neighbors and the local shopkeepers. Townsfolk knew Brigid was doing her best. People would continue to be kind. Still, Moira and even Danny's father's new wife, the Mistress Logan, prodded her.

"We all know that you love him still, Brigid. No one would think the less of you if you married another. Not now. Not after so long. It's been

159

almost two years. Danny's gone, or might as well be. All this time…and not a word from him."

Moire sadly shook her head. She was pregnant again but so emaciated, that except for a little protrusion of her stomach, it barely showed. She looked tired. She and Gerald had named their first child Deidre. The wee stillborn lass was born a month prematurely after Danny's capture. Moire said if the new babe was a boy, she would name him Daniel after his uncle.

"'Tis not even the respect of being the grieving widow that ye have. You are so young, Brigid. Do what is best for *you*. Yer bloody father is drinkin' his life away. *He* should be carin' for yer ma and the little ones. Times are hard and getting harder."

Moire told her she was daft. Danny might have been lost at sea. Mayhaps dead of disease. Gone from them to a better place. No, Brigid told her that wasn't so. She'd know in her heart if he were dead. But even as she spoke of it, she felt dizzy and then…the chill at her center core.

Brigid could not control the Sight. When it came upon her, she went numb, unable to respond. She saw his face…Danny was so close to her…she almost felt the warmth of his breath. He was more handsome than when last she saw him a year ago. His shoulders were broader but his face harder. Brigid reached to touch his cheek but he seemed to pull away from her. Then she realized that he could not see her. Panicked, she heard his voice saying her name. His name echoed in her head but she could not make a sound.

Her eyes went black and she could no longer see him…but still he called her…Brigid felt herself fading into the vision. Then, suddenly, Moire's voice drew her back. The other woman kept one hand on Brigid's shoulder as she shook her gently. Brigid gasped for air.

She was shivering uncontrollably. The Sight. There was no escaping it. She knew it for certain now. Brigid Devlin would never gaze on her true love's face again.

"Are you all right? Dear Jesus, let it go, Lass. It's me, Brigid. His own sister. Do you think I want our Danny to have met such a fate? But I love you as if I were your sister, too. Another few months and you would have been so."

Moire wiped away the tears rolling down her own cheeks and hugged Brigid to her. The girl felt like ice.

"'Tis just...ye must do what ye must to survive. Who cares what anyone thinks? Ye can not give up. Danny would not want you to stand on ceremony, Brigid. Marry Pig Face O'Rourke if ye have to. He could go first, y' know. Imagine that...to have the O'Rourke place for yourself."

Brigid cringed. She would not sink that low. Besides, where would the other snout-faced O'Rourke's go? She knew Moire meant well. The Carrolls had it a bit easier since Danny's father married the widow Logan. Moire tried to help the Devlins when she could with an extra scrap of meat or a bone for soup, the extra loaf of bread.

Moire did not know what exactly Brigid had seen. Brigid kept her visions to herself. She had not the heart to tell Moire or anyone else. The visions had robbed her of almost all hope of Danny returning. He had been gone so many long months. She only wished to spare his family what she knew already in her heart of hearts.

First, the date of their wedding came and went. It had been a fine day. 'Twould have been grand to have married on such a glorious day. She'd tried on the gown she had made with her own hands, weeping with grief the whole while Brigid would. But she could not weep forever. There was too much to do, too many chores. The months passed by. The seasons changed. She wrote long letters. Written them from her heart then given them to neighbors and kin en route to the Americas. And still no word from Danny. Not to her, not to his family.

The last little shred of her psyche that still believed in miracles began to shrivel and die. Things grew harder and harder to manage. 'Twas when her father began to pressure he for the first time..

"Marry the O'Rourke. Think of your family, you selfish child."

It became a daily topic. When it was not enough to harass her himself, he put her mother up to it as well. At first, Paddy Devlin resorted to the arguing and the brooding. Her mother followed with the pleading and the crying.

"Will you not do it just do it to make him leave you alone, Brigid? Your father said that the O'Rourke has promised to get us all away from here. Perhaps it would be best...do you not think so?"

Brigid did not think so. Soon after, the threats began.

So little of the father she remembered as a child was left. She hardly knew him at all. It was the drink she knew that made him argue with her mother and harass the children. A faraway look in his eyes came and never left. Paddy Devlin grew angrier and more distant.

Like a caged animal, dreaming of the wild, but no longer believing it existed. Brigid felt disgusted his behavior. He was her da but she could not help it. The cage was of his own creation. The poorer they became, the more her father drank. How dare he take money that could be spent on food and piss it away with his beer? Danny's pain at his own alcoholic father's struggle was more real to her now than ever before.

Brigid was suffocating. Not that it mattered anymore. She had turned seventeen last week and her life was over. It was too painful to hope. The only thing left was honor. Her mother was helpless with grief over her father; her father was half mad with drink. To whom else could her young brother and sister turn? Little Mary Margaret was only nine and Patrick Thomas eleven.

It was up to her to save her family's farm. At least until the wee ones could earn their way. Her mother was barely thirty but looked an old woman. Her father was rarely sober. He drank most of the day and threw up blood half the night. And when he was able to speak, his harassment continued. *Marry the O'Rourke...selfish Brigid...to pass up the chance for us all to have a roof over their head...marry the O'Rourke.*

For the first time since Danny had left, Brigid realized she was needed. She did not have Danny but she had a purpose. That sense of purpose gave her hope of existing without her true love. Somehow she would find a way to make her father leave her alone and in peace. If she could just keep the farm and the house for a bit longer. Next year would be better.

Brigid had a plan. A sure fire way to make sure they would all survive. And it didn't involve marrying Fergus O'Rourke

The whole idea hadn't come to her all at once. At first, her thought was to just take in sewing. Mending and the like. But then, it came to her. A seamstress. There were only a few women who knew the skill well enough to make a business of it.

Brigid's mother had taught her how to turn a needle years ago, but it hadn't took. It was only when she and Danny were to marry that Brigid, needing a wedding dress but having no money, began to sew one pieced together out of scraps of bleached muslin.

After Danny's disappearance, she could not help but continue. Working on the gown was like medicine. Adding a ruffle here, embroidering the hemline just so. It soothed her. Lost in the process of creation, she could forget her pain. At times, she daydreamed about Danny and what her wedding would have been like.

To everyone's surprise, with nothing to go on except a picture in her mind, the simple gown made of scraps came out beautifully. It seemed Brigid Devlin had the knack for sewing. One day, not long after, her friend Enya's cousin Molly Mulroy from over Pettigo way had asked to see the dress Molly had been raving over. Next minute, she was begging Brigid to tell her how much she would charge to sew one for her by spring.

That's when it came to her. Clear as one of her visions. Every girl wanted a wedding dress of their own, even the poorest ones. She would become a dressmaker. Brigid figured to charge for the labor and have the girl bring their own material. There was little money for frivolities like wedding finery in a famine-ridden Ireland but Brigid would charge only enough to get by.

With her mother and young Mary Margaret started helping out, they might be abler to take in work from the surrounding villages. If she had the right materials, beautiful silks, velvets…lace…yards and yards of it. Imagine the beautiful gowns she might make! Her heart felt lighter. Things were looking up.

Until this morning. The eviction notice was on the front door when her father dragged himself home from a night spent God only knew where. He began to harp on her as she tried to sweep the dirt from the kitchen hearth. Try as she may to ignore him, Brigid grew exasperated. She'd rather throw herself off the cliffs at Sleive League than consent to marry O'Rourke or anyone else she didn't love. Half drunk, Paddy Devlin accused her of wanting to wait for Danny Carroll because he'd had his way with her.

Then he slapped her. Hit her. Her own father. It was something he had never done. Not to his wife and never to his children.

The anger bubbled up inside her. It was too much. She had been patient with him; he was her da. How dare he insinuate such a horrible lie. Brigid took the feeling, wild and full of hatred, bottled up deep inside her these long sad months. It had to be unleashed or it would eat her alive. She raged at him with the kitchen broom in her hand, intent to hit him.

It was the look of terror in little Mary Margaret's eyes stopped her.

Motionless, Brigid waited with the broom poised in the air. The next action she took would determine her worth as a person more than even she realized. She felt as if her chest was going to burst. The anger flamed within her, licks of fire burning her. She wanted to hit him, to silence him no matter what it took.

Finally, she breathed. What had come over her? Dear God, it would not help to use so much precious energy for destruction. She watched her inebriated father stagger to the cot in the corner and pass out. His snoring filled the room. Pathetic creature. Brigid lowered the broom and turned away.

Composed again, Brigid silently swore she would never again allow her alcoholic father to hurt her. Nor drive her to his own evil violence. Her vow left her feeling better...spurred her to do something., anything to help their situation. Slowly her breathing became regular. Bowing her head, she muttered a Hail Mary and closed her eyes, looking for guidance.

She had heard stories...rumors, perhaps...that the Blessed Virgin sometimes appeared to the faithful to bring them hope. She had never known anyone who had seen a religious vision, but she was as faithful as anyone else. For a long time, she knelt there praying silently. The snoring finally stopped as her father turned into the pillow. No visions came. Brigid sighed.

Perhaps she had known all along that it would be up to her to do what was needed. There was still her mother and little brother and sister to worry about. Her parents could use every ounce of help she could give. Her own life would change little in the coming years. Brigid would never marry. It was Danny or no one. Her lot would be to care for what was left of the family. It was up to her to bring up her younger siblings. She would make *sure* they had a chance.

And today was the day. She could delay no longer. Today, the farm had to be reclaimed or they were to be evicted. In five days. She hated to beg, but beg she would. She would go to the bank today, throw herself upon Edwin McCarthy's mercy, and convince him to either extend the mortgage on the farm or lend her the money until her fiancee's return. This would buy her time. Certainly the man would give her the courtesy of his good will. She had known him all of her life, as had her family, and Danny's family, too.

Throwing a cloak about her shoulders, Brigid crept out into the early morning mist. There was much to be done and little time to do it.

———

He was not just a wealthy banker… he was the bank. Though not so wealthy—or foolish—as to be frivolous with his family's money, Edwin McCarthy lived a respectable public life and kept exotic tastes in private. He naturally would have preferred to take Brigid Devlin on the side. The village girls were so easily entranced by a bauble or sweetmeat. Not Brigid Devlin, however.

The rich middle-aged businessman was not unattractive. He used cologne and bathed frequently. His clothing well tailored, his boots nicely shined. Edwin inspected his trimmed and polished manicure. Perfect. And yet…Brigid Devlin—a common trollop—turned her nose up at him as if he were the village scourge.

It was true that at first, he feigned amusement. Even to himself. Frankly, it had irritated him but the faint air of humor managed to mask his underlying annoyance. Of course, the more he obsessed about it, the angrier he got.

Finally, intrigue set in. It irked him to feel this attracted to someone who clearly was doing her best to avoid him. He was humbled… yes…*humbled* enough for him to ask her permission to call on her.

Politely, infuriating so, she had told him no. The audacity. Her staunch refusal only made him more determined. Secretly, he found it oddly thrilling. A tad perverse that he should enjoy her refusals, but he did.

He began to pursue her after Sunday mass. The McCarthys still practiced Catholicism although Edwin himself strongly considered turning Protestant to further capture the British business. Interestingly, his mother would not hear of it. It was one thing to sell to them but she would not pray with them. Edwin knew better than to cross her. Most all the family's monies had come from his mother's side and the old bitch still controlled the strings.

Needless to say, Brigid did not encourage him. She was quite kind and pleasant spoken. This infuriated him even more. She was not impressed by his looks, his wealth, nor his wit, it seemed. His dreams were filled with her...he imagined her in his bed, in the bath, at his dining room table.

There came a point in time when his waking thoughts were too often of her. The girl was no great beauty but that did not diminish his desire. What could he do, he deliberated, to attract her to him? Once he had her, he would make her want him...make her submit to him...

He began to plot...to consider his situation. Single, at the age of 50, he had never married. And so what of it? *He* chose things to be that way. It did not mean he was at a loss for female companionship. Indeed, au contrare! Edwin McCarthy had an active sexual life. Quite an appetite, he was proud to say.

He made his rounds in the village, and in Ballyshannon. There were trips to Donegal, and to Dublin. Friends from University. Daughters of business associates. Giggling American debutantes on their grand tour to the Continent. He had his sampling of them all.

Yet, none particularly caught his interest. Once he had sex with them, even the well bred ones, he lost interest. As the years passed, he saw little reason to change his ways. Eventually he would marry and have a family. He had time. Men could father a child well into their later years. It was best, perhaps, that he waited. Find himself a young lass to wed and bear children. She'd certainly be fairer than some old hag he'd had around for the last fifteen or twenty years.

It was at that juncture that he had begun to entertain the idea that the intriguing Brigid Devlin may be in line for consideration as the Mrs.

Edwin McCarthy. And why not? At this point in his life he was beyond social reproach.

He was the prodigal son of one of the wealthiest families in town. Should he choose to marry an attractive young woman of questionable ancestry, it was his business. She was of hardy stock. Those peasants, unlikely his own delicate mother, literally dropped their offspring in the fields. Yes, it was high time for him to procreate.

Or so he'd been told. By his mother. The idea of childbirth actually repulsed him. Even if it were his own child. No, Edwin planned to be at the club or perhaps out hunting like his father bragged he had been during his only son's birth. Ah, yes, sex itself was pleasurable enough but the junior McCarthy would draw the same line at being party to a birthing as the senior McCarthy had. Like father, like son.

And to rid his thoughts of such a disgusting image, he brought himself comfortably back to his fantasy. The thoughts of the lush, seventeen-year-old body of his soon-to-be bride. Yes, it all would fall into place. Most certainly. Once she realized he meant to wed her, she would be putty in his hands. What girl wouldn't? Why she would probably throw herself at his feet with gratitude!

With the daydream of the pretty young object of his lust beginning to take shape, he settled comfortably into his pre-dawn carriage ride to the bank. It was the middle of April and the morning was quite pleasant. Edwin prided himself on his early arrival. Today he would arrive a full hour and a quarter before even his elderly uncle Liam, the president. There was little Edwin found more stimulating than sex except money. He made sure to butter up Liam every chance he could.

He found himself picturing the raven haired Brigid Devlin in several compromising positions and becoming quite excited by it all. The remainder of his commute went rather quickly. Now that it was all settled, he couldn't wait to proceed with his plan. Issuing his driver the command to return for him at 4 o'clock this afternoon, Edwin exited his carriage.

And could barely believe his good fortune. In the dim predawn grayness, he had to look twice. But then, oh, what a sight! For as if his dreams had been overheard, there she sat on the stoop, before his very eyes. Brigid Devlin. It was as though the Gods had heard his very thoughts and granted him his desire.

The streets were silent except for the sound of the horses' hooves on the cobblestones as his carriage made its way towards home. The early morning mists still hung low in the street. The sea winds that had blown them in had quieted. Edwin felt a stillness in the air as if something were going to happen. He was still very excited from his fantasy.

The girl sat outside the bank doors alone, looking very young. She wore what he supposed was her Sunday gown. It was a drab blue. What a prize she would be with the proper clothes, coiffed hair! He imagined it would take very little to transform her. She really was a beauty despite her breeding and appalling lack of taste.

As he approached her, Brigid drew herself up, shoulders back, ready to speak. She looked afraid and this made him feel powerful. He held up a finger to his lips. Ah, look. The girl waited in expectation. Edwin became even more excited.

As he drew out a large ring of keys and opened the great wooden door to the bank, he took a glance at the large pendulum clock in the great hall near the vault. Uncle Liam would not wander in until 8:30. As was his custom, Edwin did his best work alone and in private. Today would be no exception.

———

"Miss Devlin." Edwin McCarthy tipped his hat. "And what a pleasure seeing you here at our humble bank. What is it I might do for a lovely lady such as yourself?"

Brigid had not realized just how early the hour was when she'd left in haste before the sun was even up. Never one for procrastinating at a task, she had decided to face her family's eviction square in the face. There was no point in pretending. She had wanted to get here before the crowd. She now realized that this early was ridiculous. There was no one but she and Edwin McCarthy on the street. Brigid stared into the dark cavern of the deserted bank building

"Mr. McCarthy, I would not dream of disturbing you before the start of the business day. It can wait. I shall come back…"

"I assure you, my business day would not be disturbed by one as fair as yourself, Miss Devlin, whether at its beginning or its end. Please, won't you come in? I can attend to your needs as easily now as later. It is unfortunate that I did not think quickly enough to have my carriage wait to drive you home. Neither my coachman nor I saw you sitting in the shadows."

Brigid felt afraid. His words were innocent but there was a predatory undertone that made her skin crawl. She did not like Edwin McCarthy but she had no choice. He was her only chance.

"I had hoped…that you might be kind enough to help…to hold off the eviction notice a bit. Perhaps the bank might loan us enough for a few months mortgage? Or at least give us a little more time? Please…my family has nowhere to go."

Edwin's eyes flickered. He turned up a gaslight in the foyer. Brigid still stood in the threshold. She was not above begging, but this man gave her chills. There was an uncomfortable span of silence. Brigid backed up one step.

"I can come back later."

"Of course not. I simply will not hear of it. I can help you. Please. Come into my office. It will take only a minute."

Brigid hesitated. There were things that frightened her and this man was one of them. There was nothing to do but to be brave. She blessed herself under her breath and went inside. The great wooden door closed behind her. God would have to watch over her from this step forward. At least she prayed he was watching.

———

Edwin did not plan to rape Brigid Devlin. Not at first. He had truly been surprised to see her there outside in the shadows waiting. She really was a rather fetching girl. A bit pale of complexion but he supposed it suited her.

No, the thought first occurred to him right there in the bank, with him sitting at his desk in his stuffed leather chair. It really would be a shame to waste this golden opportunity. His office was warm. A morning attendant came in at 6 am to stoke the fires. He loosened his collar a bit.

"Please, sit. It shan't be but a moment."

Edwin expertly located the ledger in the high wooden file cabinets that lined his office. His bank held a substantial number of the mortgages on the farms and shops in Donegal and surrounding Leitrim and Sligo counties. It was a requirement of his assistant that he keep the records organized by name, year, and county. Edwin liked things at his fingertips.

He also liked his comfortable lifestyle. He learned to curb his more unsavory impulses after that one messy incident the summer he was seventeen. His father had almost not been able to buy off the magistrate. Young Edwin came daringly close to being convicted of raping the thirteen-year-old daughter of a local Presbyterian minister. Since then, he satisfied his more base instincts with local whores, prostitutes and the occasional wench.

Bored, he listened to Brigid Devlin's tale of woe. He had heard the same tale of woe at least a dozen times this week. It was necessary to divorce oneself from the actual person in order to do his job well and Edwin did his job well. One learned to listen with one ear while preparing the paperwork for the foreclosure. It saved so much time in the course of the business day.

Perhaps it was the pitiful story the girl was laying out before him. He was not the empathetic sort. Her blatant emotional display made him recognize his own stupidity at entertaining the idea of publicly *courting* the pathetic creature. His opportunistic tendencies took over. What a shame to waste the chance of sampling the peasant girl. And here she was for the having.

What *had* he been thinking…

For effect, Edwin fanned through the mortgage folder he held. The girl looked on the verge of tears. Ah, well. It really was not in the bank's best interest to allow the Devlin's any more of a grace period. Their payment history was sluggish and rather sketchy. Edwin closed the file dramatically and crossed the room, returning it to its given place.

"I'm sorry, Miss Devlin. I simply do not see how I possibly would be able to assist you at this time. Alas, your father has let too many mortgage payments lapse."

"Mr. McCarthy, I beg of you. Please. Is there not something you could do? I give you my word. You will be paid back in full."

Instead of returning to his chair, Edwin suddenly moved around the side of the wooden cherry desk to the leather chair where Brigid sat. He could not resist it when they pleaded. He grabbed her arm roughly and pulled her up to face him. His tone was thick with innuendo.

"There is always *something* a pretty lass like yourself can do, Miss Devlin."

His breath was nauseatingly sweet. Brigid was not stunned at his insinuation that she would sleep with him, but he was becoming physical. Brigid was no stranger to domestic violence, but not in her own home.

The closest she had come had been her father's drunken slap. But even during her father's most drunken states, he would not sink to physically force himself on a woman. Her ma would have put him across the table if he had. Brigid felt rage growing in the pit of her stomach.

How dare he! Too angry to speak, Brigid jerked her free arm and clawed at him blindly. She made sure her nails dug deep when she raked them across his face. She saw him touch a spot on his cheek where welts were forming before he slapped her hard across the face. Stunned, eyes watering from the blow, she staggered back. For a moment, she stopped resisting. In that split second, he forced her from the chair. Her cloak tore away.

Free of the cumbersome woolen garment, Brigid spun around and elbowed McCarthy. He groaned in pain but it was not enough to stop him. McCarthy restrained her with an arm across her neck. Brigid kicked her boot upright, putting a heel into her attacker's groin. Brigid clawed free and tried to run. Her throat was raw but her scream rang out. There was simply no one within earshot to hear her.

He grabbed her again before she reached his office door. Fist in her hair, he yanked her backwards and she screamed in pain. He dragged her back towards his desk. Only after he punched her square in the jaw did Brigid succumb. Pain shot through her and she briefly lost consciousness.

By then, Edwin had thrown her across the desk, hiked up her skirts and raped her. Brigid woke to more pain and the horrible humiliation of what had happened.

McCarthy finished, and pushed Brigid to the floor. Spent, he leaned against the massive desk and began to laugh. Brigid lay quietly. No tears came. She felt numbed, dead almost. She knew what sex was, for God's sake. From a toddler, she had experienced the sounds of her parents in the night and the perpetual breeding cycles of the farm animals. The new calf and the ever-present barn kittens didn't happen by accident.

But this was different. A violent assault, not an act of nature.

"Well, then, Miss Devlin, Brigid, is it?" The bastard began to busy himself straightening his clothing. Brigid forced herself to watch him. He had brutalized her. She would have to live with his crime for the rest of her life.

"Now, then, I suppose I *could* see about that little matter. Of course, it is very likely we would have to have a few more of these, er…shall we call them *meetings* before anything definite decision…"

Anger heightened her sense of survival and crystalized her thinking. The selfish bastard. The stinking selfish monster. The son of a bitch had raped her once and planned to rape her again. The knot in her stomach loosened. She did not know from where it came but a soft light flow of positive energy filled her. Edwin McCarthy would never do this to another woman.

It was as he bent to pull up his trousers that young Brigid found her physical strength. Conditioned by years of farm work, her muscles were not that of a frail housemaid. McCarthy's back was to her. Pulling herself up by the corner of the desk, she stealthily reached over the ledge. Her fingers closed around the first thing big enough to do damage. He never saw her lunge toward him. Her aim was true. The heavy quartz rock the banker had improvised as a paperweight hit him hard in the temple.

Edwin McCarthy fell face down onto the floor. Everything fell silent. Breath heaving, Brigid nudged the motionless body with her boot. It made her want to vomit. Repulsive. Yet, down deep she felt a surge of power. He had no right. Her actions were in self-defense. She would be no man's victim.

She had little knowledge of healing arts, but he appeared unconscious. A trickle of blood had formed at his left temple. Brigid refused to get any closer. If he had ceased to breathe 'twas his own making. Edwin McCarthy was quite possibly dead. She had done it but she didn't care.

Stolen in an act of evil, she had lost the virginity she had long saved for Danny. Brigid felt defiled. It was not as if there were a choice. The God she believed in was merciful and good. He would understand. She hoped Edwin McCarthy *was* dead and may his black soul rot in hell.

Brigid straightened her skirts and got to her feet. What was she thinking…dear God, she must get out of here. Despite her panic, the massive wooden filing cabinets that lined the walls of Edwin McCarthy's office reminded her of why she'd come here in the first place. The mortgage. She had to find the deed.

Quickly and quietly as she could, Brigid methodically pulled open drawers until she came to the cabinet with the letter "D." It was not difficult to find the deed for the Devlin farm and eliminate every trace of paperwork mentioning the Devlin property. Returning the file folder to its place, Brigid soundlessly closed the drawer.

Edwin McCarthy had still not moved. Brigid picked up her cloak from where it had fallen on the floor and wrapped it around her. Turning around, she took one quick glance around the room. Except for Edwin McCarthy lying on the floor, there was no sign she had even been here. The deed for the farm tucked firmly in her bodice, Brigid slid back out into the main corridor of the building. Not a soul in sight.

Brigid prayed an earnest Ave of thanks.

No one noticed the young girl leaving the bank through the side door at seven forty-five that still gray morning. It began to drizzle shortly after but by then Brigid had found her way home. No one asked her where she had been. She never told a single soul.

Edwin McCarthy's uncle Liam arrived at the bank round eight fifteen and found his nephew face down and cold on the marble floor of his office. Naturally, he assumed that a common thief had broken in to vandalize the premises, killing his beloved nephew who surprised him in the act. Not a copper taken. The constable thought it a likely story, as well, and that is how it appeared in the paper the following day. "God bless our Edwin," said the obituary. "In Death, he saved the day."

The eviction notice on the Devlin's front door disappeared. No one questioned the miraculous windfall that enabled them to settle their debt on the farm. Everyone knew Brigid. She had worked out some arrangement, to be sure, for wasn't she a fine girl and an outstanding daughter? If anyone doubted the family's story, not a word of speculation was uttered.

Even her parents, bless their unsuspecting souls, assumed she had fixed things in an upright fashion. Her mother was tickled that she herself held a property deed. The Devlin family were property owners free and clear. It mattered not that the Devlin homestead was a meager parcel with very little acreage and only a small bit of usable farmland. It was still theirs.

Her father stopped badgering her to marry the O'Rourke. Once he realized he would not be tossed from his home, he seemed a bit more of the old Da. Things slowly improved. Paddy Devlin began to drink a bit less and help about the farm again. Ma looked happier. For a time, Brigid felt her load lighten.

True to her word, Brigid took in odd bits of sewing. Things were a bit slow to start, but she had even received a second order for a wedding outfit. It was to be designed around a piece of lace from the bride's mother's own wedding dress. She was not ready to call herself a dressmaker, but one day she hoped to do so. She felt a kinship with the poet and the composer for the act of creating a garment was an art.

Two months went by. Brigid told no one what had happened that morning at the bank. At first, except for the nightmares, she thought she had gotten away with all of it. Everyone, from the constable to the McCarthy family seemed overwhelmingly satisfied with the motive of attempted robbery. Edwin, not particularly well liked in life, became an unlikely hero in death. Brigid would be charged for no crime. No one suspected her. They were barely aware she even existed.

As the weeks went by, something else unexpected happened. Her waist grew larger and her cheeks fuller. Brigid Devlin had not gotten away with murder. *A life for a life.* Edwin McCarthy was dead but Brigid Devlin was with child.

And four and a half months later, as she bled to death in childbirth with the very life trickling out of her, she thought it again.

A life for a life.

"A boy, a boy, Brigid. Try to fight it. We need you. Please. Come back to us."

It was her mother. She was needed. A boy? Oh yes, the child. Her responsibility. Her heart quickened. The child would need her. To go back would be hard. Danny would never want her but that was not the child's fault. She must fight this ever growing sense of sleepy contentment that crept inside her, replacing the pain. Her mother's voice faded...was that the sound of a baby's cry? Was it her baby? No...

What *was* that?

Brigid heard it first in the distance. No, not a baby.

'Twas the pipes. Their faint thunderous drone made her heart ache with both joy and longing. To hear the bagpipes...across the meadow. The mists parted and a bridge lay ahead. The sound grew. Her heart slowed.

Someday, he would come to her. It would not be long. She called to him. *Danny...Danny.* That shadow ahead...no, not Danny. But someone she loved. She felt it envelop her. Brigid knew those features...her grandmother...Honorrah Carroll. She had died when Brigid was eight

A life for a life.

Brigid clearly saw her grammy's tender smile and knew she was dying. It was easier not to breathe. A cord, a faint cord...holding her back, making her not want to go along. *Danny.* He was still alive. Perhaps if he understood that she had been raped...he could forgive her...

Nay, Brigid, 'tis not for you.

Honnorah Carroll reached out her fingertips to touch Brigid's own hesitant ones. The older woman's face was unlined, radiant, almost young but her eyes were filled with the wisdom of time. Gently, she shook her head. Brigid knew what she would say.

It is done now. It is your time. You must let go.

Brigid looked back, towards life. It was hard to see. She could not remember much of what life had been like. Like a reflected image in a disturbed pool of water, fragments of people and places wavered in a blur. Someday, the pool would clear again but it would be she who would be the one waiting to reach out and touch the fingertips of another loved one. She must try to reach out to him.

Danny, I will be there for you on the other side of the bridge. Look for me there. Listen for the pipes...

She could wait no longer. She felt the gentle tug on her soul. Brigid turned to face her grandmother's loving face. The message was there, in silent love that needed no words. Time stopped having meaning. She knew her soul was leaving her body. Her heart was at peace. She and Danny would be together again. In another time, in another life.

A life for a life.

Brigid formed a picture of Danny in her mind. This was all that she could take with her. He had been the one...her soul mate. The faces of the others would be forgotten, to be reacquainted with again as familiar souls behind in the guise of strangers, but not he. She would know him always.

A light was ahead. Familiar voices in the distance. Her heart leaped. There was family waiting. Releasing her last breath, she blew back a kiss for her beloved Danny. The Sight had been right after all. Brigid Devlin squeezed tightly her grandmother's hand and passed over. She was not yet eighteen years old.

———

Two months after Brigid's death, Danny Carroll trudged into the village of Ballycraig. He had come from the North, traveling on foot. It had not been an unpleasant trip despite the possibility of inclement weather. The weather was milder in Ireland this time of year. Friday O'Donnell was deposited among his clan in Gweedore for safe keeping—at least until the situation in America quieted down. The trip had taken him a full day less than normal. He could not wait to see Brigid.

He arrived at the Devlin farm just as Brigid's mother was feeding the hens. Mrs. Devlin looked at him as if she had seen a ghost. When she broke out crying, he knew something was wrong. A thousand thoughts ran rampant through his mind. Had Brigid found another?

Still, he was unprepared for what Mrs. Devlin told him. Though a dozen times he'd thought himself dead since he had left this place, he never thought the same of Brigid.

His mouth opened in a soundless scream that went on for a long time. Mr. Devlin came out into the yard. Danny had dropped to his knees, his face in his hands. The older man bent and laid a hand on his shoulder.

"Danny Carroll. You are a sight for sore eyes. There, there, Laddie. 'Tis just…well, we never thought to see you again." He paused, his voice saddened. "The missus has told ye. Aye, she's gone. Two months. Seems hard to believe. She said you would come back someday." The older man shook his head. "Canna say that I believed her. But I regret that…and a lot more. Alas, my beautiful Brigid. Gone."

Young Patrick Thomas and little Mary Margaret had come out to the yard as well. Both had grown in his absence but remembered him and ran to hug him. Then they all were crying and Danny most of all. Mrs. Devlin went inside and came out in a bit with a packet of letters. She wiped her eyes on her apron.

"These three letters are for you, Lad. Once the…" The older woman hesitated. "I mean, a few months ago, she stopped mailing them. Understand, Danny…no one, not even yer own sister, knew if ye were dead or alive. Brigid never stopped writing to you, though, nor believing in ye. Know that if ye know nothing else. She loved you, Laddie."

Mrs. Devlin, eyes reddened, glared at her husband. "More so, than *some* realized at the time. 'Twere not easy the past two years. She managed to save the farm for us, dear God only knows how so. Nor is it for me to judge. She was a wonderful daughter, Danny Carroll."

She took Danny's hand before handing him the bound envelopes. "She loved you to the end. It was your name that she called."

Fresh tears filled Danny's eyes. Blindly he took the ribbon wrapped packet. Brigid's faded blue hair ribbon. Recognition broke what was left of his heart. Clutching the letters to him, he sobbed and sobbed like a wee babe. Mrs. Devlin patted his shoulder. The rest of Brigid's family stood wordlessly in a moment of mourning for her loss.

Finally, when he could not longer weep or even speak above a whisper, Danny was ready to listen. He numbly followed the Devlins inside. A fire was in the hearth. The cottage was clean, tidy. The family had fared better than most.

Danny wondered what had transpired. Somehow, they had managed to save the property from being foreclosed. Or rather, from what her ma had said, Brigid had saved it. How he could not imagine. The poverty and destitution he had left behind in America were nothing compared to what was left of Ireland. His trek south from Gweedor had reacquainted him to the misery and troubles of his homeland.

But he could not think about that now. Brigid's mother was crying again, haltingly telling how she had passed. A baby…there had been a baby. *A baby.* Mother of God…Brigid had died in *childbirth*. He listened, his anger grew. She had betrayed him. All this way, he had come for her to betray him.

Mrs. Devlin saw his face and knew what he must think. "Danny, try to understand. Even I do not know what happened. She refused to talk of it. Told us she would raise the child as her own…that all was not as it must seem."

Danny looked at her. Did the woman think him an addled brain-damaged fool? It did not take a scholar to figure out she had cheated on him with another. He would not even have the satisfaction of accusing her to her face for she had abandoned him to a place where even he couldn't follow her. Dead bearing a son whose father's name she would not divulge. Not even to her parents.

Danny could not believe what he was hearing. His emotions were boiling over and his thinking fragmented. She had duped her parents as well. It did not make sense. "Where is she buried?"

His tone was hard as steel, but Danny held the slender packet of letters as tenderly if they were a delicate rose. He wanted to rip them, shred them, into a million pieces. But he could not. He would not. Slipping the letters into a pocket, Danny suddenly became conscious of his embarrassingly public display of emotions. He roughly wiped at his eye with his coat sleeves.

"In the graveyard at Saint Anne's. But Danny…"

His chest hurt so that he could barely breathe. "Yes, Mam."

"Ye must listen to me and believe me. Harden not your heart. There was no one else. You must believe that."

"What of the child?"

"Aye, a lovely sweet lad. Just a babe. Her da and I are raising him like our own. She never told us, ye see, of the father. Just said it weren't the child's fault so we were to love him or her as our own. So a Devlin he is."

Young Mary Margaret had gone into the house and come back with a wee infant wrapped in a bunting. He was wailing but the shock of raven hair that curled on top of his head was the same color his mother's had been. A son. Brigid had a son and now she was dead. Young Mary offered him up.

"His name is Danny."

He held the small child and could feel himself tearing up again. He smelled the sweet infant scent and on top of that, the aura of the child's mother. A piece of her would live on…

He kissed the baby's head and gently handed him back to Mary Margaret. Danny knew he must go to her despite what she had done. Exhausted from the emotional turmoil, he hugged Mrs. Devlin and shook her husband's hand. He affectionately ruffled the hair of the wee ones. This would have been his family had he and Brigid married.

"Will ye not stay? For supper at the least."

Danny thanked them but he could not stand to be there anymore. Brigid was gone and a piece of him with her. There was nothing else to say. He needed to walk. Weary beyond belief, but unable to stop himself, he slowly made his way back into the village and toward the church. Many the times he and Brigid had walked this path. Danny felt himself begin to thaw. The warmth softened his thoughts.

Nothing had changed except now he walked it alone.

The morning light came through the trees as he opened the wrought iron gate of the small Catholic cemetery. He saw the Devlin family plot in the far right of the churchyard, cattycorner to the Carroll grave sites. A simple cross graced the still fresh mound. Its simplicity humbled him. Danny approached the overturned earth. She rested here. His beloved Brigid.

What if he had he made it back sooner?

Sooner? His anger returned.. What was he to have done? Swam back to Ireland? Jesus, she was pregnant with another man's child. *That* did not happen overnight. Had she not the decency to wait a bit longer? He began to sob anew, wracking soundless sobs that made him gulp for air.

The letters in his hand…

A sudden feeling of calmness entered his stomach and became centered there. Here, at the graveside of his own true love. Here where he thought his heart would finally break, he felt at peace. Danny swore he could sense her there. He looked down at the rocks and loosely packed dirt. The earth was fresh and damp.

The reality of death. Never to see her smile or hear her gentle laugh again. May her soul rest in peace.

Mrs. Devlin had said there was no one else. How could that be? She was pregnant. But then why was there no husband or at least a name of the baby's father? And for not even her family to know the answers! This was a puzzlement that bothered Danny. The letters…he again became conscious of their weight in his pocket. Perhaps they held some clue.

He spread his cloak on the damp ground. There were three wax sealed letters addressed to him, written on thin parchment in Brigid's hand. Slitting open the first seal with his blade, his fear abated. Nothing worse could happen, could it?

Eyes red rimmed and blurring, but anxious to see even a word that could shed light on what had happened, Danny opened the top envelope and began to read. The first letter was written within the past four months. She was dead for two.

These were Brigid's last worldly thoughts and they were to him. Tears flowed, but they cleared his vision this time. And though the ground was moist and cool, its dampness sinking into the cloth knees of his britches, Danny stayed there bent in penance until he had read every sentence.

He knelt and put his forehead to the earth to be nearer to her. The first word of the familiar prayer came easily. *Hail Mary, full of grace, the Lord is with Thee.* He prayed an Ave, the most simple of prayers, over young Brigid Devlin's grave. It was what she had asked him to do in the last letter.

Tearing a corner from his shirt, he placed in its center a small bit of earth from the spot where she rested. He put it, folded neatly, inside the packet of letters. And then, bending one last time, close to where he knew her dear sweet face lay looking up at him, Danny kissed the cold earth.

"I will love you all the days of my life, Brigid Devlin. And I shall look for ye when the pipes call me home. God rest you, sweet Brigid. May you sleep in peace until I come to thee."

It was all he could do. And while it was not enough, could never be enough, it would have to be.

Danny Carroll wasted no time. He never even went to see his family. There was nothing left. Journeying from Ballycraig that same day, he continued traveling south to Galway. Two days later, he sailed for America.

In 1881, Daniel Carroll became a naturalized American citizen. He never again returned to Ireland. Nothing left for him there, he told his children, later his grandchildren. Aye, but 'tis a grand place, he'd add slyly, with a wink and a smile. Brigid's letters were kept locked in a metal strongbox. Danny never discussed her with anyone. Not even Doolin.

But once a year, for many years, on the feast of St. Brigid, a single red rose appeared on the grave of Brigid Devlin, in the parish cemetery of St. Anne's in Ballycraig, Ireland. After a few years, it became a bit of a legend. No one ever admitted to playing any part in its appearance. The residents of Ballycraig were fond of any good mystery surrounding a grave yard. It did not take long for it to become local folklore. Stories grew up around it, as is the nature of those things.

Somewhere in about 1886, a monument appeared to replace the simple cross that marked the Devlin plot. A small sitting stone made in the shape of a bridge with the words *Wait for me on the other side* etched above the arch. Intertwined across the bridge and bordering the words, there were Celtic symbols and knots. Truth be it known, the new priest, Father Flannery, was aghast that no one knew who was behind it. Someone who would not identify themselves was paying the local stone mason to carve the new tombstone and put it in place.

It drove Father daffy but the Devlins, strange folks, were not in the least bit bothered. Even said 'twas a fine thing. In fact, the family seemed pleased as punch when they met with the stone mason to make sure all of the Devlin birth names and dates were correct.

Old Mr. Devlin had passed on by then, but Mrs. Devlin and little Mary Margaret were still at home. Young Patrick Thomas had taken a wife and the two were running the farm. The new Mrs. Devlin, her Christian name Kathleen, was helping to raise young Danny along with two young lads of her own.

Odd thing too, when Brigid's son, young Danny Devlin, turned the age of eighteen, there in the mail packet all the way from America, wasn't there a silver pocketwatch. Imagine! A silver watch. Strange, too. The card signed simply "a Friend." And what would young Devlin be doing with the likes of a friend in America? Himself never even setting foot out of Ballycraig. Such foolishness!

Still, the people of Ballycraig couldn't help but chatter about such a strange occurrences. The ongoing rumor, a mite time limited, that Nellie O'Shaunessey had slept with the Presbyterian minister, faded by the wayside. But not the stories surrounding Brigid Devlin's grave.

Years went by. At some point, the roses ceased to appear every Feburary 2nd. It didn't matter. Local gossip kept them as fresh and alive in the townsfolk's minds as firmly as if they still being placed there on

St. Brigid's Day. Rumors still surfaced now and then regarding their bearer's identity. But no one really knew and that was the delight of it.

Time passed. Very few people remembered exactly what had transpired in the year 1875. Gossip became rumor, rumor story and story myth. Gossiping tongues ceased to wag but the myth of the St. Brigid's Day Roses took on a life of its own.

Such was the nature of the Irish.

————

Tommy Terrance O'Toole sat in the middle of the crowded New York pub. It was a far cry from the pubs in rural Ireland, especially those he had seen in his long days. Quite upper class to his estimation. The buxom waitress in quasi-period dress resembled a punk medieval wench as she brought him yet another mug of Guinness. Tommy winked at her and watched the doorway for a glimpse of Maggie Carroll's curly red hair.

It would not be long.

Next to him, at the quiet table in the rear of the establishment, lay a packet of old letters, very old indeed. The thin parchment was well preserved despite their age. Someone had lovingly cared for them for their entire life. They were bound with an old blue ribbon that Tommy absentmindedly fooled with while he drank his tankard. He felt every one of his one hundred and forty odd years, but he also felt a glimmer of something else.

Peace. Things were coming to a close. The little man let a sigh escape. Coming to a close, but not over yet. There was still much to do. Human nature was fickle. He still had yet to get those two within a hundred and fifty miles of each other let alone to Ireland together.

The good news was he was pretty sure that once they stepped on Irish soil, fate would take over, the curse would be lifted and his punishment complete. Well, sure as a minor Immortal being could be, that is.

He frowned. She was late. That figured. Well, so it was a little more complicated than that. Anything that had to do with love was bound to be. Especially when it came to humans. The leprechaun drained the last of the succulent dark beer. Ah. There were some things fairies did better. In fact most things. Making ale wasn't one of them.

He'd miss beer in Tir Nan Og. Perhaps he could learn how to brew a small batch between now and the time he sat sail. Tapping his foot to *The Galway Piper*, Tommy pondered the art of brewmeistering. He almost missed the red-haired woman entering the door.

He didn't, however. The glint of copper hair caught his eye. Taking a moment, Tommy watched the maitre d' sort through a tall stack of reservations and notes. Finding the one he sought, the man pointed to the back of the bar. The Galway Piper led into a lively reel.

By the time Maggie Carroll made her way to the small table in the dimly lit back of Hoolie's, it was empty. Odd. The waitress had said her party was there. She looked back to the maitre d' and he nodded. It was the right table. Maggie sat down. An empty Guinness mug and a stack of old folded letters tied with a ribbon. Maggie looked closer. A note lay next to them.

"Dear Maggie..."

It was for her. She picked up the note and read further.

> *So sorry. Do understand. I have been unexpectedly called away. 'Twas such a shame to have missed you but never the mind...*
>
> *The point is this, Lassie. These letters belong to you. They are part of your past, your family's heritage, and yet they are also part of another's past as well. In bearing these letters to you I have fulfilled, at least in part, a debt owed to your great great grandfather, Danny Carroll. The rest must come of its own will. I can do no more but wait.*
>
> *Mayhaps what you seek you shall find if you seek with open heart and mind. Slan...*
>
> *Tommy Terrance O'Toole*

—————

Ballycraig, 29 May 1875

Dear Danny,
The days are beginning to grow longer and the world more beautiful. Oh, if ye were here to see the daffodils blooming all over the meadow. It is late spring, Danny. Remember that last day when we walked home from church...it seems so long ago but I know it is not. I feel so old. So mortal. So afraid of what lies ahead.

I know in my heart I will never see you again. I suppose I have known it a long time now but I had prayed I was somehow wrong. Some day, you shall come back. I know you laugh when I speak of the Sight, but somehow, I know these things. I want to be there, with all my heart and soul. I wish I could be...

Perhaps, it is for the best, dear Danny, for there are things you do not know. Things that have happened. You would not want me now. For as the days grow longer, I grow more and more remorseful. I regret to tell you...for you shall hate me, but when you return, you shall deserve to know the truth.

Know that I had no choice. Da was drowning in drink and Ma in sorrow. The bank would have taken the farm. There was no one to turn to, Danny. Everyone was too busy turning to me.

My peace has been made with God. You see, there was naught to do but what was done. You and no other shall know what passed that day. When you think of what I have done, know that Edwin McCarthy assaulted and forced himself upon me. I went to the bank to beg him to not foreclose on the farm. For the sake of Ma and the children. And it was there...

Forgive me, Danny. He would have done it again. I saw it in his eyes. And as he came at me with his threats, I couldna bear it again. I hit him with a paperweight...a rock he had on his desk..

I killed him, Danny, and I am not sorry for my sin. I believe God understands that he was evil. It was in the papers the next day. No one knows but me and now you, Danny. I had no choice, Danny. It was not my intent to kill him but neither do I regret it. I was not the first one that Edwin McCarthy violated. But I swear you this...I was the last.

God watch over us both, Danny. I love you always.

Brigid

———

Ballycraig 16 June 1875

Dear Danny,
As I write this by candlelight, I wish I could reach out to touch your face. Just once more. There are times, when I drift between the hours of awakeness and asleep, that I can almost see you. Your face becomes clear, like a reflection in a pool of water, but only for a moment before it wavers and is gone.

To think that all the years of our young lives that we laughed and played in Ballycraig, I took your dear face for granted.

It has surely been a lesson to me. There is little I take for granted now. There is much that has been taught me, yet so much more that I do not understand. God took you from me, but he has given me something back. In some odd way, there is a bit of poetic justice in all this.

A life for a life, Danny Carroll. Edwin McCarthy assaulted and raped me so I killed him. But the irony is this. Within me he planted his seed. I shall bear a child sometime by January...my child. A life for a life.

A new life for a new year. Perhaps if I were a different sort, I might hate the child. I suppose I have reason by rights. Still, I cannot hate a wee bairn even for the sins of his wicked father. Please understand. This has naught to do with our love for each other, Danny. Do not let it. Promise me. Do not dampen the light that shines bright for me now when I need most its candle. Love the child as mine, for mine he will be. He will be all that is left of me when I am gone.

If something happens to me, Danny, please watch over him.

Promise me in honor of all that we had between us that you will see he is alright.

All my Love,
Brigid

———

Ballycraig 16ᵗʰ October 1875

Dear Danny,
It is funny. Wishful I know...but still, even after all these months of not hearing from you, I wait with the thought that perhaps today will be the day. Thinking perhaps I was wrong, the Sight mistaken. Perhaps today you will come to me. Or tomorrow...

But you do not come. I do not know if I will ever get used to being without you.

Time is moving on...

We are growing older. How long is it since last we saw each other? It seems forever some days, only yesterday on others.

It is hard for me these days. The babe weighs heavy. I have taken in sewing now for a bit. It is paying off a little here and there. I made my third wedding outfit for Millie Monaghan from down by the river.

Ah, Danny, things are looking up now. If you were back, things would almost be perfect. Sometimes...I wish...I wish I could leave here to look for you in America. Maybe you would forgive me...

Then, I remember. It is not just me. There is more to think of than my selfishness. How would my parents survive? Da has finally straightened up a bit and is more like himself all round. Ma is grand. She's helping as much as she can with the sewing. She looks a new woman these days. The little ones are help as well. And then there is wee Danny. Well, if he is a boy that is...aye, that is what his name shall be.

Ah, Danny, our time is passing. The Sight does not lie. So short yet it is nearly gone now. Who would have thought that Sunday at church that our lives would be changed forever? Forgive me and think well of me.

When the old biddies begin to gossip, look ahead proudly and know that you knew the real truth. Stand behind my parents so they do not feel as shamed. We shall not see each other again but look for me in every sunrise and every flower. Tread soft upon my grave and whisper that you love me so I will sleep in peace.

This shall be my last letter, Danny, love. Until you come to me...

All My Love...
Your Brigid

Chapter Fifteen

Cinneamhain
(pronounced *Kinnevin*; English "Fated")

In New York, there are places where the tourists go and places tourists only wish they could go. Hoolie's in the center of New York was a closely guarded treasure known on both sides of the Atlantic. The newly immigrated Irish as well as those long settled in the Americas had managed to find their way there since the 1870s. They knew the real thing when they saw it.

Hoolie's was a bit of a legend. Those tourists who did wander in by accident knew they had found something special.

Its regulars described the traditional Irish pub as having its heart in Eire and its feet in America. The pleasant mixture of Irish brogues and lilts wove a pattern through the variety of American and other worldly dialects. Today, the pub was swarming with people. Most of them were Irish or of Irish descent. Though not all looked it on the surface, Irish blood runs deep.

Looking like a hole in the wall from the busy city street, Hoolie's scarlet red door hid a cavernous maze of rooms housing a variety of entertainments including pool tables, musicians, a library and several bars. The downstairs lobby led into the main. The polished veneer shone and the glass behind the bar reflected the pride of many devoted owners throughout the years. Overlooking the bar area was a large balcony.

Hoolie's was pretty much a family affair—the Muldoon family to be exact. Local legend had it that there had been a Muldoon by blood behind the bar since its opening well over a hundred years ago. Hoolie's had been wetting Irish whistles in New York since 1870.

The smell of beer had settled into the wood, giving off a pungent aroma of hops that was intoxicating in scent alone. And the music! Traditional Irish music permeated every nook and cranny. Fiddles and pipes, bodhrans and tin whistles, all wafting together in harmonic symphony. Galen breathed it all in as he entered one of his most favorite Irish haunts.

Hoolie's wasn't fancy but it sure as hell had class.

Erin's America magazine rated the bar as one of the best kept Irish secrets in the colonies. Galen agreed. When he was missing home, he headed to the dark security of Hoolie's. It wasn't Ireland, but it sure as hell was the next best thing. You never knew who you might run into at Hoolie's.

Galen himself had encountered all sorts of folks. From his mother's hairdresser to Bono. More than once, Galen had ducked to avoid an old schoolmate or a particularly obnoxious business associate. Galen had even been present in one of the music rooms when Irish born Elvis Costello gave an impromptu a capella performance of *Wilde Mountain Time*.

He had arrived back in the city quicker than he had expected. The drive back from northeastern Pennsylvania had been uneventful. A lack of decent tea on the road made him grab a 24 oz. American coffee for his morning stimulant. Galen had set the cruise control on 69 and kept a watchful eye out for police cruisers.

The Americans were safer drivers than the Irish. His countrymen, and women too, were mad for speed. His da claimed that this was the very reason that God saw to it that most of the Irish continued to travel by foot. Few pedestrians suffered mortal injury when they collided with each other.

Stretching his long limbs, Galen was thankful to be out of the cramped quarters of the car. He raked his fingers through his short dark hair. The cladaugh ring on his right ring finger was given to him by his mother on his 18th birthday. The card had read…"Friendship, Love, and Loyalty. These three things I hope for thee."

Yeah, he hoped for that too, but Galen didn't plan on giving his heart easily or carelessly. He had seen too many cases of love gone ballistic. He grinned, thinking of his parents. They might fire a few missiles at each other now and then, but they truly loved each other. World War III had apparently settled down once his dad started watching his diet and exercising. Good thing too, Ireland being a neutral country.

Despite their bickering and threats to leave each other, the two would remain together for the rest of their lives. A match made in heaven. Galen envied them. Still, he wasn't sure he'd ever meet a woman with whom he would care to spend the rest of his life. Ma and Da had had more than a few rows but they were passionate for each other even at their age.

It was a wonder.

Galen wasn't getting any younger but he wasn't willing to risk a bad marriage to soothe his mid-life anxieties. He snatched a quick glimpse of himself in the wall mirror as he entered the foyer of Hoolie's. Not bad. No grey hair yet. A few well placed crinkles near the eyes. He still had a little time left on the vine, he supposed. He wouldn't turn bad overnight.

The bar was packed. A pipe band had arrived ahead of him and had set up camp in the corner of the room. Chances are they would all soon be treated to an impromptu concert. Galen loved New York in the waning days of winter. Spring was about to burst. New York couldn't wait to thaw out of its concrete coldness.

It was nearing St. Patrick's Day. Paddy's Day in New York was more like a season than a day. In the Irish parts of town, especially, it was one more excuse to have a wearin' o' the green and drag out the Clancy Brothers CD. Green beer flowed for at least two weeks before and after. Everyone with even a faint taint of Irish blood reveled in their knowledge that once, they too, came from that most magical of all places, Ireland.

Tonight was no exception.

Hoolie's was full of energy. Galen felt the excitement as he entered. Like a mild jolt of electricity. He stopped, in the corridor, before going into the main room where the bar was located. He had one thought and it was enlightening. Galen took a deep breath. He was going to meet Maggie Carroll.

He felt another jolt, low in his belly. Perspiration beaded on his normally calm and cool brow. His heart was pounding and his face warm. He knew himself well. This was his body's way of letting him know he was charged up about something.

Insight hit him like a ton of bricks.

It was because of Maggie Carroll. How stupid he was. His stomach was doing flip flops. His brain was mush. Galen had never been an excitable person, but right now he felt like he could crawl out of his skin.

Sweet Jesus...and all this because of Maggie Carroll? The trip back from his joyride to Pennsylvania had given him ample time to think. He knew it was foolish. Ridiculous. Still...he had a feeling if his ma been there, she'd have told him he'd been shot in the arse with Cupid's arrow.

Galen quickened his step. Truth be told, he felt great. This was the most fun he'd had in ages. God, he hoped she was in there. She was an itch that needed scratching.

The low murmur of the bustling bar increased in volume as he approached the hostess. The pretty freckle-faced brunette was dressed in a fetching innkeeper's bodice and skirt while the barmaids racing from table to table wore classy updated versions of traditional serving wench attire. He could hear the strains of "Wilde Colonial Boy" waft through the crowded pub. His was so warm, flushed with anticipation, that he felt feverish.

Eyes beginning to adjust to the eternal twilight of pub lighting, Galen decided to forgo the hostess and help himself. God, the place was hopping, but then, when wasn't it? A quartet of long raven-haired beauties was taking the stage in the far corner. They looked more like sisters than any possible coincidence could have produced. Good. There was no better harmony of voice than between that of family members.

One held a fiddle, another a bodhran, and the third a mandolin. The fourth grabbed the mike and introduced the girls as the Sisters of

Shannon. They launched into "Whiskey in the Jar." Their voices blended like a bottle of Jamison's. They sounded good. Good enough to be making records. Well, and wasn't Hoolie's the place to start?

It must be an open mike day. New York was one of the only places short of Ireland with enough crowds to make up a rowdy audience this early in the evening. Galen hit the bar and caught the eye of Johnny Muldoon. The big bearded redhead looked more like a Viking than a New Yorker. Winking, Galen saw him grab a mug and craft a perfectly foamed Guinness.

Walking towards Galen, he stretched his long arm over a crowd three deep to hand the draft to his friend. "On the house, Laddie."

Galen tipped his finger to his forehead in thanks. Johnny Muldoon was an old friend since Galen's earliest days in the city. He was even the godfather of one of Johnny's seven children. Little Michael Galen Muldoon was now four and a notorious soccer player on whom Galen doted whenever he had the opportunity. Last month, Mikie, to the dismay of his preschool teacher, had been practicing his soccer kicks during playtime using Oreos from his snack.

Next year, red haired and freckled, "Mikie G," as the family nicknamed him, would be entering kindergarten. May the saints preserve his teachers at St. Martha's Elementary, Galen thought.

The ale hit the spot. He took a long drink and turned his attention to looking for Maggie Carroll. Galen realized he was half in lust with a voice on the phone and an essay of 300 words or less. His businessman's practicality took its first shot at the romantic that dwelled deep within his soul.

He must be crazy. At the first available opportunity, he would have to schedule an opportunity to have his head examined.

But first thing's first. Maggie Carroll.

The Sisters of Shannon had started their next number. *I know my love by his way of walking...I know my love by his way of talking.* A Corrs' number. They were doing a nice job of it, too. Galen scanned the room. Galen didn't for one moment believe that Maggie Carroll would remotely recognize him, but he had a feeling he would recognize her. His heart was beating like the rhythm of the bodhran that drove the song.

What the hell was he getting himself into this time?

———

Maggie had tears streaming down her face. She read every letter through once and then again. The parchment-like paper was so fragile she feared it would tear but it did not. She calculated mentally. Saints preserve us…as her Grammy would say…if these letters were no hoax, they were almost 130 years old!

Was that even possible? Maggie was beginning to doubt her sanity.

She lost awareness of the present, of the people and music around her. The foreignness of the great city around her faded into the background. She was alone with the story of her great great grandfather and a woman who once loved him. Brigid Devlin. Devlin…

Where had she heard that name before?

The tragedy of the young girl's plight reached across the century and tugged at Maggie's heart strings. Danny Carroll, her great great grandfather, had probably never gone back to Ireland. Or if he had, he had not stayed there. For here she was, in the flesh, Maggie Carroll, a direct descendant on this side of the Atlantic. If this story were true, what did it mean to her and to the descendants of Brigid Devlin?

Da Da *Da* Da *Da* Da *Da.*

Maggie heard the muffled ringer that played the ultimately corny version of "When Irish Eyes Are Smiling." She had voice mail. One of her pet peeves in life was people who took cell phone calls in public places. She hesitated then reached deep in her purse to turn the damn thing off. She had more than enough to digest here without some new element being thrown into the plot.

Who the hell was Brigid Devlin? For that matter, who the hell is Tommy Terrance O'Toole? Why had he left her these letters? What sins was he atoning for?

Maggie's eyes dried. Her catlike sense of curiosity was winning. There was a mystery of sorts here. Devlin…Devlin.

The name made her neurons dance. Devlin. Dear God, almighty. She knew. Galen Devlin. *No way.* That would be too weird for words.

Like the faint who descend into the world of foggy gray unconsciousness for a brief period before reentering the light, Maggie blinked and began to be aware of her surroundings again.

She refused to be intimidated by the curve ball she had been thrown. Au contraire! Coincidences aside, Maggie loved a good mystery. These letters promised all the makings of one. Questions needing answers popped into her head. Thomas Terrance O'Toole had been right about one thing. Brigid realized the importance of these letters in her quest to find her Irish descendants. She wouldn't rest until she put together the pieces of the puzzle.

What happened to Brigid? Why had Danny Carroll left her in the first place? They sounded so in love and yet, the horror of what had happened to her had defiled her forever even in her own eyes. This woman could have been her own great great grandmother. The depth of the relationship that Brigid Devlin was describing was one of substance.

And what had happened to the child?

The music washed over her and she came back to the present. Tenderly, she folded the letters back into their original forms and carefully retied the faded blue bow. They were hers to keep apparently. Painstakingly preserved.

Ballycraig, Ireland. The map of Ireland flashed across her mental canvas. West…perhaps, more northwest really.

Da Da *Da* Da *Da* Da *Da.*

Drat. There it was again. Someone really wanted her and bad. Breaking down, she pulled the phone from her purse and scanned through the message options. The call back number looked familiar but not enough to jog her memory into identifying it.

Ms. Carroll…This is Martha from O'Carrick Traveling Tours…Mr. Devlin requests the honor of taking you to dinner at Hoolie's Pub and Restaurant. Any cab in the city knows where it is or call me when you retrieve this message. It's not too far from the Emerald. Eight o'clock. Call me at 509-9489 to confirm.

The turmoil hit almost immediately. Maggie Carroll felt the world spiraling out of control. It was like being in line for the roller coaster one minute and waking up coming down the first hill the next. Her mind flashed to the Tower card in her Tarot deck. She wasn't sure what to do next…confirm the date, look at her watch, run for the bathroom to fix her face…

She became conscious of the fact that she had stopped breathing when the lightheadedness hit. Ok. Breathe in. Breathe out. She looked at her watch. She had a little time…not much. Good thing she'd picked up that message.

Relax. She needed to steady herself and quick.

It was as if she entered an alternate universe. Galen Devlin. The sexy Irish voice. Devlin. Like the Devlin in Brigid Devlin. This Galen Devlin was going to meet her here. Right here. For dinner.

Maggie considered the odds. She was in New York. A hop, skip, and a jump across the Atlantic to Ireland. Here in a pub, an Irish pub no less. Some eccentric Irishman, from who knows where, just left her a packet of letters written by a century old lover of her great great grandfather's with the same name as the Irish lad who was meeting her here. A packet of letters that, by the way, if authenticated, would be worth a small fortune at auction but even more importantly, would be forever priceless to her family.

She was dreaming, right?

Maggie wasn't much of a drinker, but this called for one. Her letters safely tucked away in the deep pockets of her coat, she decided to explore. There was another act taking the stage. Must be an open mic.

Four beautiful young girls were taking the stage.

"We are Sisters of the Shannon. *Hello, New York!*"

The crowd cheered. Maggie wandered closer. They really were sisters. Sounded like a Corrs numbers. She liked the Corrs' modern takes on the old traditional melodies. These girls were sound-alikes, their harmonies so tightly woven that Maggie found herself swaying to the beat of the bodhran. Unable to sit, she stood at the edge of the crowd, foot tapping, enjoying the show.

"G'day. My name is Diedre. I play lead guitar and the pipes and in case you are wondering, aye, these really are my sisters."

Maggie laughed along with the rest of the crowd. Another of the sisters moved into the mic. This one carried the bodhran. A picture of a griffin playing a harp covered the skin of the drum.

"My name is Grace on bodhran. My sister Gwenyth is on fiddle and Lilly on the mandolin and the tin whistle."

The group broke into a spirited rendition of "I Know My Love." Maggie was in heaven. She glanced at her watch. Seven thirty. Plenty of time. Her full glass of ale would be her timer. When it was gone, she'd make for the hostess and find this Galen Devlin.

I know my love by his way of talking...I know my love by his way of walking...I know my love, dressed in a suit of blue...

Would she know him? The ale was slowly doing its work. Or was it something else? Maggie wasn't much of a drinker but she could hold her own in a crowded bar. Her head felt clouded, like she'd had four ales instead of one. Maggie figured it must be intoxication with her surrounding. By the time her mug was half empty, Maggie was having a grand time singing along with the Sisters.

Then uncharacteristically, Maggie stood up and began clapping her hands. The sisters took notice and encouraged her. Draining her mug, Maggie could feel the flush of the alcohol but something else, too. Maggie wasn't sure what came over her. An almost tinkling of bells, the smell of something exotic...like heather or honeysuckle...

One minute her mug was empty, the next she was somehow onstage, singing high harmony with Diedre to "Black Is the Colour." Cheeks flushed with adventure, Maggie Carroll was having the time of her life. Borrowing Diedre's acoustic guitar, she began to strum the chords to the song she had written from the words she'd submitted to the contest. She wasn't much of a guitar player but somehow her fingers managed to strum the right chords at the right time. The sisters picked out a harmony and joined in. It was a simple song.

"Oh, come back to Ireland, come back with me...come back to the green rolling hills and the sea..."

Across the bar, Galen Devlin's ears perked up. Those words. He'd heard them before...where? Head twisting, his radar tuned in the direction of the stage. It was then he saw her. Red hair and all.

And he knew. Maggie Carroll. It had to be. She was as Martha had said.

"Come back to the music…Come back to the dance…"
It was her story…she had turned it into a song.
"Now I'm yearning to see Ireland's coastline so dear…where the sea meets the rocks and the air's fresh and clear. My heart reaches back…"

Galen couldn't breathe. He was paralyzed. The four girls on stage were beautiful to be sure…but it was the red-headed woman who had his full attention. It had to be Maggie Carroll. The words she had written had mesmerized him on paper. But in song…*her* song…they took his breath away.

His heart thumped so loud he feared the woman next to him could hear it. He waited, until the song was done. Then he waited a little longer while she hugged the four sisters with the dark hair and pale skin.

It was when she left the stage, amidst the clapping and cheers, Galen made his move. He reached her as she passed him then just as suddenly turned. Flushed, her mug empty in her right hand, less than an arm's length apart, they looked into each other's eyes. Galen knew. It hit him like a ton of bricks. She *had* to know.

The red head grinned. Flushed, chest heaving with excitement, she could barely believe she just did what she did. What in God's name possessed her to get up on that stage…granted it was fun…but…

"Maggie Carroll, I am Galen Devlin. I believe we have a date for dinner."

Martha was right. The girl was more beautiful close up than he'd imagined. Her eyes were like green pools.

"You *are* Maggie Carroll. You have to be."

She looked at him again. Blinked and understood. *Omygod…he was Galen Devlin.* Her eyes found his level and stayed there. Somewhere, from within she located her voice and extended her hand.

Maggie stared at his handsome Gaelic face and dark hair. The last few hours had been almost magical. The last few months as well. Now a tall Irish version of Mel Gibson was standing in front of her telling her they have a date for dinner. No one would believe this in a million years.

OmyGod…he was kissing her hand. Who kissed hands these days?

Hell, if she wasn't living this, *she* wouldn't even believe it. This guy was drop dead gorgeous *and* he just kissed her hand. Further words escaped her except for the obvious. So the obvious it was.

"Galen Devlin, I *am* Maggie Carroll. Dinner sounds like as good a place to start as any."

———

Life was good. Oh and wasn't Tommy Terrance O'Toole well pleased with himself?

Perched in the balcony, overlooking the main bar, he nursed another ale and had he been able to reach around his stout torso, would have altogether given himself a well deserved pat on the back. It had been easy to slip away in the crowd, not a smidgen of magic required. A little lad like himself was easily lost track of within a sea of tourists and patrons starting to build for the evening trade.

He'd wandered upstairs and had settled in. It wouldn't be long now.

It was happy hour and now wasn't that just dandy, Tommy thought, because he himself was one happy leprechaun. He sang a little song in his head. *'Tis close to ending… 'Tis almost over…My true love crossed the misty sea…In Tir Na Nog, she waits for me.*

Tommy felt the excitement building as he watched Maggie read each yellowed letter.

He barely stopped himself from doing a slipjig when Galen Devlin finally entered Hoolie's. Had he not had that last ale, well, he would not have been adverse to kicking up his heals. He sighed contentedly. Tommy had front row seats for the grand finale. A gentle nudge or two was all that was needed. Just enough to bump them into a path of unavoidable harmonic collision, er, convergence. A few more weeks…

At least they were in the same room. 'Twere only a matter of time.

In any event, for Betsy's sake, Thomas was on the right track.. Matchmaking wasn't what it was in his day, but well, now that it was all just about said and done, you might say he had a knack for it, now couldn't you? Delightful business, this steering two young hearts in the direction of each other.

Would the Queen be pleased? Pleased enough to set him free? To let him sail?

Pretty thing, that Maggie Carroll. Danny Carroll had been a comely lad, if he remembered correctly. A red head, too. Ran in the family. Looked to be a spitfire, just like her great great granddad. He felt oddly proud. Tough breed, those Irish women.

Galen Devlin had been intercepted by a tall glorious looking blonde who looked hell bent on singlehandedly screwing up Tommy's whole bloody plan by hooking her shapely little arm through the handsome Irishman's free one. Tommy felt his left eye twitch. His left eye always twitched when he got nervous. Oh, he hoped he wasn't going to have to turn her heel…

Tommy considered charming a tall kilted bagpiper in the direction of the blonde. It would be a nonviolent alternative that would satisfy his need to do something, anything other than idly sit here and watch his bloody life's work for the last one hundred and thirty some odd years go down the blimey drain.

And then, wonder of wonders, he watched as Galen extracted himself from the spiderwoman's clutches. He caught the bagpiper, who had no wedding ring, veering in the direction of Maggie. She had apparently finished reading the last letter, because they were no longer on the table. A new act, a group of sisters, was taking the stage.

Tommy did what he knew best. He halted things with a glamour. A wave visible only to those knowing magic. There seemed to be a silent tinkling in the air, like chimes barely heard…and the smell of clover and honeysuckle. Or perhaps it was ginger and hyacinths. Rather pleasant. Like a memory one remembered with the senses rather than the mind. The same glamour felt different, smelled different, even if two people were experiencing it at the same time.

The bagpiper on a mission forgot midstream that he wanted to try to pick up the redhead who looked like she'd been crying. He instead headed towards the blonde who'd just been dumped by the tall dark haired Irishman. Tommy breathed a sigh of relief. Ah but *that* was a close one.

Maggie Carroll was another story altogether. Tommy watched as she drained her mug of ale. She was dancing and clapping her hands to the music. Her excitement energized other patrons in the bar and the happy hour frenzy began to spill onto the dance floor. His enchantment certainly had a gleeful effect on the lass.

Ah, well, when you're good, you're good, he thought, turning to hail his waitress for another mug. My, my but she held her liquor well, he was thinking to himself. He recanted his words when he turned around and saw Maggie.

Maggie Carroll was on the stage with the Sisters of the Shannon. Did his glamour have anything to do with it? He hadn't anticipated this nor attempted it. The girl was musical, sure, but could she pull this off? Things were about to get interesting...

"Tommy."

The leprechaun thought he'd heard his name. How silly. No one knew him and he didn't see anyone...

"Tommy."

The elf turned. Sitting directly in front of him, across the narrow booth, was Queen Maeve.

"Your Majesty." Tommy scurried to rise, but the Queen ushered him sit.

"Shhhh...do not call attention to yourself, Little One."

Tommy saw she was dressed in a sort of long saffron yellow dress, soft and flowing, but not one out of place in modern society. She looked eternally young, unlined, unblemished. Her hair was still red as flames. Maeve was as regal dressed in the clothes of a commoner as she was in her gowns of satin and gossamer.

But Tommy could see the toll time had taken on her. She had thinned over the years since they had first met. A faint glow illuminated her skin to almost transparency.

"Are you well, Tommy?"

"Aye. That I am, Your Highness. As you can see..." He patted his stomach. "I seem to find my way to the table more than not."

"And, so, know you why I have come, Thomas Terrance O'Toole?"

"Aye. That I do."

"Your time is up. Have you righted the wrong?"

The sweat broke on Tommy's brow and he began to shake. His time was up? What did she mean? But there was more to be done! He had not yet managed to get Maggie and Galen together! He thought he had as long as he needed...it was so close...so close.

"Oh Come Back to Ireland...Come back with me...Come back to the green rolling hills and the sea...Come back to the music..."

Tommy looked down. For Pete's sake, it was Maggie Carroll singing. He hadn't put that in the glamour. And if he hadn't put it in the magic, it meant she was making the magic herself.

And she wasn't half bad either, he decided.

"But, your Excellence...I did not realize that I was under a time constraint! I need more time! Look, look down there...they are within inches of each other, Queen Mauve."

The two looked down and indeed, there was Galen Devlin moving towards the stage where Maggie Devlin was singing. Tommy wished harder than he had ever wished before for anything. He was a creature of magic. Surely his wishing had some type of charm connected to it.

"Why, look at them...so close and I have but to nudge them. Give me a week, just a few days...I promise, I will somehow manage, Your Highness, to get them to Ireland."

"To Ireland, Tommy?"

"Aye, it won't be long. It is almost time for the contest and then, you see, Maggie Carroll is sure to be the winner. Do you hear her song? She wrote it for the contest that Galen thought up to build up business at O'Carrick Traveling Tours, er...well, sort of wrote it...aye, then perhaps it was more like a story and then she must have taken in and turned it into a song. She does that, you see. Maggie, I mean."

The fairy stopped for a breath.

"My heart reaches back and it touches the past...Some dreams live forever...Some loves always last..."

Tommy felt the room begin to spin about him. He looked at Maeve, seated across from him, and while they did not seem to be moving, the vortex around them continued to swirl. He could hear Maggie Carroll and the four sisters harmonizing as Maggie's song ended. The music and their voices began to crescendo into one single chord of sound.

"Oh, Come back to Ireland...With Me..."

———

The last thing that Tommy saw in Hoolie's Bar was Maggie Carroll descending the stage and Galen Devlin walking towards her. He remembered thinking, yes, finally they will meet and then to Ireland. It won't be long...

Then, he closed his eyes. He had to close them to make the spinning stop. It felt like two too many ales on Saturday night. His stomach was about to turn. He willed the sensation to stop.

Suddenly, it did. Tommy instantly knew where they were. It wasn't just a smell or a sound. It was a feeling he would know anywhere.

The Irish mist was in his face. A song grew in his heart. Opening both eyes, Tommy saw Queen Maeve was next to him, her saffron dress now covered by a long cloak that she wrapped against the breeze. It was dark. Tommy wasn't sure of the time. He wasn't sure of the date. He wasn't even sure of the year.

But he knew where he was. He could smell it. The clear scent of salt air, blowing across the docks. The soft scuffling sound of water lapping at the wooden bough of the ships. The flapping of the sails.

He dared look. It was as he had long dreamed.

The Celestial Myst.

"Tommy, 'tis your time to go."

Tommy shook his head. He thought he heard the Queen telling him it was time for him to go. How silly...

"Master Thomas Terrance O'Toole, I release you from your said bondage to me by virtue of your good intent and diligent efforts to right the wrong that was committed..."

Tommy tugged on the Queen's cape.

"But, Your Excellence."

"What is it, Tommy?"

"I wasn't done yet. I haven't got Maggie Devlin back over to Ireland, you see. Mind you, I am confident that it will happen within the next few days. She and the Irishman just need a little more time..."

"Tommy O' Toole, you are a fey and foolish elf but deep inside, you have a heart of pure gold. Your burden is borne, Thomas. You may lay it down now."

Tommy looked up. On the deck of the *Celestial Myst*, he saw someone waving. It was difficult to see into the darkness. But he peered hard and tried to make out the face…

Could it be? Was it his own love…his dear sweet Betsy?

"But, Queen Maeve…"

"There are no *but's*, Tommy. You have done what you could. And done it well. You are a being of pride and honor. But, know this. 'Tis not *for* you to see them home. Your foolishness separated young Brigid and Danny so very long ago, but it did not keep them apart. Fate and the evilness of Man managed to do that without your help."

The beautiful Fairy Queen paused. "But now, Tommy…whatever happens between Maggie Carroll and Galen Devlin, well, that they must choose themselves. Aye, 'twould not have even been for you to bring them together, not really…but…" The Queen's eyes grew misty for a moment. "Nay, I suppose it could not have been overlooked."

Maeve drew a circle in the dirt with her staff. She murmured a few soft words, and a swirling light appeared within the circle's diameter. When it cleared, Tommy saw Galen and Maggie. They were seated in Hoolie's.

"You have done as much as you can. Perhaps even more…but we shall let that be. See for yourself, Thomas Terrance O'Toole!"

Tommy looked deeply into the circle of light. He saw the young couple's plates pushed to the side. They had eaten apparently, the prearranged dinner. The red-haired woman and dark-haired man's heads were bent over something. Tommy leaned closer.

He saw the blue ribbon, faded, curled and forgotten. It was the letters. Brigid Devlin's letters. The two were reading them together. His heart lightened. He did not need to see their faces. Pride swelled in his chest.

"Tommy, you are crying."

"Ah, 'tis but the sea salt, Your Highness, stinging these old eyes." The wizened old leprechaun wiped away the wetness. "And look, Queen Maeve, there ahead! Do you not see the ship?"

Tommy paused and peered into the dim horizon then turned, face puzzled, to his Queen. "Why, look...I believe it is my darling Betsy waving to me. Could it be? Could she have made the trip?"

The fairy queen smiled. "She has. Not even I could have stopped her. It is many the long year that your missus has waited to cuff your ears for your shenanigans."

"Is it time, then?"

"Aye, Tommy. 'Tis time."

Tommy drew himself up gallantly, offering his arm to the beautiful lady.

"Shall we walk together then, to the dinghy, Your Excellence?"

Her hood hid her face in shadows. Tommy did not hear her answer at first.

"Queen Maeve?"

"Nay, Tommy. It is your time. It is not yet mine."

"But...there are none of us left! I thought...there can't be more. I thought I was the last one..."

Maeve threw back her hood. Her red tresses streamed in the light of the moon that had come from behind a cloud. Suddenly, the *Celestial Myst* was bathed in a sea of silvery light. Mauve smiled a bittersweet smile. One that Tommy would not soon forget.

"Ah, sure but of course there are those of us left here, Tommy! And, until the last of us rights our wrongs, I shall stay to oversee that indeed those wrongs are righted."

The Queen flashed him a smile, beautiful in its radiance.

"Ah, but Tommy, perhaps when it is my turn, would you be kind enough to return here to make the last trip home with me? It would make me happy to think you would."

"Nothing would be a greater honor, My Queen."

And with that, Tommy Terrance O' Toole bowed deep and low to his Queen one last time. He did not look back as he stepped into the little rowboat that ferried him to the deck of the colossal sailing vessel that would take him to Tir Na Nog. In truth, he was a bit afraid, afraid it would all evaporate away like a summer rain.

It was only when he reached the upper decks and his own Missus's warm loving arms that Tommy dared turn and peer back across the moonlit bay. But by then, like all things of gossamer shimmer do once you look away, the Queen had disappeared.

Tommy smiled. The circle had been closed. Facing out to sea, he felt as if time had slipped into a perfect Celtic knot that once wrapped into and around itself would go on forever. The past, the present, the future…all connected in one flowing form.

All as it should be.